batw

deviant

ADRIAN McKINTY

Amulet Books
New York

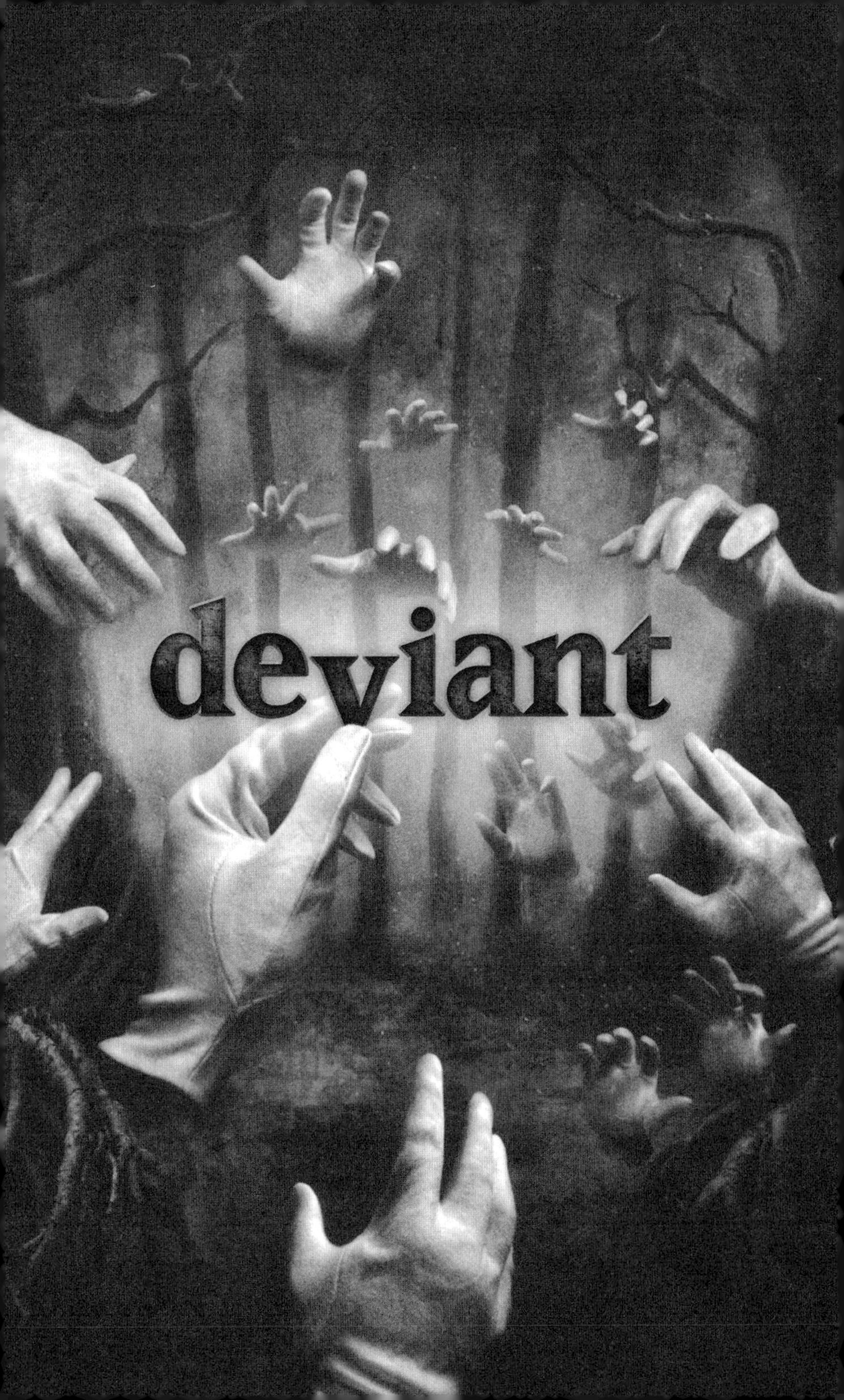
deviant

Library of Congress Cataloging-in-Publication Data

McKinty, Adrian.
Deviant / Adrian McKinty.
p. cm.
Summary: Fourteen-year-old Danny Lopez reviews the path that led him from Las Vegas, Nevada, to an experimental school near Colorado Springs and then to his imminent death at the hands of a cat-killer ready for bigger prey.
ISBN 978-0-8109-8420-2 (alk. paper)
[1. Moving, Household—Fiction. 2. Junior high schools—Fiction. 3. Schools—Fiction. 4. Stepfathers—Fiction. 5. Family life—Colorado—Fiction. 6. Secret societies—Fiction. 7. Psychopaths—Fiction. 8. Colorado Springs (Colo.)—Fiction.] I. Title.
PZ7.M4786915De 2011
[Fic]—dc22
2010023465

Text copyright © 2011 Adrian McKinty
Book design by Maria T. Middleton

Printed and bound in U.S.A.
10 9 8 7 6 5 4 3 2 1

Amulet Books are available at special discounts when purchased in quantity for premiums and promotions as well as fundraising or educational use. Special editions can also be created to specification. For details, contact specialsales@abramsbooks.com or the address below.

THE ART OF BOOKS SINCE 1949
115 West 18th Street
New York NY 10011
www.abramsbooks.com

"For I will consider my cat Jeoffry . . .
For he keeps the Lord's watch in the
night against the adversary . . . For he
counteracts the Devil, who is death,
by brisking about the life."

—Christopher Smart, from *Jubilate Agno* (1758)

PART ONE

The Letters of Indrid Cold

Letter 1

I offer you nothing less than the gnosis of the universe. Countless civilizations have flourished, grown, reached an apogee, faded, and died. If the history of the earth is to be believed (and I have grave doubts about this history) most of these societies fell by their own hand, the Mallarmé point coming long before the final collapse. The Mallarmé point, of course, has had many names across many different cultures. For me it was best expressed by Stéphane Mallarmé, who observed at the end of the nineteenth century (if such a century ever existed): "La chair est triste, hélas! et j'ai lu tous les livres." In English this phrase is best translated as: "My heart is sick, alas, and I have read all the books."

I, Indrid Cold, have not read "all the books," but I have seen through this sentiment to the truth beyond. The world is hollow, empty, and without meaning.

However, the gnosis, the secret history of the earth, reveals a different story.

ONE

Cat Killer

The mangled sounds of civilization faded slowly as he walked into the black nothingness of the desert.

His boots crunched sand, the snow slid off his coat. He moved carefully through the scrub and ground cactus and turned at last into the rock canyon. Here he was shielded from the traffic noise and the arc lamps on the federal prisons that lit up much of the lower mountain. He kept moving west until the ambient light dimmed and the stars began showing themselves. Finally he reached that place on the trail where all was quiet and even the Union Pacific trains were nothing but a distant rumble in the dark.

They were gone now, the people, their talk, their city.

He was alone.

What is it about silence that frightens us so? he wondered. Is it the prospect of being left with one's own thoughts? For some this was a torment, a dreadful confrontation with the terrible emptiness within.

He never felt that.

He liked quiet.

He shrugged. It was unimportant. He had a job to do in this place.

For the Ute Indians this natural amphitheater between great red sandstone columns was a holy place. Among these inanimate rocks the Ute chiefs and medicine men had worshipped and made offerings, pledging themselves to unknown gods in forgotten ceremonies. And before the Ute there were other peoples who had venerated this spot. For thousands of years the Native Americans had been coming here. And before the Indians, before people, this was a seabed and dinosaurs had walked the shore.

He wondered what "God" had been doing then. Watching the dull herds of stegosauruses, waiting for something more interesting to come along. God's patience, like his love and wisdom, must also be infinite, he thought dubiously.

He coughed. His blood was rich with adrenaline and his tongue was dry, bitter, thick in his mouth. He was shaking. As he shone his flashlight between the sandstone henges, the beam wobbled involuntarily.

"Is anybody there?" he called.

There was no reply and snow damped the echo, making his voice sound weird—strained, high-pitched, the way it had been before he'd gone to his speech pathologist, Miss Leahy.

He forced it down an octave and tried again. "Is anyone there?"

And this time it was a little better.

"Is . . . ," he began a third time, and stopped.

There was no one there.

It was snowing just hard enough to keep everyone indoors. This *was* a popular location though. The long-distance runners from the US Olympic Training Center sometimes came out this way, and the alert battalion of the Tenth Special Forces Division often hit the mountain trails first thing in the morning. Sooner or later someone would certainly find the sacrifice. That wasn't the problem; the problem was getting them to take notice of it. Out here there were always a lot of small animal corpses: possums, squirrels, raccoons . . . and if he didn't display the corpse correctly, the soldiers would probably take it for a coyote kill.

He looked at the bag in his left hand. "See? You think it's easy, but it's not that easy," he said.

He poked the bag with his finger and the cat thrashed weakly against the sides. There was a little fight left in it, but not much.

"Well, I suppose we better get started," he said.

He set the bag on the sand and took off his backpack.

He breathed the night air and looked at the stars. The Dipper had moved in the sky, but the moon was still hiding itself.

"I wonder what time it is," he muttered.

He looked at the luminous hands on his watch. Twelve! Already twelve! He was troubled, but not really that surprised. All aspects of this plan had taken him much longer than he had bargained for. Longer to get his gear, longer to get to the girl's house.

And then of course her parents had decided not to go to the cinema after all.

Foiled at the very first attempt!

He had headed home utterly dejected.

But then he had spotted the stray, merely by chance next to the Dumpster behind the gas station.

A small black-and-white tomcat who was trusting, *far too trusting*, of humans.

He wondered if the Master would be happy with this. Would he commend him for his improvisation?

And maybe it wasn't a stray. Maybe it belonged to someone who right now was calling the police . . .

A slight stir of panic.

A quickening of the pulse.

But then he calmed himself.

No one had seen him. No one would ever find him here.

Even so, the next time he would have a backup plan.

He breathed deeply and shone the flashlight around the rocky amphitheater until he found the famous "sacrifice stone" that was covered with ancient symbols and modern graffiti.

"There it is," he said aloud.

He walked over, placed the backpack on the rock, unzipped the central pocket, and took out his multi-tool.

On a whim he turned the flashlight off.

Total darkness.

He liked that.

Mr. Boyle, the mathematics teacher, claimed that on planets whose spin was fast, night did not last very long and in binary star systems there were planets with no night at all—as one sun set, another rose.

What a hideous prospect, he thought.

He turned the flashlight back on, picked up the cat bag, unlooped the string from the top, reached in, and grabbed the animal. The cat cried. Not a hiss but a full-bodied cry of pain and terror.

He grinned. "Oh but you haven't seen the half of it, my little friend," he said.

It clawed at him but he was holding it by the scruff of the neck and wearing the thick falconer's glove the Master had bought on eBay. A cat could scratch and bite him but couldn't penetrate the thick leather. He watched as the animal desperately tried to harm him. It didn't have a chance.

The cat fought pointlessly for a minute and then gave a great screech of terror.

"Ssshhh," he said and pushed it down onto the rock, holding it tightly by the neck. He squeezed on its carotid, choking the flow of oxygen to its brain. The cat ceased fighting and stared at him out of almond-shaped, starlight-reflecting eyes.

"Well, now, cat, I'll bet you have no idea what's in store, do you?" he said.

The cat hissed.

"What's the matter? Don't you know who I am?"

The cat hissed again and he squeezed harder.

"I'll tell you who I am. I am the object of your transfiguration. I deliver you from this vale of tears."

With his left hand around the cat's throat he picked up the penknife multi-tool with his right.

He tried to unhook the blade but he found that this was awkward in the dark.

He pushed hard on the knife blade, but it wouldn't come. One-handed, he couldn't quite get purchase on the blade tip and was unable to lever it out.

"Always something unexpected," he muttered.

Next time he would open the multi-tool first and place the blade on the rock, ready to go.

The cat began shivering. Convulsing. What was the matter with the thing? Was it having a heart attack? Did cats have heart attacks?

He once again tried to hook the blade out on the rock but still it wouldn't come.

"Oh, this is ridiculous," he muttered. "Come on."

He pushed and pushed, but what was needed was an opposable thumb. He considered his options for a moment. The best thing to do was to put the cat back in the bag and start it all again with the multi-tool open.

Yes.

He shoved the cat back inside the canvas sack. "Only a reprieve, not a pardon; don't get any ideas, cat," he said.

He shook off his gauntlet and with both hands working the problem this time the multi-tool blade came easily. "There we go," he muttered when finally the blade was out.

It was long, sharp, pointed, serrated—perfect for skinning a small mammal.

"Reprieve over," he said, excitement making his voice sound high and strange.

He put on the glove again and carefully reached into the bag and got the cat around the throat.

This time it didn't even fight but merely lay there limp and trembling.

He imagined the deliciously pitiful yell, the blood pouring over the sacrifice stone, the light dying from the cat's eyes, the smell of fear and intestinal gases . . . his spine tingled, his attention wandered, his grip slackened, the cat seized its opportunity.

Probably a pampered indoor cat wouldn't have stood a chance against the cat killer, but this particular creature had lives aplenty yet. It was a stray that had been adopted by the inmates of the Cobalt Colorado Minimum Security Prison. It stayed there during the day in one cell or another and at night made its way through the wire to hunt all over town. They called it Houdini after the great escapologist.

Houdini felt the pressure ease on his throat and he sensed

that the human's attention was elsewhere. Just a little more. Just a little more. He let the muscles in his neck slacken. His whole body flopped, becoming as flexible and pliant as a water balloon. His stomach slid through the thick gauntlet fingers, then his shoulders, then the back of his neck, then one ear, then another.

Gravity did the rest.

The cat killer looked at the blade glinting in the starlight. The effect pleased him. It was nice to be outside. So much purer. So much crisper. Killing indoors lacked poetry. The Ute had been right to come here, and of course when Abraham had come to sacrifice Isaac it was in a place like this.

There hadn't been a sacrifice here for a thousand years, but perhaps above him and around him the legions of the dead were watching in approval.

The cat killer swayed back on his heels, high on endorphins, his eyes glazed.

"And now, my beauty, the moment of truth has—"

He looked down, surprised.

There was no cat.

He swung the flashlight in all directions, but it did no good; the animal had gone.

He howled in frustration.

He howled and smashed his fist on the rock.

The Master would not be pleased.

Oh no, he would not be pleased at all.

Perhaps he would tell him only about the girl's parents canceling the trip to the cinema. He need not know about any of this.

Yes, he thought. That's what I'll do. And next time . . .

Next time nothing will escape me.

TWO

Leaving Las Vegas

Snow was falling on the Empire State Building and the pyramid of the Luxor. The taxi driver shivered as he loaded suitcases into the trunk. The poor guy was only wearing a T-shirt, Danny noticed. People forgot how cold it could get here in January.

"Dan, are you sure you don't want to come in the car?" Walt asked.

The taxi driver slammed the trunk, got in the driver's seat, and warmed his hands over the vents.

Danny shook his head. "If there's traffic, I'll probably beat you anyway," he said.

Walt closed the passenger door. "OK, son, but don't dillydally. If we miss the flight, your mother will skin us alive."

"Sure," Danny replied.

The taxi drove down Prince Scotty Street and turned on Westminster Avenue.

"Make sure you take good care of Jeff!" Danny shouted after them, but they didn't hear.

He stared at the sky. Normally by now the deep blue would be filled with crisscrossing vapor trails until it resembled every bored-senseless drawing he'd ever done on PaintBox; but today it was gray, low, foreboding.

He laid down his best skateboard—Sunflower—and looked back at the Strip. From the empty lot next to their house he could see all the way from the Luxor up to Circus Circus. The pyramid, the castle, the New York skyline, Paris . . . It didn't look weird to him—it was familiar, comforting.

He wondered when he'd be back here again.

Probably not for years and years.

He kicked with his right foot and rolled down the hill.

He cruised through the junction feeling the cold wind in his ears and nostrils. On Hacienda he could see mountains to the east. That's where we're going, he said to himself without enthusiasm.

In fact, his mother was already there.

He kicked again and looked at his watch—10:44. He'd have to get moving if he was going to beat the taxi. The best route was west on Swenson because the other slip roads to Wayne Newton Boulevard were complicated; but then again it would also be nice to see something of the old neighborhood before he left.

He went north. He switched to goofy-foot and kicked with his left, then centered himself in the middle of Sunflower, one sneaker on either side of the blue grip tape on the deck.

"Bye, Danny," Mrs. Connor said.

"Bye," he replied.

"We'll all miss you," she said.

He doubted that. Joe and Tommy Connor had done nothing but chase him and beat the crap out of him since they had moved here from North Las Vegas two years ago. Claire Connor was nice sometimes, but the brothers were the worst.

He zipped the front of his black hoodie and pulled it over his head. He leaned to port and the board turned left on Maryland. This part of town was bad news. Empty lots, garbage in the yards, pine boards nailed over broken windows, stripped cars and pickups. The population here was transient and he'd never gotten to know any of the kids.

On Escondido someone had tipped a shopping cart full of beer cans upside down in the middle of the street and left it there. At two cents a can, that was about five bucks' worth going to waste. A sheet of pasteboard drywall was lying in front of it. Danny could easily steer around it, but the drywall could possibly be a vert, so he decided to ollie it instead. He hit the ramp and kicked the tail down while jumping and sliding his front foot toward the nose. Almost magically Sunflower lifted off the ground. Momentum carried board and boy over the shopping cart, and skill brought them together again on the road.

He landed horizontal on the blacktop and freewheeled farther downhill.

Danny knew it would cost him minutes, but for old times' sake he cut through an alley and skated to the Tropicana Wash. It had been a while since a river had once flowed here, and he pushed past tires, stray dogs, and some kind of improvised homeless camp. The recession was already squeezing Vegas harder than other parts of the country. Maybe they were getting out just in time, Danny thought. He skated up the forty-degree bank and hit the street near the Hard Rock Hotel.

He looked at his watch. It was time to go. He maxed the volume on his iPod, laid down Sunflower, and kicked hard all the way to McCarran Airport.

Walt had gotten there first, but only just.

Danny spotted him at the Frontier desk and walked over.

"Hi, Danny, we're all set. So ya gonna miss the old place?" Walt asked.

"I guess," he said, but he didn't really know how he was feeling. Sad, maybe. Confused. Nervous.

Danny said good-bye to Jeff as the Frontier Air check-in lady took him to the oversized baggage area. Danny didn't like the way she was swinging the cat carrier left and right in her hand. He unplugged Winds of Plague and said, "Excuse me, ma'am, he's very old; can you be super careful with him?"

"Of course," the lady said, and swung the carrier about a little bit less.

"You wanna get a coffee?" Walt asked. He seemed tired. Danny knew he was only fifty, but he looked a lot older than that. He kept his hair long, almost to his shoulders, and it was so streaked with gray now that really it was better to say that it was gray hair streaked black. His face was wrinkled and that little pug boxer's nose of his looked uncomfortable and awkward on that big, flat face. Sometimes Danny wondered what his mom saw in him. He was thin, wiry, almost frail, and by his own admission a screwup. He'd gone to Annapolis, and if he'd stayed in the Navy for six more years he'd be on half pay by now living on easy street, and if he'd stayed on at the Glynn Casino he could be earning big bucks too, but he had screwed up that job just like he had screwed up half a dozen others since.

Walt was Danny's stepdad, of course; his real father was a married guy living in Illinois with a whole other family and kids. Juanita—Danny's mom—never talked about him, but that was the information he'd been able to get from his aunts over the years. Some guy who had lied to her and made her promises and got her pregnant and then skedaddled. Danny was an only child, but sometimes he thought about those half brothers and sisters out there. How many of them were there? Were there boys? Girls? Whereabouts in Illinois? Chicago?

When he visited his cousins in L.A., he was jealous of their bunk beds and private games, secret handshakes and jokes. They always included him in the games (he was a year older than Jose, and Jose kind of looked up to him), but when the weekend was over it was back to Vegas and his big, spacious, comfortable, lonely bedroom.

"You know, I'm not really supposed to drink coffee," Danny said.

Walt put his arm around Danny's shoulders. "Come on, let's just sit and talk. We never get a chance to talk. Let me get you a chocolate-chip muffin. What do you say?"

Danny sighed and they sat at the Starbucks near the luggage carousel.

Of course they didn't talk. Walt was absorbed in his thoughts and Danny spent the time wondering if he should adjust the grip tape on Sunflower. His foot had almost slipped on that vert earlier.

"Danny," Walt said in a conspiratorial whisper.

His eyes had narrowed and he had a reckless grin on his face that Danny had seen one or two times before.

"Danny, do you see that fellow over there?"

Walt had gone to some fancy New England boarding school and sometimes his voice adopted a slightly more patrician accent than normal, and he used phrases like "do you see that fellow . . ."

"What fellow?" Danny sneered.

"That fellow. He's going to try something, watch, just watch."

"I'm not interested, Walt. Leave me alone."

"When are you going to start calling me Dad? Huh? Ever?" Walt said angrily.

The Walt/Dad thing was just another one of his tactics,

but one that tended to work. Danny was guilt-tripped into silence.

"You see that character over there with the blond hair and the twitches? He's been looking at that little black suitcase going round and round for the last fifteen minutes. Everyone else has got their bags and gone. That one's unclaimed, and you know why it's unclaimed?"

"*No se.*"

"Because whoever owned the suitcase didn't travel with it. They didn't make the flight, but the bag did. And that dude over there is going to steal it."

The word "steal" made Danny cringe.

A month ago he'd been caught stealing a Snickers bar from the 7-Eleven. The cops had dragged him home and embarrassed him in front of Walt and his mother.

His mom had made a big deal out of it.

And when JJ's basketball money had gone missing from the locker room and people had accused him, his mom had not believed that he was innocent.

They were all so high-and-mighty about it.

"What are you going to do about it if he does take it? Turn him in? It's a victimless crime, isn't it? It's insured, right?" Danny said.

"I'm going to stop him before he gets into trouble," Walt said.

"No, you're not. Just sit down."

Walt began walking toward the baggage carousel.

"No. Walt, don't do it!" Danny pleaded, swallowing the

muffin, grabbing Sunflower, and trying to catch him before it was too late.

Walt picked the suitcase off the carousel and began carrying it over to the United desk. Before he'd gotten ten yards, two men in dark suits with earpieces and sunglasses appeared from the crowd and walked briskly to either side of him.

"Is this your suitcase, sir?" one of the men asked.

"Nope," Walt said with that smile of his that Danny hated so very much.

The men drew semiautomatic pistols from shoulder holsters inside their jackets and pointed them at Walt.

"We're informing you, sir, that you are under arrest for possession of illegal narcotics with intent to deal," the second of the two men said.

"I was just trying to take it to the United desk," Walt said.

Danny had the satisfaction of seeing Walt cuffed and taken to airport security, but it ceased to be funny half an hour later when they missed their plane.

Danny may have stolen a Snickers bar, but Walt was the real idiot. He pulled stunts like this all the time. He was the real screwup, not him.

When the cops questioned Danny about it, he said nothing.

"Tell them I was going to return the suitcase, Danny," Walt begged, but Danny kept his mouth shut, refusing even to confirm that his name was Danny Lopez.

They were taken to the security area.

Time passed.

Cops with mustaches.

Lady cops with offers of soda.

Phone calls: from Mom, from one of Walt's Navy buddies who was now a lawyer someplace, finally from Mr. Glynn himself, of the famous Glynn Casino and Resort. Mr. Glynn explained to the cops that Walt's wife, Juanita, was now a vice president in his organization and since Mr. Glynn was a hugely important man in Las Vegas, the police finally saw sense and chose to believe Walt's story.

Muttering "stupid hippie" to themselves, they let them go.

Back in the terminal, Walt was seething. "Why didn't you tell them I was trying to *prevent* a crime, Danny?"

"Because I didn't want to."

"Why not?"

"I was exercising my constitutional right."

"You have a real attitude problem."

"Do I?"

"You know, I was the one who didn't want you to go to that school. I was the holdout. I wanted you to go to public school. I was on your side, but now I see that your mother was right. You need to learn obedience and respect . . ."

On and on it went.

Danny tuned it out.

They boarded a midnight flight so empty that Jeff was allowed to fly in the cabin with them. Jeff was a brown and orange tabby with scar tissue over his left eye and a chunk of fur missing on his left rear leg. He'd probably lived for two or three years in and around the Tropicana Wash until Danny had adopted him. He was a survivor. Six or seven hours in a cat carrier wasn't enough to disturb his equanimity, and seeing Jeffrey's coolness made Danny chill too.

He closed his eyes and every second brought them closer to a new world over the Rocky Mountains to a new town, with new kids, a new house, a whole new blacktop to explore and skate. Just a little while longer and he'd be reunited with his mom and maybe things would be better.

THREE

The New Student

Through the break in the clouds Venus rises pale and yellow in the evening sky. It means nothing to him. He knows the real color of things. He walks on the far side of the mirror. He walks in the captive land. This Earth is counterfeit. Filled with false fossils, bogus shale deposits, lies. That snow is a lie. These trees were electrons grown on the moon.

His phone is ringing.

The tone tells him it's a text.

He lets the text come.

The path leads down into the forest.

"Lead me, wind," he says. "Lead me, polestar."

He follows the trail through virgin snow. He walks to the cliff edge. He stops at the famous cliff-side View Point. He can see a hundred miles from up here.

But he doesn't look.

He closes his eyes.

He imagines himself standing at the end of the universe.

All the worlds have gone, counterfeit or not.

Even the machines are gone now. It's late. The suns have died and the artificial suns have burned their fuel and guttered out. Darkness reigns and the best efforts of the finest minds are for naught. The last of the artificial life forms has given up the ghost as weakly as the last of the organics. The second law of thermodynamics has proved unstoppable.

Everything decays. Given enough time, even atoms break down into random protons, neutrons, and electrons, separated from one another by unimaginable spaces.

Matter itself falls apart at the very end.

Nothing remains.

He sees all this and he is awed.

The universe is still.

A trillion years pass.

And then another trillion.

And then another.

And that's how the story ends. There is no twist. There is no hope. There is only nothing. An eternity of nothing.

Only he can see a way out . . .

Only he . . .

Only . . .

Snow falls on his face. He opens his eyes. In one hand there is a hunting knife. In the other is a phone. He catches the moon in the blade. He reads the text: NW STDNT DNNY LPZ. GD 9.

A new student?

That will make exactly one hundred.

He wonders if Danny owns a cat.

FOUR

The Girl Next Door

Danny's mother woke him with a kiss on the cheek. She hadn't done that for years. He rubbed his eyes. She was wearing her work suit: an expensive-looking ensemble consisting of a black jacket, white blouse, black skirt, and low-heeled shoes. She looked pretty: In the week she'd been away she'd gotten her hair cut short—something he hadn't noticed the night before at the airport.

He knew he should tell her that she looked nice, that it would make her feel good, but he was still harboring a lingering resentment toward her. Why did they have to come here for her job, just when he was starting to make friends at Grover Cleveland? He took the middle path, neither praising her looks nor complaining.

How long had he been asleep? "What day is it?" he asked.

His mom laughed. "Well, there's good news and bad news."

"What's the good news?"

"It's Sunday."

"What's the bad news?"

"You've got school tomorrow."

She tugged back the curtains and he noticed that she was holding something in her hand.

"What's that?" he asked.

"I brought you breakfast in bed," she said, placing a bowl of cereal carefully on the wobbly IKEA bedside table. Juanita was smart but no handyman.

Still, Danny was proud of her.

She'd started off as a cleaner in Mr. Glynn's signature casino on the Strip. She'd gone to night school and learned how to be a blackjack dealer. She was a good dealer: sharp, observant, patient. After a couple of years she'd been promoted to senior dealer and then pit boss, and finally she had moved up the hierarchy to become one of the few female house managers. Juanita had excellent people skills; she was tactful, fair, firm, and though she was only five foot three she could be intimidating when she needed to be. She was good at her job and when they were looking for a manager for Mr. Glynn's new Indian casino in Cobalt, Colorado, Juanita had seemed like an ideal fit. As well as being one of Mr. Glynn's best employees, she was half Cherokee . . .

"I've got to go, honey. Please remind your father that he's seeing Mr. Randall this afternoon."

"Mr. who?"

"Randall. Remind him. I've written the address on a Post-it on the fridge. Forty-four Correctional Institution Road. You'll remind him?"

"Yes."

"Do you like your room, darling? You have a view."

Danny stared at the bare walls for a second and then leaned across and looked out the window. The house was on a rise with a few other homes on either side and beyond the houses a dense, seemingly endless forest that crawled up to a pair of snowcapped mountains.

It gave him the creeps. Anything could be out there in those trees. Brown bears, black bears, wolves, coyotes, escaped mental patients . . .

"I was talking to Aunt Louisa," his mother continued. "She said that the boys are so jealous that you'll be snowboarding."

Danny shook his head. "I don't know if I'll be snowboarding," he said grumpily. "Who said anything about snowboarding?"

"Well, I just assumed because of your skateboard."

Danny shook his head. "Don't assume."

"Danny," she said in a disciplinary tone.

"Sorry," he muttered after the longest pause he thought he could get away with.

"Look, hon, I should be heading off. Don't forget to remind your father. We don't want to let down Mr. Glynn."

"Don't worry, I'll tell Walt."

His mother smiled.

Her eyes were brown like her skin, and her lips today were a deep red. She had brown feline-shaped eyes and straight heavy eyebrows that didn't arch at all. She was beautiful and smart and kind and she had a great job. Walt was lucky to have her. She was far too good for him.

"You've got to work on a Sunday?" Danny asked.

"I do. The grand opening is in three weeks; you wouldn't believe the stuff that hasn't been done yet . . . I have to go. By the way, Jeffrey's under your bed."

Danny looked under the bed and, sure enough, there was Jeff. "He must be freaked," Danny said.

"He'll get over it," his mom said, and left.

He heard her clunk down the stairs.

He looked out the window to see what kind of car she was driving. It had been so late, he hadn't even noticed it when she picked him up at the airport.

A brand-new Volvo XC90. Just like the ones that cruised the Strip on a Friday night. Cool. They really were moving up in the world.

Danny coaxed Jeff out from underneath the bed and set the cat next to him while he ate the cereal Juanita had brought.

It was Cocoa Krispies rather than Cocoa Pebbles, but that was OK; she'd at least made the effort to get his favorite.

Jeff meowed and Danny put a little chocolate milk on his spoon and let Jeff drink. He'd read somewhere that cats couldn't digest chocolate, but old Jeff was so tough he could deal with anything.

"You could deal with a bear, couldn't you?" he said.

While Jeff curled into a warm spot on the bed, Danny finished the cereal and went for a brief reconnaissance of the house.

Upstairs there were three big bedrooms, two with en suite toilets, all of them with views. Just how much was Glynn paying her? Downstairs there was a gigantic living room with a panoramic view of the street and the mountain beyond, a dining room, a kitchen, and two more bathrooms. The house had been decorated in a kind of Western motif: paintings of cattle drives, lonely vistas, cowboys. There were mounted antlers above the stone fireplace and a couple of fake-looking Navajo sand pictures, which probably meant they were real.

There was a big spot where something was missing on the dining room wall, and a little detective work revealed it to be a painting of a noble savage–style Indian standing over a dead buffalo. His mother had placed it down in the basement. Was it offensive? Obviously to her, but Danny couldn't really see the problem. The Indian looked pretty bad-ass standing on top of the bison he'd just killed with a bow and arrow.

There was a small study and a bookcase that contained only phone books, a front yard where you couldn't do much, and a large back garden with a thin layer of snow on it.

The forest began right at the backyard fence. Danny opened the back door and examined the snow with his bare foot. He'd only encountered snow a few times in his life. He didn't like it before, and he doubted if he'd like it now.

In Vegas when snow fell, it disappeared soon after it touched the ground; it didn't generally lie around like this.

"Hmm," he said, touching the stuff skeptically with his big toe.

He closed the back door.

He was still hungry. He went to the kitchen and after opening a million cupboards he found the Cocoa Krispies box and got milk from the refrigerator.

"Hello?" a voice said.

He turned. Much to his surprise, there was a girl standing in the hall. A scrawny character, about thirteen with short blond, spiky hair, a red dress, redder cheeks, a thick unzipped black coat, red tights, boots. If she'd been wearing a white dress, Aunt Isabella would have been crossing herself and muttering things about the faerie folk or La Llorona.

"Who are you?" Danny asked.

"Who are you?" the girl said.

"Danny."

"I thought so," the girl said dispassionately, and walked into the kitchen. Her eyes were the same green as the trees, and he saw that her crazy hair was actually a kind of brownish blond. The way she'd gelled it and spiked it up looked a bit ridiculous.

"So, who are you?" Danny asked, putting down the Cocoa Krispies box.

"Tony. Antonia, actually, but I like Tony. Whatcha eating?"

"Uh, I haven't totally decided yet, uh, Antonia."

"Tony, please!"

Tony widened the fridge door and they both looked in. It was packed full of stuff. Sodas, fruit, eggs, cheese, candy bars. Danny grabbed a can of Dr Pepper and Tony got a gigantic bar of hazelnut chocolate that must have come from Sam's Club or Trader Joe's.

"Do you want a Dr Pepper or something?" Danny asked.

"Do you drink coffee?"

"Sure," he lied, wondering how to make it. Something to do with the French press, he thought. "Are you sure you don't want a Dr Pepper? There's a six-pack in there."

"No, thanks," she said disdainfully.

Coffee, he thought. Hot water and crushed beans? His mom took instant, but Walt had a whole complicated system. He lit a ring on the stove, filled the kettle, and put it on it. Meanwhile, Tony had spied Sunflower lying on the table. She picked it up.

"Is this yours?" she asked.

Danny's brow furrowed. There was a possibility that girls in Colorado might not like boys who painted one of Van Gogh's sunflowers on the deck of their skateboard. In fact—like the girls in Vegas—there was a possibility that Colorado girls might not like skateboarders at all, that they considered skateboarders on the dork side of the great dork/cool-guy divide.

"Um," he said, grabbing a coffee mug from an empty shelf and trying to clean dust out of the bottom of it.

Tony put the skateboard on the table deck-side down. She spun the plastic wheels with one of her fingers.

"Can I have a glass of milk?" she asked.

"Instead of the coffee?"

"Yeah."

"Great, sure."

Danny sighed with relief, turned off the gas, and poured milk into the coffee cup. She came over and took it from him.

"Thank you."

"You're welcome."

"So you live here in Colorado now," she announced rather than asked.

There was no point denying it. "Yeah," Danny said.

After two more slugs of Dr Pepper he was completely awake but he was still a little reluctant to ask where she lived, in case the answer was inside the mountain or Aunt Isabella's Land of the Faeries or something.

"Can I have a piece of that chocolate?" he asked as a way of placating her. It wasn't a traditional method of warding off La Llorona but you tried anything in such cases.

"My mom got you this," Tony said, passing him the bar.

"She did?"

"Yes. She sent a gift basket. Welcoming present when we thought you were all coming. But just your mom came.

My mom says you're going to be living here now and that you're going to be going to our school."

"Does she now?" Danny said, snapping off a square and putting it in his mouth. It was hazelnutty and good.

Tony grabbed the chocolate back. "Yeah, she does," Tony muttered, rather savagely biting into the chocolate bar instead of breaking a bit off.

"What else does your mother say?"

"She says your mom is going to be working in that Indian Casino they're building."

"That's true."

"Most people round here don't like that casino."

"Really?"

"Yes."

The kitchen didn't have anyplace to sit. Danny pointed at the living room. "You wanna take a seat in there?"

"OK, but at some point I should be going back. I don't really know you or anything; you could be like one of those people from *America's Most Wanted* for all I know," she said, sitting at the large oak living room table.

That made Danny a little annoyed. It rubbed him the wrong way, especially considering the fact that only a few hours earlier he'd been waiting for Walt outside a holding cell at McCarran Airport. "Hey, I didn't ask you to come in. In fact, I didn't even hear you knock," he said.

Just then Jeffrey wandered in and began rubbing himself against Tony's legs. She bent down and stroked him, and like the traitor he was he began to purr.

"You've got a cat," she said.

"Don't let anyone ever tell you you're not observant."

"He's kind of a bit squirrelly-looking."

Danny was incensed. "He's a tough street cat! I found him in the Tropicana Wash."

"He's cute. And he doesn't look so tough to me," she said, stroking his belly.

"He killed a snake once," Danny said, increasingly annoyed at Jeff's purring.

"You're going to hate school," she said, apropos of nothing.

Danny didn't like conversations where people jumped around so much. It was like reading the spam comments on his YouTube skateboard channel. Half of them didn't make any sense; they should have just held their breath and their keystrokes.

"Why am I going to hate school?"

"You just are," she said with real satisfaction.

"Maybe I love school."

"No, I can tell, you don't. And certainly not this one."

Her face had a pale, slightly asymmetrical, weird quality to it. She was definitely pretty, but not in that obvious American way, that way you saw at the beauty pageants at Mandalay Bay.

"What are you thinking about?" she asked, catching him looking at her.

"Oh, um, nothing really. I like your hair."

"I like your board," she said.

"You do?"

"Tell me about it?"

"Do you skateboard?" he asked quickly.

"No."

He shook his head. "You wouldn't be interested."

She broke off an impossibly big chunk of chocolate and shoved it in her mouth. "Tryyyyyy meeeee," she said, and scooted the chocolate bar back across the table.

Danny laughed. "You're pretty funny," he said.

"To look at," she added, and he laughed some more.

He flipped the board over. "Nevada Skateboard Company, 2008, polymer wheels, wood deck, stainless-steel ball bearings and supports, only a few hundred ever made before the company went bankrupt. Five hundred bucks apiece, but I got it eighty percent off. Perfect balance, bump grips, an eight-inch-wide—"

"What's that picture?"

"Oh, I did that myself, it's not very good. I used to do art. It's one of Van Gogh's sunflowers, you know? But actually I kind of called the board Sunflower after a Beach Boys album. Walt's into the Beach Boys. They were a group from a million years ago and he played it all the time and it got into my brain or something."

"Who's Walt?"

Danny shook his head. "Stepdad, I guess."

She nodded sagely. She understood. Her parents were

still married, but many of the kids at school were from separated homes. She didn't want to pry further, but Danny offered the information anyway. "They're married and everything. Two years now. At the Little Chapel of the West if you can believe it. That was horrible . . . Anyway, they're married. But they asked me if I just wanted to keep Mom's name and I said yeah. So that's why she's Juanita Brown and I'm Danny Lopez, before anybody talks or says anything or, uh, anything."

He'd said all this very quickly and now he paused to take a deep breath.

"Well, I suppose it's my turn," Tony said. "I'm from the Springs, born and bred. My dad works at NORAD, in Cheyenne Mountain; my mom's an admin assistant for Focus on the Family. My dad's also an elder over at the Faith Cathedral, but I don't think he gets paid for that."

"NORAD—that sounds pretty cool."

"Yeah, I guess, I don't know. We're not allowed to go there. Oh, I have a sister, like a big sister, she's eighteen, Alexa, she's cool, she's in college. Kinda near Vegas, actually. Arizona State. And I have a cat called Snowflake. My grandparents live in Texas and Florida and I snowboard. So I'm sort of a board chick too, but the mountain bullies are such dicks. I kind of think of myself as a hippie surfer girl without the ocean, you know?"

Danny didn't know, but he nodded anyway.

"Your English is pretty good," Tony said.

"WTF? So's yours," Danny said furiously.

Tony looked embarrassed. She covered her mouth and swallowed a big chunk of chocolate. Her cheeks were burning. "I didn't mean anything by that, it's just that, I don't know, I never met anybody whose mom was Mexican, that's all."

"My mom's American. Her dad was a Cherokee, and his people have been here for ten thousand years. And my grandma's from Texas, so don't start any of that crap with me."

Tony reached across the table and grabbed his hand. Her fingers were tiny, cold, delicate.

She squeezed his palm. "I'm really, really sorry. I didn't mean to hurt your feelings. That was a dumb thing to say. It's pretty white-bread around here, worse than the Springs even. I don't know what I was thinking."

The green of her eyes wavered in front of him for a second or two and then melted his resistance. He knew that sometimes he was a bit too quick to fly off the handle.

"*De nada, ese,*" he said.

"What does that mean?" she said suspiciously.

"It means 'it's chill, sista.'"

She let go of his hand and stood up.

"Good, OK, well, now that I've checked out the scene and alienated you forever, I have to go back. This is an unofficial scouting mission on your family, unsanctioned by the rest of the street, but I must deliver my report before church."

"What are you going to tell them?" Danny asked.

"What else? The truth. You're into heavy metal, devil worship, and you have dug a portal to hell right here in the living room."

Danny smiled. "Don't forget the human sacrifices."

"Human sacrifices, check."

"Which house do you live in?"

"The one on the other side of the road. The pink monstrosity," she said, pointing to a newish McMansion almost exactly like the ones you'd see in Seven Hills. Four or five bedrooms, triple garage, black Tudor-style wood boards over pinkish white stucco.

"That is a big house," Danny said with mild satirical intent.

"No bigger than yours," Tony replied. "Anyway, I gotta go."

"I'll walk out with you," Danny said.

"In that?" she said, pointing at his clothes.

Danny realized that he'd been wearing blue pajama pants with race cars on them and an old T-shirt with a fading image of Kurt Cobain, who had died before he'd even been born.

"I guess it is kind of lame," he said more to himself than to Tony.

"No, it's not lame, I just thought you'd be too cold," Tony said quickly.

Danny found a coat in the closet, pulled on a pair of sneakers, and walked Tony across the road. The sun was coming out and the snow was melting but it was still chilly.

Around freezing, he thought. They stopped in front of her house.

"How high up are we here?" he wondered out loud.

"The Springs is six thousand feet, we're another thousand on top of that."

"Wow. And it snows how much?"

"It can snow every month from September to June."

"Yikes . . . OK, uh, so, bye, I guess I'll see you at school tomorrow?" Danny asked.

Tony smiled. "You might not recognize me . . . no hair gel allowed. Actually, I better shower it out before church anyway . . . And of course I'll be in my uniform. You're not a genius, are you?"

Danny shook his head. "I don't think so, why?"

"Well, then, you should be in my class, 9B. We get tested every month; the kids that do better go to 9A, the others 9B," she said, smiling sweetly.

"So you're not a genius either," he surmised.

She walked down the path and opened her front door. "I kinda am, actually. I started the year in the eighth grade, 8B, and I've worked my way up . . . See ya," she said, then gave a little wave, opened her front door, and went inside.

"See ya," Danny replied, and began whistling. He was still whistling an hour later when Walt came down for breakfast.

FIVE

The Prison

Walt turned off the electric razor and looked at Danny. "How come you're so cheerful?" he wondered.

"I don't know. I guess I'm happy that we're not in jail, maybe," Danny said.

Walt reddened. "Yeah, sorry about that, I probably shouldn't have gotten involved," he muttered. "You check out the house? Pretty groovy, isn't it?"

Walt said things like "daddy-o" and "groovy" like it was the olden days. He was right, though. It certainly was a lot bigger than their Vegas home. Danny didn't really think much about money, but now he saw that the move here probably meant a huge pay raise for his mother. This house, the car—it changed things. Danny thought of himself as an outsider, a street kid from East L.A. like his cousins, not as some comfortable, middle-class boy from suburban Nevada or Colorado. But in a day he'd gone from laughing at *South Park* to living in South Park.

"The house is OK," he said.

"You wanna stay here, or you wanna come with me?"

"What? Where are you going?"

"To see that Randall guy. I'm starting work tomorrow and they want me to come over today."

"Mom took the car."

"You haven't seen the Tesla? We got the use of it for a month. The casino is giving away two of them as opening-week prizes, you know, 'cause of the whole Tesla thing. Brilliant idea. That Glynn guy is smart. They wanted her to drive it around. She didn't like it, but I think you'll be impressed!"

Danny pulled on his leather jacket, grabbed Sunflower, and followed Walt outside to the garage. When they opened the garage door Danny *was* impressed, but it was important that he didn't let Walt see.

"Don't these things run out after like twenty minutes?" Danny asked, looking at the red Tesla Electric Roadster parked in the left port of the two-car garage.

"A hundred and fifty miles per charge. Totally silent running," Walt said, looking at Danny significantly.

Which is useful why? Danny thought, but didn't say anything.

Walt tied his long graying hair back in a ponytail and got in on the driver's side. Danny got in next to him. Walt plugged the strange address he'd been given—44 Correctional Institution Road—into the GPS, and off they went.

The Tesla was fast and sleek, and despite himself Danny felt seventeen shades of awesome riding in it. They drove quickly through what turned out to be the surprisingly small town of Cobalt. It was little more than a glorified crossroads, four streets, a couple of hundred houses, a 7-Eleven, a garage, a bakery, a Denny's.

"I think that's your school," Walt said, pointing to half a dozen redbrick buildings cleared from the forest.

"I hope not," Danny said.

Walt winked at him. "Meaning to talk to you about this. Listen, son, you gotta float under the radar; just stick it out for a few months until we're settled. You don't have to stay there forever."

Danny didn't like Walt's tone. He wasn't going to be part of a conspiracy to put one over on his mother. "I'll stick out the school if you stick out the job, Walt," Danny said.

Walt bristled. "Don't give me that goddamn look, son, I'm not a total screwup, you know."

"We'll see," Danny said under his breath.

The GPS took them to Correctional Institution Road in about ten minutes. Its odd name did not turn out to be much of a mystery.

In the space of about five miles they rolled past correctional institution after correctional institution. Federal prisons, state prisons, maximum-security prisons, minimum-security prisons, and a terrifying bunkerlike place called ADX Cobalt or, to give it the full name on the sign, "The United States Penitentiary Administrative Maximum Facility of Cobalt, Colorado."

This was the famous Supermax prison that Walt thought he'd seen a documentary about on the National Geographic Channel. "This place has got the worst of the worst. All the terrorists you can think of, serial killers, you name it. They only get out one hour a day or something. Did you see that documentary?"

"No, I hate that channel," Danny said.

"You should watch it. It's good. You learn stuff. They had this whole thing about Stonehenge last week, did you see that one?"

Danny ignored him and looked out the window at the ADX, fascinated by the coils of razor wire, lookout towers, an alleged antiaircraft battery, and even a moat.

"Oh yeah," Walt continued, unfazed. "Apparently, before the Stonehenge they said there was a wood henge and before that there was a dirt henge . . . Wait! I think this is it."

Number 44 Correctional Institution Road was right next to the Supermax. It also appeared to be a prison, but not quite as intimidating as its neighbor. It was surrounded by a wire fence, which disconcertingly had holes in it, and beyond the fence the inmates appeared to live in what looked like mobile homes. A small sign said COBALT COLORADO FCF, 44 CORRECTIONAL INSTITUTION ROAD.

"Are you sure this is the right address?" Danny asked. It

wouldn't be the first time that Walt had gotten something like this wrong.

"I'm pretty sure," Walt said dubiously, driving up to a wooden hut at the prison entrance. A none-too-sturdy metal bar ran across the road, and a sign said PRESS FOR SERVICE.

"I'll do it," Danny muttered. He got out of the Tesla and laid down his board, but the road, wasn't cement—it was just compacted dirt. Disgusted, he picked Sunflower up and walked to the hut. He pushed the button.

"Yes?" a voice said through an intercom.

"We're here to see, uh, a Mr. Randall?"

"What's your name?"

"I guess . . . Brown."

"Come on up."

The swing bar lifted vertically. Danny got back in the Tesla and they drove through the gate.

A man with a shotgun in a guard tower (which looked to Danny like one of those lifeguard towers in Santa Monica) waved them on, and they were inside the prison.

A skinny-looking guy in a pair of orange overalls came out of one of the trailers and nodded to them. He was about thirty-five, with long red hair (almost as long as Walt's) and a goatee. He pointed to a parking space in front of the trailer he had just exited. They pulled into it and got out of the Tesla.

"Hi there," the man said. "I'm Bob Randall."

"Walt Brown. This is my son, Danny," Walt said.

They shook hands.

"So you're the new foreman?" Bob said.

"I guess so, um, I don't really know a lot about it . . . my wife got me this gig," Walt said a little uneasily.

Bob laughed. "No worries, it's a piece of cake. I do everything. You're just the exterior liaison for liability issues. We can go into my office and talk. You want a coffee or something?"

"Sure," Walt said.

"What about you, kid, you want a soda?"

"You got Dr Pepper?"

"I don't think so . . . I'll look. Come inside. We got *Mad* magazine. You like *Mad*, or are you too old for that?"

They went inside the trailer. It was a small office jammed with papers, an ancient computer, a Stone Age printer. There was a funky smell and the bars across the window made it a little hard to see. Bob rummaged in a minifridge and produced a can of Coke, which Danny accepted. There was a huge pile of old magazines, among which Danny found *Surfer* and *Surfer's Journal*—two odd publications to find a thousand miles from the sea.

He started reading anyway while Walt and Bob talked.

"So, I'm not really getting what's going on here. This is a prison, right? What are we doing here?" Walt said, sipping his coffee.

"I guess they didn't tell you much of anything?"

"My wife works at the new casino they're building in Cobalt. I think her boss, Mr. Glynn, pulled a few strings . . ."

"Yeah, that makes sense. That's the job. The whole casino itself was more or less built by work gangs from the various prisons in and around Cobalt. Our crew will be building the road. It's pretty easy stuff. It says on your résumé that you were an engineer in the Navy."

"Yeah. Long time ago."

Bob picked up on Walt's worried expression.

"Don't sweat it. I run the crew. You'll be fine."

A nervous-looking cat came in and hung around Bob's legs.

"Who's the cat?" Danny asked.

"That's Houdini. We adopted him. Great little guy. He used to come and go all the time, although lately he's been reluctant to leave my sight."

Danny picked up Houdini and stroked his neck.

"So it's basically all prisons around here?" Walt asked.

"The Springs is a bit more interesting. Colorado Springs has the Air Force Academy, NORAD, the US Olympic Training Center, Focus on the Family, Fort Carson, and prisons. Up here it's all prisons. From Cobalt all the way to Manitou, nothing but correctional institutions."

"So you guys, it's like cheap labor, union-busting, that kind of thing?"

"It's not so cheap when you've got maximum-security prisoners; you need a lot of guards. But it's a pretty cost-effective process with a minimum-security prison like ours. Most of these guys are in the last six months of their sentence. They're not going to do anything to jeopardize their release. And working outside the prison is a privilege, so they do a pretty good job."

Walt was still troubled. "I don't have a lot of experience with this kind of thing," he confessed.

Bob shook his head. "Don't worry. We got one guy who ran his own construction firm, and everyone else is a pro . . . about a hundred years' experience on this crew, easy."

Houdini went to sleep on Bob's bed.

Danny thumbed through *Surfer's Journal* and *Surfer* and finally picked up the *Colorado Springs Gazette*.

A headline on the lower part of the fold immediately caught his eye:

MISSING COBALT CAT FOUND EVISCERATED
(turn to page 3)

Danny turned to page 3.

Rebecca Pigeon, 60, a lifelong Cobalt resident, was devastated to learn Thursday that her missing three-year-old cat, Spartacus, had been found dead. A group of Girl Scouts discovered the cat eviscerated on Gray Street. Animal welfare officer Kevin Hud said that the cat was almost certainly the victim of a coyote. "There's been a lot of hysteria about wolves lately. This was not a wolf attack. This was a lone predator, probably a coyote."

The cat's heart was missing, but quickly damping down any untoward explanation, Mr. Hud told the *Gazette* that coyotes will often eat the organ meat first. "It was probably startled and unable to finish its meal," Mr. Hud explained and went on to ask all of Cobalt, Manitou Springs, and western Colorado Springs residents to keep a close eye on their pets for a week or two until the coyote moved on to new territory.

"Danny!"

Danny looked up. Bob and Walt were on their feet and staring at him.

"Danny, I've been talking to you . . . We're ready to go," Walt said.

"Uh, OK."

"You can borrow those 'zines if you want," Bob said.

"Yeah, thanks, we don't have TV yet," Danny replied.

He grabbed a few magazines, said good-bye to Houdini, and walked with them outside.

"Nice wheels, by the way," Bob said.

"Yeah, Tesla Roadster. Apparently, Glynn's trying to play up the Tesla link because the new casino is right next to the scientist Nikola Tesla's old laboratory. The casino's giving away the Roadster as a prize and we get to drive it until they do. You like it?" Walt asked.

"It's the future, man," Bob said.

They said good-bye to him and drove out of the prison.

Back on Correctional Institution Road, Danny noticed another hole in the fence of Cobalt Colorado FCF, which made him think that minimum security really meant the bare minimum. Grover Cleveland Middle School back in Vegas had better defenses.

When they got home, Juanita was back already and baking a chicken in the oven.

An hour later at dinner, Walt filled Juanita in on Bob, the prison, and his job. He seemed excited, and Danny knew that this would make his mom happy.

Danny ate his dinner hungrily, folding strips of chicken and spoonfuls of rice into the tortillas his mom must have gotten from a local supermarket, because they didn't taste homemade. Which meant that they had Mexican food in Colorado.

"Mom?" Danny said after finishing his plate. "Can I ask you a question?"

Juanita looked at Walt, but he didn't know what was coming.

"Some people say the casino isn't very popular round here."

"Who said that?" Juanita asked.

"The girl across the street. I think they're kind of religious or something. She's nice, though."

Juanita thought for a moment. "Well, I don't know, there are going to be people who are resistant to us making money from gambling, and if that's their religion that's OK."

"Do you think it's OK to make money from gambling?" Danny asked.

"People have freedom of choice. No one forces them to fly to Las Vegas. No one's going to force them to drive up that long road from Colorado Springs. And let me tell you something else. Mr. Glynn is building this casino for the Ute and Cherokee Nations. He'll run it, but it's going to be theirs. The people around here have gotten pretty rich taking Ute and Cherokee land and building prisons all over them, and if the Utes and Cherokees wanna take some of that money back by building a casino, I think that's a very good thing."

Danny nodded.

"OK?" Juanita said.

"Sure," he muttered. "I don't really care. It was just something that girl said."

He stared out the window at the snowflakes. He looked at his mother. She was tired. She was holding a glass of iced vodka tonic against her forehead with her left hand. "Mom, do you *feel* Cherokee?" Danny asked.

Juanita put down her glass and looked at him. "Yes. Yes, I do."

"But you're only half Cherokee though, really, and I'm only a quarter," Danny protested. "A quarter Cherokee, a quarter Mexican, and half God-knows-what."

Juanita had had this conversation before. She wasn't going to be sucked into it. Danny appeared to be fishing around for a potential argument to alleviate his boredom.

"My dad was Cherokee, and that makes me Cherokee, and it makes you Cherokee if you want to be," Juanita said gently.

Danny shook his head. "I don't want to be."

"Why not?" Walt asked loudly, butting in like it was his business. Danny looked at Walt's place setting to see how many beers he'd had. Only one bottle of Heineken. There was no point trying to bait him. "I couldn't care less about it," Danny said, addressing his mom, not Walt. "This is the twenty-first century, we're, like, going to Mars and stuff this century, you know? That Stonehenge stuff? Nobody cares about that anymore. That's the past. It's all dead and gone."

Juanita didn't get the Stonehenge reference, and Walt just shrugged and took a bite of his tortilla. "This is delicious, honey," he said.

Later, when it was pitch-black outside and so cold it hurt your face even at the open window, Juanita came into Danny's bedroom.

Jeffrey jumped onto her lap and she stroked him absently and looked at Danny until he put down the copy of *Surfer* magazine.

"What?" he said.

"Nothing. How was your day?" Juanita asked.

"Fine, boring."

"Are you OK, Danny?"

"I'm OK. It was kinda weird with the cops yesterday and actually going inside a prison today."

"That is weird. You should keep a journal."

His mother was always trying to get him to write and read more.

"Uh, no, I'll just check out these magazines, OK?"

"OK, I'll go," she said, and as she stood, Jeffrey hopped

off her lap. She walked over to the door, turned the handle. Danny didn't want her to go just yet. "Oh, Mom, can you tell me about La Llorona? The Cherokee La Llorona," he asked casually while turning the page of his magazine.

"La Llorona? Aren't you too old to believe in that nonsense?" Juanita said.

"Of course, but I was just wondering . . ."

"Well, I don't really know that much about it. You should ask your aunts if you want the real story . . ."

"What do you know?"

"OK, um, well, when the Cherokee came to the mountains, they found a race of people already living here. But gradually the spirits fled, and when the white men came, they were all gone, except for La Llorona, the mother goddess, who haunted the mountains."

"That's not the bit I want to hear about," Danny interrupted. "Tell me about the cat. There's a bit about a cat, isn't there?"

"A lynx took her baby. You know what a lynx is?"

"Of course."

"She hated cats. She killed cats wherever she could find them."

"That's what I thought."

"What put this into your head?" Juanita asked, ruffling his hair.

"Nothing, really . . . That girl across the street, she's sort of a bit weird-looking, but Jeffrey went right over to her, so she can't be bad."

Juanita nodded. Danny had not yet had a real girlfriend, but this was the sort of confused thinking she was expecting to see when a girl he liked appeared on the scene.

She smiled and said nothing and left.

Danny lay for a while and turned off the light.

That night his dreams were vivid.

He thought of the men in the prison. He thought of the girl next door. He thought of the spirit men of the mountains.

He woke shivering. Freezing. He had left his window open and snow was coming in. "Jeff?" he said, half expecting to see him, hackles up, backed into a corner, terrified at some unseen creature.

But Jeff was still sleeping peacefully at the bottom of his bed, untroubled by coyotes or bears or snow or anything else.

The house was quiet.

Danny looked out at the blackness of the woods. Not a single light anywhere. A dark world, strange, unknown, almost unknowable.

The hairs on his neck were pricking up. "Calm down," he whispered to himself. "There's nothing out there."

He closed the window and pulled across the heavy blue curtains. Everything was normal, everything was as it should be. And yet he couldn't shake the feeling that something *was* there, something—or someone—was watching, waiting . . .

Letter II

I was walking in a field once after the spring thaw. A buried electricity cable had become unearthed. Five cows were lying dead next to the cable. They had mistaken it for a salt lick. I tried to imagine the scene. First one cow licks the cable and is electrocuted. The others are perhaps alarmed, but then they forget and one by one they too try the new salt lick. None of them learned from the other's misfortune. None of them tried to avoid death. Their dead eyes were black and vacant. They communicated no mystery.

I paid a visit to a slaughterhouse after that. Have you ever been? On a school trip, perhaps? The cows walk placidly to their fate. True, some appear to be nervous, but there is seldom panic. The stun gun is very loud, but they grow used to it.

We are like that.

The great herd of humanity walks unthinkingly through life to their eventual annihilation.

No one warns the person behind them in the line that the great silence is coming like an eclipse, like an oil slick, like an executioner. Down into the trapdoor floor we all go, hooded, gagged, screaming. Into the great dark. Into the nothing.

You, I feel, understand this.

You are different from the others.

You have potential.

I've got my eye on you.

SIX

Direct Instruction

The windows of Mr. Lebkuchen's office were tinted so that
it was difficult to see through them to what would have
been a spectacular view of Pikes Peak beyond. The room
was bare but for a few esoteric charts and a pristine wooden
desk behind which Mr. Lebkuchen sat in an uncomfortable-
looking ergonomic chair. Danny fidgeted in his school
uniform of black blazer, black pants, white shirt, green
tie, black socks, black shoes. He actually didn't mind the
uniform too much. Although he hadn't worn a uniform at
Grover Cleveland, he had at the Las Vegas Primary School
for the Arts. He was only fidgeting because this interview
had been going on for almost fifteen minutes now, mostly
with Mr. Lebkuchen talking about how extraordinary it
was to accept a student in the middle of the year and if it

hadn't been for the personal intervention of Juanita's boss, Mr. Glynn . . .

Danny's parents were on either side of him. His mom in her smart work clothes and Walt—incredibly—in a suit and tie, the first time Danny had seen him so attired since the wedding. He'd even shaved and tied his graying hair in a ponytail behind his head.

Danny was uneasy. Mr. Lebkuchen looked like a fairly decent guy: late twenties, close-cropped curly blond hair, blue eyes behind rimless John Lennon glasses, and a smudgy Play-Doh friendly face. He wasn't very tall, smiled a lot, and was obviously enthusiastic about his job. He was wearing white gloves, which was a bit eccentric, but the problem wasn't Mr. Lebkuchen. The problem was the words coming out of Mr. Lebkuchen's mouth.

"So you see, Mr. and Mrs. Brown, that's been Danny's main issue, I think. It's not his fault that he's not progressing; it's the fault of his teachers, the fault of the whole educational system. Here at Cobalt Junior High we use the system of Direct Instruction that was developed by Siegfried Engelmann at the University of Oregon. It's now used by two dozen charter schools across the country. Our method is a modified version of the Slavin approach from Baltimore, which has saved many failing Baltimore schools and which has been used by the Bureau of Indian Affairs to completely transform Native American schools."

Who says I'm not progressing? Danny wanted to protest, but didn't.

"How does it work?" Juanita asked.

"Well, it's very simple. Breathtakingly simple, really. Can I give you the standard school pitch? It'll sound a bit canned, but it covers everything," Mr. Lebkuchen said, rapping a gloved knuckle on the desk.

"Sure," Juanita said.

"OK. Here goes. Cobalt Junior High Charter School is a publicly funded, tuition-free charter school running the DI system. Founded in 2008, our school serves students from Cobalt, Manitou Springs, and the entire Colorado Springs area. The mission of CJHCS is to provide a content-rich, academically rigorous education with a well-defined, sequential curriculum in a safe, orderly, and caring environment. With an initial intake of just forty, now we have three grades, one hundred students, and are oversubscribed by fifty percent—in just three short years we've become one of the best public schools in the state."

Mr. Lebkuchen gasped for breath and pretended to wipe sweat from his forehead.

"Got that? OK then, pitch over, now the basics of DI. All our lessons, every day, are planned in advance. Planned and printed by the Association of DI Schools. Teachers read from a set script, and the children follow along from a script of their own. This is the Direct Instruction method. It sounds strange, but it's been tested and it's foolproof. Our results speak for themselves. It's a little bit hard to describe, so let me show you one of our books," Lebkuchen said, passing across a reading booklet for the month of January. Every lesson was indeed laid out in advance: what the teacher had to say in one script in red and what the children had to do in blue. Juanita passed it to Walt, who passed it to Danny, who passed it to an invisible shredder on Mr. Lebkuchen's desk.

"We do intensive reading, mathematics, science, history, and geography," Lebkuchen continued. "No music, no art, no dance, no silly subjects. We do the three Rs here. By law we are not allowed to teach religious instruction, and by law we have to do PE, but I think that a lot of that is wasted time, especially since we don't have a gym, and we've got to minibus the kids into Colorado Springs."

"No music?" Walt said, aghast.

"No, Mr. Brown, kids can do that on their own time. However, we are starting an extensive after-school program that includes music and art."

"Oh, well, that's OK then," Walt said, relieved.

"We begin the day with two hours of reading. Then we have a spelling and vocabulary test. Then mathematics. More reading. Social sciences, more reading."

"That sounds wonderful," Juanita said, and for some reason added in a whisper, "Danny is not a big reader at the moment."

Danny felt betrayed by this and looked at the floor. Mr. Lebkuchen smiled. "He will be. We're only a junior high, so we appreciate that we'll be losing Danny in June, but by that time he will be among the elite readers for his grade in this state," Mr. Lebkuchen said confidently.

"Well, that all seems great," Walt said.

"Excuse me just one moment," Lebkuchen said. He lifted a microphone and CD player from beneath his desk and put them in front of him. He turned on the microphone and a mild feedback loop went through the school. He inserted Aaron Copland's "Fanfare for the Common Man" into the CD player, and it began playing through the school's loudspeakers. When it reached its climax, Mr. Lebkuchen read from a piece of paper: "Math stars for the second week of January: Jane Morris 7A, Peter Farthing 8A, Marcella Hernandez 9A . . . well done, everyone. I expect that you all will continue to work hard."

He turned off the microphone, put the CD player back beneath his desk, and smiled. "Our math stars," he said, slightly apologetically.

"Yes," Juanita said and, looking at Danny, added, "Maybe that will be you in a couple of weeks."

Nothing could have excited Danny less, but he nodded and faked a smile.

"Now, you may have noticed how quiet it is in our school. We run the silent system here. No talking is allowed at any time—not in the classroom, not in the corridors, not at recess. The only communication is vertically, between student and teacher and between teachers and me. I don't permit triangulation, and by that I mean horizontal communication between students or even between teachers. Danny, if you have a complaint or a problem, bring it to me, and I will deal with it."

"The kids aren't allowed to talk to one another?" Walt

said, not entirely sure he had understood what Mr. Lebkuchen was saying.

"Precisely. School is for work. They can talk or play as much as they like outside these walls, but from nine until three thirty, they are here to work. No triangulation means increased focus on what they are here to do."

"Do you find, I mean, do the kids . . . silence seems . . ." Danny's mom couldn't phrase her objection the way she wanted to, and her voice trailed off.

Mr. Lebkuchen smiled. "It takes some getting used to, of course. It's harder on the teachers, actually."

"The teachers have to be quiet too?" Walt asked.

"Oh yes. You could hear a pin drop in this school. And in the staff room, the lunchroom . . . it's wonderful. We have almost no discipline problems; silence, it turns out, is conducive to work. That's why the monastic model worked so well, and I think that's why they used to have signs that said 'Shh' in libraries. Of course, nowadays you can't hear yourself think over the noise of iPods and computers in public libraries. No iPods allowed in the school, by the way. OK, young man? I'm sure you've got one?"

Danny nodded.

"Well, none here, please. And no phones. Not that they would work anyway."

"What do you mean?" Walt asked.

"It was an idea I took from the Denver Public Library. They have a cell-phone jammer to stop people from talking on their phones inside the building. I mean, kids are kids of course, and they'll always find a way around any system."

"I'm still not getting it," Walt said.

"We discovered that they were texting each other on their cell phones, but now we've installed a jammer and put a stop to that."

"Oh, I see," Walt said.

"We're still a new school, so some of the things we're trying are probably going to seem strange." Mr. Lebkuchen's cheeks colored slightly as he explained. "For example, one of the ideas we took from the Baltimore pilot project was the gloves."

He twiddled his fingers for a moment.

"Gloves?" Juanita asked.

"Yes, all our students wear white gloves all the time. We can spot immediately children who have been playing in the dirt or (excuse my coarseness) picking their noses. The gloves promote hygiene, discipline, and responsibility. You'd be surprised how this one little cosmetic change can transform an environment. Of course, many public schools have a uniform code these days, but we're only one of half a dozen in North America whose code includes gloves."

Juanita looked skeptical and Mr. Lebkuchen, smiling, picked up on that. "As I've said, it may seem strange, but our results speak for themselves. We tested twelfth in the country in the Uniform Reading Test. Twelfth in the country! And that was against private schools. We beat

Phillips Exeter, Colorado Academy . . . many others. In June last year we got a citation for excellence from First Lady Michelle Obama. And remember, many of our children could barely read at all when they came here."

Juanita nodded, but Walt had decided that he didn't like Mr. Lebkuchen or his school or his methods. The lack of music, the uniforms, gloves, silence, scripts for teachers . . . by themselves that didn't amount to much, but taken as a whole it was over-the-top. He knew he'd only get one go at this, so he launched an attack that he knew might hit home with Juanita. "That's all very well, Principal Lebkuchen, and strangely enough I went to Phillips Exeter myself, but one of the things I didn't appreciate at that school was its lack of diversity. One thousand little white boys does not reflect America."

Mr. Lebkuchen smiled and shook his head. "Oh, I completely agree. First of all, we're a small school. Danny will be our hundredth pupil, I believe. I know all of them by name, most of their parents by name too. And we're coed here. Girls and boys are going to have to work together in the real world, so why shouldn't they start in school? And thirdly, we are very diverse. We're about ten percent Latino, we have Native American students from the Cherokee and Ute Nations, and we also have a couple of African American kids from Colorado Springs."

"Hmm," Walt said as Juanita patted him on the leg.

"And what's your background, if you don't mind me asking?" Walt wondered.

"Mixed-up!" Mr. Lebkuchen said with a laugh. "I was born at the hospital in Fort Carson, Colorado, not a million miles from here—my father was in the US Army—and I actually spent my early years in Okinawa, Japan."

"How lovely," Juanita said, embarrassed by Walt's question.

"It was certainly an experience. Anyway, after Japan we ended up in Denver; I went to East High School and then Columbia University and Teachers College in New York. I taught in the New York City public schools for three years before coming back to Colorado. I did some private tutoring and then I found out about this place, the old Cobalt Tesla Elementary, which had closed down in the late 2000s because of a lack of students."

"It seems to be doing OK now," Juanita said.

"Yes! Before we opened, most Cobalt and Manitou parents wanted to send their kids to one of the bigger schools in the Springs, but now my phone is ringing off the hook with parents from as far away as Denver who want to send their children here."

"We're very grateful you took Danny," Juanita said.

"You can thank Mr. Glynn for that. He's sponsored our school since the beginning."

Yeah, ever since he wanted to build a casino just up the road, Danny thought.

They talked for five more minutes, Mr. Lebkuchen explaining homework, demerits, notes for being late, notes for illnesses, and so on. Juanita and Walt assured the principal that Danny would be good, would come on time, and would do his homework. Mr. Lebkuchen said that he was sure that Danny would be an asset to the school and soon he would become a math star or a reading star or both.

Mr. Lebkuchen gave him a pair of white gloves to put on. Thus ridiculously clad, Danny was taken, along with his parents, down a pristine corridor decorated with the kind of watercolor landscapes you saw in cancer wards or insane asylums.

They stopped outside 9B and Mr. Lebkuchen said, "Miss Benson's great . . . you'll like her."

He entered without knocking. All the students immediately stood up.

"Sit, sit," Mr. Lebkuchen said affably.

"Good morning, Miss Benson," Mr. Lebkuchen said.

"Good morning, Principal Lebkuchen," Miss Benson replied.

Room 9B was an airy space that faced the playground and the mountains. Miss Benson was a forty-year-old white lady with brown eyes, brown glasses, and black hair cut medium length. She had an unmemorable face but spoke with a Southern twang that Danny found pleasing.

"We have a new student, Miss Benson. I trust that you can accommodate him," Mr. Lebkuchen said.

"Of course, Principal Lebkuchen."

There were about fifteen kids in the class. Danny recognized Tony, but when he gave her a little wave she did not wave back.

"Boys and girls, this is Daniel Brown," Principal Lebkuchen said, getting both parts of his name wrong. "He has recently moved here from Nevada. This is his first day, and I'm sure you'll treat him with the respect and warmth we've all come to expect from students of CJHCS. Miss Benson, over to you. I suggest you hand him a workbook and throw him right in at the deep end."

"Thank you, Principal Lebkuchen," Miss Benson said, and gave him a little nod of the head. Mr. Lebkuchen ushered Juanita and Walt to the door.

"*Bye, love you,*" Danny's mom mouthed as they left.

"Welcome to 9B. Sit down here, please," Miss Benson said, pointing to a desk directly in front of her, where he couldn't really see any of his fellow students. He was given the reading script for the day and in a minute he was following along.

They were reading *Oliver Twist*, which, apparently, was about a boy who lived in England ages ago.

The class was pretty straightforward. Each student took a turn reading out loud, and the teacher asked pre-prepared questions about nouns, verbs, vocabulary. You could read the questions in advance, so you'd have to be particularly dense to get one wrong—especially the vocabulary ones.

When it was Danny's turn to read, he had no trouble. Miss Benson asked him to speak up a bit, but that was about it.

After an hour of this, at exactly twelve o'clock, it was

lunchtime. There were no bells. Kids filed silently out of class and walked on the right-hand side of the corridor to the canteen.

Danny sat with his class at a long table, and the table server went up and brought back the same food for everyone, plus a juice box of either apple or orange juice. The only words spoken in the whole canteen were the servers asking kids in turn if they wanted apple or orange juice and the kids saying "orange" or "apple" in a weird whisper.

No one started eating until all the kids had been served and when one of the lunch ladies rang a handbell. Then everyone noiselessly began.

Lunch that day was chicken breast, boiled potatoes, collard greens, and a fruit salad for dessert. This is worse than the prison I was in yesterday, Danny thought, but of course, like everyone else, he said nothing.

The teachers sat in the same hall as the kids and ate the same food and they, too, said nothing, but they at least were permitted to read a book or a newspaper.

A little dark-haired, moonfaced kid was sitting opposite Danny. The kid was pale, scrawny, and fidgety with squat, toothbrushy eyebrows. When Danny looked up from his meal, the kid nodded to him significantly. Danny didn't know what to make of it, so he just nodded back.

One table over, Tony finally gave him a wave. Danny grinned and returned the wave, relieved that he hadn't been getting snubbed earlier. Tony's hair was combed into a straight bob. He was surprised to find that he liked it much better than when it was all spiky the day before. In fact, he discovered Tony was actually very pretty.

When everyone had finished their food, the kids filed out of the canteen into the playground, leaving the servers to clean the table.

The playground was little bigger than a couple of basketball courts. Some of the boys began kicking a soccer ball around; some of the girls played with them or played their own game, which was like a cross between hopscotch and freeze tag. Many of the seventh-graders went over to a small jungle gym that had swings, a slide, and a climbing wall; some of the kids just sat down and read.

Danny shivered. The sun was shining but it was still quite cold, at least for him.

"Man, this sucks," he said to himself.

The Las Vegas Primary School for the Arts, where he'd gone for a couple of semesters (until they'd kicked him out for not doing his drawing assignments), had even had a skate park on the grounds, where he could practice his moves at lunchtime.

There was no question of even free skating around this place.

At least he could see the supposedly famous mountain of Pikes Peak as it loomed ominously over the playground, its whole top third covered with snow.

The rest of the view was impressive too. The sky was clear and he could see the Front Range curving south, he imagined, all the way to New Mexico.

"I wish I was in New Mexico right now," he muttered. "New Mexico or real Mexico or anywhere."

A shadow in front of him.

The scrawny little moonfaced kid again.

"Yeah?" Danny said.

The kid gave him something.

"What's this?" Danny whispered. The kid put his fingers to his lips and pointed to the teachers on playground duty gloomily walking around.

Danny gave him the thumbs-up sign and the kid walked away.

Danny looked at the object in his hand.

It seemed a bit like an old-fashioned pager, with a small screen and beneath that nine alphanumeric buttons like on a cell phone.

Letters began appearing on the screen. It was a text.

trn yr back frm t tchrs & othr kds go t fir tree nr t fence!

Danny understood. Turn your back from the other kids and the teachers. He walked to what he hoped was a fir tree near the perimeter fence.

More text:

gd. hi im tom tony sz yr cool u cn txt me bk using t keys, kp yr bk trnd frm tchrs & othr kids, kp an eye out, blue bttn is snd.

Danny knew what to do. He had texted frequently on his mobile phone, but this was a little more difficult, especially with the stupid gloves on.

this place is crzy, tom, he keyed, and hit the blue button. Tom smiled at him.

u don knw t hlf of it kid, Tom texted.

They spent the entire break secretly texting each other. Danny had the feeling that Tom was texting other kids, too, perhaps letting them share in the conversation. He didn't mind. He'd been in enough schools to know that there were few secrets. He supposed it was like being on a ship; very soon, everybody knew everything about everybody else. The quicker the illusion of privacy got broken, the better.

Tony, however, did not appear to join in the conversation, because she was playing some kind of elaborate skipping game with a group of girls.

Danny told Tom he was an only child from Las Vegas and his name was really Lopez. Danny learned that Tom was also an only child, from Colorado Springs. Tom's dad was a lawyer but also a reservist in the Judge Advocate General's Office who'd recently been called up and sent to Afghanistan, which Danny thought was bad-ass.

As break was coming to an end, the kids began lining up at the edge of the playground in their classes. 9A, 9B, 8A, 8B, 7A, 7B.

When recess was finally over, a teacher gently blew a whistle and everyone went quietly back to class.

It was history after lunch, and Danny and the rest of the kids spent the time memorizing the names of sixteenth-century explorers.

At the end of the day, they picked up *Oliver Twist* where

they'd left off, and finally at three thirty sharp, Miss Benson said, "Thank you, children. Don't forget to read pages sixty through eighty for homework. We will be having our usual pop quiz tomorrow. Get home safe, be respectful to your parents, and I will see you here on Tuesday."

Danny threw his stuff into his bag and was about to run out of the class, but of course there was a system for that, too. The children left in rows, starting from the window. Sitting in front of Miss Benson's desk, he was one of the last to leave and both Tony and Tom had gone before him.

He hugged the right-hand wall and followed the mass of pupils to the entrance. As he walked through the big wooden double exit door, he—like almost every kid there—exhaled.

There were school buses for kids who lived in Manitou Springs and Colorado Springs but not for the local students. His mom had offered to meet him, but Danny had figured out the geography of Cobalt pretty quickly. There were only half a dozen streets in the whole town, and it was a short walk home. He pulled the stupid gloves off his hands and shoved them in his pockets and then loosened his tie and top button.

Left, he thought, up the hill, and then the first right at the—

"Hi," Tony said.

Hearing a voice after all that quiet startled him.

Nonplussed, he turned and then smiled at her. "Hi," he

replied. "That pager thing that Tom gave me was pretty awesome—"

Tony shook her head and said in a whisper, "Let's not discuss that here. We can talk on the way."

To avoid the big bend on Alameda they took a shortcut back across the school playground, but this was a move that apparently had been anticipated. Before they could reach the gate at the far side of the basketball court a tall boy with a long face, light brown hair, and a mouth full of big tombstone teeth grabbed Danny by the arm and began dragging him to a school building. The boy had a tan line across his face where his baseball cap had stopped, and he looked uncomfortably like one of those zebras that just stare at you in the San Diego Zoo. "This way," the boy said.

"What do you think you're doing?" Danny cried, but the boy had gigantic fingers and a powerful grip.

Danny knew he was outgunned. He was a little small for his age, and this kid was massive. He pulled down with his wrists and tried to kick him, but it didn't do any good.

"Leave him alone, Todd!" Tony protested.

Todd ignored her.

Danny let himself be led. He had been in this precise situation before, and it held few terrors for him now.

Waiting around the back of the building were three more kids. A girl from 9A with red hair in pigtails, very pale skin, and a rodentlike cast to her face, and two snarky-looking boys from 9B (his own class). One had green eyes and Flight of the Conchords specs and black hair combed rigidly across his forehead in an old-fashioned kind of way. Not a nice face—the face of a farter who always blames it on the kid sitting next to him. The other boy was tall with blond hair and dark brown eyes.

"So you're in trouble already," the boy with the glasses said.

"Stop it, Hector. Leave him alone!" Tony said.

"You keep out of this!" the redheaded girl muttered.

Danny got one arm free from Todd and tried to free the other by pulling down hard.

"Hold his arms, Todd," the second boy from 9B said, and Todd grabbed Danny's wrists in one of his big paws and pinned them behind his back.

"What are you doing, man?" Danny yelled. "Don't touch me!"

The second boy searched in Danny's pockets and came out with a couple of bucks, a pen, a set of keys, and the text-messaging pager that Tom had given him. The boy threw the money and the pen on the ground and put the pager in his pocket. He turned to Tony. "Now we can read whatever you send. So your little lame-ass group of losers better watch its step!"

"Charlie, leave him alone. Hector, tell Charlie to give him that back," Tony attempted.

Hector looked a little embarrassed. "You can't really take his stuff, Charlie," he said.

"I'll take whatever I want," Charlie said.

"He'll take whatever he wants," the girl echoed in a high-pitched, mocking voice.

"You better watch out, Rebecca!" Tony said, her face red with fury.

Tony stared at Rebecca, Danny struggled against Todd, and Todd stared into space like a character in a TV show whose lines were finished.

"What is going on here?"

A deep, furious voice.

Everyone turned. One of the teachers was looking at them. Danny opened his mouth to speak, then checked himself, remembering that he was still on school grounds.

"What is going on here?!" the teacher demanded again.

None of the other kids felt that they could speak either.

"You can talk!" the teacher said. He was an older man with a red beard and a crumpled checked suit.

"Sir, we're not allowed to talk to you; that would be triangulating," Rebecca said.

The teacher looked furious. "You! Let him go," he said to Todd.

Todd released Danny's arms.

"Now, you. What's your name?" the teacher asked Danny.

"Danny Lopez," Danny said. "I'm new."

"What's going on here, Danny?" the teacher asked.

"Nothing. We were playing," Danny muttered.

"Yeah, we were just playing," Rebecca said in that

annoying singsong voice that would have gotten her a slap in the face if she'd been at Grover Cleveland.

"Come on, Danny, let's go," Tony said, and led him away from the others.

They exited through the rear gate, and when they were clear of the school and halfway up Alameda she stopped and looked at him.

"Are you OK?" she asked.

Danny kept walking and she ran to catch up. "Are you OK?" she asked again.

"I'm fine."

"Don't worry about those guys. Hector and Charlie think they're tough, but they're not."

"Hector and Charlie are the ones from our class?"

"Yeah. Todd's from 8B and Rebecca's from 8A. Tom's been keeping an eye on them, don't worry . . . we're on top of it. We think there's about a dozen of them altogether. They've got a secret club. It's so lame. We think Charlie's running it."

"Charlie's the blond one?"

"Yeah. He thinks he's so handsome. I guess he is, in a cartoony kind of way, like Fred from *Scooby-Doo* or something."

"They're in a secret club?"

"Yeah, can you imagine? Lame City. You can see them on the playground acting all dorky. They have their own sign language. *Sign language* . . . I mean, like, how sad can you get? We're miles ahead of them."

"How many are in *your* secret group?" Danny said, with a slight mocking edge to his voice.

"Not as many as them, but we're more exclusive. There's me and Tom, and Olivia Quintera and Cooper Reid and you, and I think Carol Brennan left. She and Tom fell out or something. I don't know about her."

"But haven't I screwed it up for you guys now? Now they've got the pager; they'll be able to read *your* texts. Your whole communication system is ruined."

Tony laughed. "No, they won't be able to do anything. I'll call Tom tonight and he'll sync a different encryption system and when they try to read our texts tomorrow they'll just get junk. Might even be funny to watch them."

Tony smiled and gave him a little punch on the shoulder.

She wanted Danny to laugh, but he didn't feel like laughing. This was all a bit much for him to take in—secret societies with different ways of communicating, bullies, reading programs, silence, scripts, gloves, and all this on his first day. His head was pounding and he felt humiliated. He'd been roughed up in front of two girls.

He blinked hard. Oh no. He actually felt like he was going to cry.

All he wanted to do was get away. From school, from Tony, from Colorado.

She was talking. Her lips were moving, but the drumming in his head was so loud he didn't hear what she was saying.

He rubbed his eyes, took a deep breath. This was not the time to ride the pity pony. He couldn't run away—they both took the same route home—he had to keep it together until he got to the house. Then he could go to his room, close the door . . .

Tony continued with her explanation of whatever it was she was explaining. "There's only six of us, and we're all in 9B. We don't have anyone in grade eight or seven, but their club is mostly grades seven and eight. Olivia thinks—"

"Who's Olivia?"

"She was sitting behind you."

"I didn't notice her. I was afraid to look back."

Tony laughed, and her laugh made him feel a little better. "Oh, you can look back. Miss Benson—her name's Laura, by the way—she only pretends to follow along in the book; she's really reading a magazine behind her desk. Usually *People*."

"So who was that big red-shirt guy?"

"Oh, don't worry about him. He's OK. His dad's a janitor at the MFC."

"What's that?"

"Metropolitan Faith Cathedral. It's the big church around here. My parents go there too. Actually, I go there with them. Lots of people do. My dad's an elder. Don't worry about it. Don't worry about any of it."

"What about those other kids?"

"Hector's OK, really. Don't stress about him. Not as smart as Tom. He's OK. But Charlie . . . He thinks he's made of awesome. He's from South Carolina or somewhere originally. Transferred here from Citadel Prep last term. By the way, if you want to get on his nerves, ask him what his dad does."

"What does his dad do?"

Tony grinned. "He runs the *Dr. Quinn, Medicine Woman* tours of Colorado Springs. Drives people around in the bus."

"Dr. what?"

"It was a show from the nineties. They filmed in L.A., I guess, but it takes place here, so a lot of tourists come out for it. Especially from Japan. It's kind of embarrassing, really, because there's nothing to see. You know?"

They turned right on Manitou Road. The houses thinned out there and the sidewalk became narrow. Pinecones and needles crunched under their feet.

"We used to go out. Charlie and me. Not anymore. I'm so over him," Tony said, and continued to disprove this by talking about Charlie until Manitou Road bent to the left and the houses began again.

"Hey, what's that?" Tony asked.

There was a work crew up ahead. Tony was looking at them in fascination, and as she did so Danny examined her. Her neck had a little mole on it just beneath her chin and her eyes had a strange aquamarine tinge to the irises. She caught him looking. He coughed. "So what are you saying? There's several secret clubs or something?"

"Oh yeah, about four or five. Most of them are stupid, but the SSU is pretty serious. Tom thinks—"

"Danny! Danny, over here!"

"There's someone calling you," Tony said.

It was Walt. He was standing next to a gang of six men in orange overalls, each of whom had a chain running between his ankles. The men were being watched by a prison guard in a cowboy hat who was holding a pump-action shotgun across his body and blowing bubblegum bubbles.

"Danny, over here!" Walt called again. Bob was with him, operating some kind of earth-pounding machine. Bob was also wearing a pair of orange overalls. He turned the machine off when he saw Danny.

"You better go over," Tony said.

"You go home . . . I'll talk to you later," Danny muttered quickly.

"No, I'd like to meet your dad," Tony said breezily.

"No, just go home, please," Danny insisted, but Tony was having none of it. She walked across the road, and Danny reluctantly followed.

Walt introduced himself, Bob, and the members of his work crew. The guard with the shotgun didn't seem to care that all the men had downed their tools to chat.

"This is Vern," Walt said, and Vern touched two fingers to his cowboy hat.

"Wow, so this is a real chain gang," Tony said, impressed.

Bob laughed. "Yup, I guess, technically speaking, it is, although we're not chained together; that would make it too hard to work."

"Pretty rad," Tony said.

"What do you do, young lady?" Bob asked. The sun had

brought out Bob's orange freckles and he didn't look much like a hardened con.

She grinned. "I'm at junior high!"

"Junior high? I felt sure you were a doctor or a lawyer or something," Bob said.

"No, not yet, but my dad works at NORAD."

"Really? NORAD? He ever see any UFOs? I hear they track lots of UFOs there all the time," Bob said.

"He's not allowed to talk about it," Tony said happily.

"You're one of the prisoners?" Danny asked Bob, feeling both horrified and also a little bit impressed. He'd thought Bob was a warden or a foreman or something.

"Yup," Bob said.

"Is this your boy, Walt?" one of the other convicts asked. A big guy with a beard and a New York accent.

"Yes, this is my son, Danny," Walt replied.

"No, I'm not," Danny muttered inaudibly.

"So, Danny, how was your first day at school?" Walt asked.

By now Danny's cheeks were burning. His father worked with criminals. Tony's father worked at NORAD. The criminals were talking to Tony. There was a man guarding them with a shotgun.

"It was OK," Danny said.

"I remember my first day at school—many first days at many schools—it's always a bitch . . . oh, 'scuse my French, young lady," Bob said.

"Don't worry about me," Tony said.

"You're in Danny's class?" Walt asked.

"Yes, we live opposite you," Tony said.

Walt turned to Bob. "These kids are at Cobalt Junior High. It's a charter school, supposed to be one of the best in the country," he said with pride.

Bob nodded. "Yeah, I know the place . . . or rather, I know of it. I've never actually been to Colorado Springs, despite living here for the last five years," Bob said, and winked at them.

"How do you know about it?" Tony asked.

"There's still a gigantic Tesla coil in there, isn't there? One of the biggest in the country. I don't think they've taken it out," Bob said.

"Oh, that thing. Yeah, it's still there in the science room. It looks weird. Our science teacher, Mr. Burke, loves it," Tony said.

"What's a Tesla coil?" one of the other men asked.

"Uh, we should probably be heading on now. We've got *Oliver Twist* to read and I'm real excited to see if he manages to get more gruel," Danny said.

Walt nodded. "Oh yeah, of course, homework . . . and actually, you know, we should be getting back to it, right, Vern?"

"I suppose so," Vern said unenthusiastically.

The men nodded and grunted in agreement.

"Bye!" Bob and Walt said almost simultaneously.

"Be careful on the roads," Walt said.

"Be better than careful," Bob said. "Be smart."

"Bye," Tony replied.

Danny said nothing. He led Tony quickly back to the sidewalk as the sound of pneumatic machines shattered the quiet of the Colorado day.

"That was cool seeing your dad like that," Tony said.

"Uh-huh," Danny muttered.

"I liked that Bob guy, he was funny," Tony said.

"Was he?" Danny said, and lapsed into silence for the rest of the walk home.

When they came to Johnson Close, their own little cul-de-sac, Tony sensed that Danny wanted to be by himself. He'd seemed OK, but now she wondered if she'd done the right thing, telling Tom to let him into the Watchers. Danny was a bit moody and they couldn't kick him out now that he'd taken one for the team at the hands of Charlie and Todd. But then again, maybe it was just first-day blues.

She said good-bye to him and walked up her garden path.

"Bye," Danny said quietly.

He hadn't meant to be weird. He'd been looking at the road, thinking.

Now that he could evaluate the blacktop, he saw that the sidewalks weren't great but the roads were new and freshly laid.

He rummaged in his pocket, found the front-door key, and went inside his house.

He knew there was homework, but he didn't feel like homework. His computer hadn't arrived yet, nor his Xbox. They didn't even have TV.

He checked the weather. A slab of gray cloud was covering the entire sky, the ceiling a few hundred feet above his head. It looked like it might snow, but it didn't matter. He had to get out. He stripped off the awful uniform, pulled on his black jean shorts, his Raiders beanie, his red Converse high-tops, his brown hoodie. He looked at himself in the mirror on the back of the dresser. His bangs were almost covering his brown eyes. He wondered if he was good-looking. He was small and dark. Certainly not up there with the likes of Charlie, but definitely more handsome than that Tom dude.

"Jeff!" he called, but Jeffrey was sleeping.

He went upstairs and got Sunflower.

He took it outside and pulled the beanie low over his eyes.

"To hell with all of them," he said, and pushed off.

He skated downhill from Johnson Close to Manitou Road. His father's work crew had moved on, so he didn't have to deliberately ignore them. He flipped his iPod to a '90s shuffle and heard songs he didn't know by Pavement and They Might Be Giants.

He skated a long time. From Manitou Road to Alameda and all the way out of town.

He skated for miles.

He skated until he forgot about being roughed up.

Until he forgot about the chain gang.

Until he forgot about the school.

He skated east through Manitou Springs along West Colorado Avenue. He skated over the Monument Valley

Freeway and Fountain Creek. He skated deep into the Springs, all the way to the Greyhound terminal on South Weber Street.

The sidewalks here were wide and they had Starbucks and diners and coffee shops and pubs, but he kept going east on Pikes Peak Avenue past a school for the blind and a big park that had a massive memorial to all the fallen firefighters of America. He kept going east past a couple of charter schools and then, because it was getting dark, he changed direction and went north and west, past the US Olympic Training Center and finally back downtown to the Greyhound bus depot.

Light snow was falling now and a bus was idling in the parking lot with a sign above the driver's seat that said LOS ANGELES.

The driver himself was outside smoking with a couple of passengers, everyone coughing in the cold night air.

How easy it would be to slip onboard.

To take a seat at the back, to sit there with his beanie pulled down, pretending to sleep. In seven or eight hours they'd be in Nevada or Arizona. Either would be fine. And maybe he could make it undiscovered all the way to the terminal in downtown L.A.

He thought about it for a moment. Aunt Ines would take him in. He'd talk to her in Spanish about the school, about the other kids, about the silence, the gloves. She'd be freaked. She'd look after him. She'd give him rice and beans, and his cousins Marco and Lucien would show him the gang signs and teach him to read the graffiti.

All he had to do was hop aboard.

He walked to the steps. Looked inside the bus. A dozen empty seats. One right at the back.

But after a full minute's hesitation, he shook his head.

No, it wouldn't do.

His mother would be scared out of her mind.

Even Walt would be upset.

And anyway, that's what a coward did—quitting school after one day because a couple of punk kids were mean to him.

The driver and the other passengers came back from their smoke break and got on board. The Greyhound's door closed with a pneumatic hiss.

Danny's cell phone rang. He was surprised. He didn't even know it worked in Colorado.

"Hello?"

"Where are you, Danny?" his mom asked, worried.

"I skated to Colorado Springs."

"That must be ten miles away! Danny, what were you thinking?"

"It's downhill and I wanted to see it."

"How will you get home? It's pitch-black out."

"I'll skate home, I'll be fine."

"Where are you, exactly? Your dad and I will pick you up."

"No, don't do that."

"It's snowing. How will you even skate in the snow?"

"Don't fuss. I'll be fine."

"Where are you? Tell me exactly where you are."

Danny sighed. It actually would be cool if his mother came for him. He was already freezing and it was uphill the whole way back.

The Greyhound bus pulled out, growling like a wounded dinosaur.

"I'm close to the bus station," Danny said. "The Greyhound bus station. If you take Colorado Avenue all the way in, I'll see you."

"We'll look it up on Google Maps. Wait for us."

He hung up and waited. Between the snow clouds, stars hung low in the pollution-free Colorado sky except in that patch of night occupied by the void of Pikes Peak.

It was quiet. The streets were empty. The stores were all closed. He felt lonely. He hadn't seen Jeffrey all day. Wasn't seeing anyone, 'cept for a random kid on a bike.

He picked up his board and hugged it.

The board was his transport but also his shield.

"Sunflower," he said to himself.

He shivered.

"The shorts were probably a mistake," he muttered to the streetlamps and the crescent moon.

He yawned.

The boy watching him yawned too.

It had been hard trailing Danny all the way from Cobalt and halfway around the Springs. Boring, too. Just for a minute there he'd thought that Danny was going to jump on the Greyhound and take it wherever it was going. (Wouldn't be the first kid who attempted to run away from home after freshman day at CJHCS.) But he hadn't. He just called someone on his phone instead.

The boy leaned against the alley wall and rubbed his mittens and stamped his feet until an SUV pulled up and Danny got inside.

"That's that, then," the boy said, and got out his own mobile phone. He speed-dialed a number. "I can't follow him anymore," the boy said. "He's in a car. Going back to Cobalt, I suppose. But I wouldn't worry about him. He doesn't seem that interesting."

He hung up the phone, tightened the scarf about his neck, turned on his bike lights, and began the long ride home.

A Conversation
with the Demons

Are they real? Sometimes he thinks they're not, that he made them up to serve his ends; other times he talks to them.

Like now.

"Out here, in the woods, I can feel you."

"We can feel you, too."

"Where are you from?"

"We're old."

"How old?"

"We've been here forever. We watched the human race grow up. We walk with you. We're behind you, in your shadow, at your back where the sun is sprawled with the red gore of the horizon."

"It's late. Let me do this quickly. I have to be getting back."

"No, tarry awhile; watch with us. Look west. Watch as the sun drowns in the penumbra of the earth's curve . . . There. Do you hear the quiet? It's nearly our time. It's nearly our time and the creatures know and they are sure afraid."

He trembles and turns on his flashlight.

The hikers are gone. The hunters are gone. The rangers are gone. Just a pair of flashlight beams and a scared reflection in the ice.

His hands are shaking. On his sleeve there's dried white spit.

"Get on with it," the Master says.

A deep breath and then he's squeezing and the cat is clawing, hissing, drowning in the air.

The cat's eyes becoming his eyes.

And in a minute it's finished. He starts to tremble all over. "And this is still only the beginning," he hears himself say.

Letter III

Do you still believe in the faerie stories, Antonia? Heaven, hell. The good guys get a prize, the bad guys get punished. It's all very convenient, isn't it? And what do they know? Those men who wrote the holy books before anyone even realized that the world was round.

No, you reject that, don't you?

Even if, as I've observed, you faithfully attend church services.

You are going through the motions, aren't you?

You are like me.

A skeptic. A doubter.

Except that I have gone deeper.

I have gone to the deepest level and I have explored the abyss and I have returned with news.

I have been where no one else has been.

I am a necronaut.

Death is not a closed box.

Yes, Death is annihilation.

For the many.

But for the few . . .

For the very few who have glimpsed the pattern?

Consider yourself fortunate that you and I have come into contact.

Luck, not brains or imagination, has been your salvation.

EIGHT

Something Wicked This Way Comes

Wind in the canyons. Wind in the sierra. Vultures rising on the thermals. Danny knew it was a dream. He'd had it before. The air was dry and carried a hint of salt. He wanted to wake up. But he couldn't. The sky was incandescent blue.

He was tired. Thirsty. He'd skated up Las Vegas Boulevard all the way to the 15.

It was two years earlier. It wasn't a dream then. It was real. It was June 20. A day before the wedding.

Hot at six A.M. The Santa Ana blowing across the Mojave.

His backpack on his shoulder. His thumb out.

The heat haze making the road bend.

A thousand vehicles passed by.

A car slowed. An old car. A '70s Chevy convertible. Red.

"Where you going, son?" a man asked, winding down the passenger-side window.

"Chicago."

"How old are you?"

"Eighteen."

"Take you as far as Salt Lake."

"OK."

Danny got in. The man was in his forties, wearing a white shirt with short sleeves and a thin black tie. He had a graying flattop. He was smoking.

Half an hour went by in highway and blue sky.

"So what's in Chicago?"

"My father. My real father. I've never actually met him. My real dad, that is," Danny confessed.

The man nodded. Drove. Adjusted his aviator sunglasses, reached into the pocket next to his seat.

This was the bad bit of the dream.

"If you could ask your real dad a question, one question, what would it be?" the man wondered.

"I don't know. I'd ask him stupid stuff, not like heavy stuff, you know."

"Like what?"

"Like, I don't know, stupid things, like I'd ask him if he thought magic really existed. I mean, what if all the magical objects on the earth were just alien technology, from some vast civilization that died out eons ago. I mean, Earth's been habitable for a couple of hundred million years, aliens are bound to have visited at some point, don't you think?"

The man smiled, drove for a while, took his sunglasses off, looked at Danny, pulled the car over to the side of the road.

"I liked your question," he said.

His eyes had narrowed. Danny noticed he was holding a small semiautomatic pistol. It was silver and Danny watched it glint in the sunlight.

"Do you believe in evil, son?" the man asked.

"I don't know," Danny said. He felt cold. Not afraid, but cold.

"I wish there were evil," the man said.

"Why?"

"Because if there were evil, at least there would be something."

The man pointed at the desert.

"You know what's out there?"

"What?"

"Indifference. Nothingness. When you die, boy, the world won't hesitate on its ellipse. On it will fall toward the sun. No one will care. Your killer will never be found. You'll be a story for a day or two, not much more."

"Mister, I—"

"Get out of the car. Go back to Vegas. It's a dangerous world, son . . . a mighty dangerous world."

The man pointed the gun at Danny.

Sometimes, in the dream, the man pulled the trigger.

"Danny."

"Uhhh."

"Danny."

Danny.

"Danny. Have you seen this?" Tony said.

"Who? What?"

"Have you seen this?" she repeated, handing him a blurry white object. Something big and noisy. Danny rubbed his eyes, sat up, checked to see that he wasn't wearing his Lily Allen T-shirt.

He wasn't.

What she was handing him turned out to be a newspaper. The *Cobalt Daily News*, a free paper that they threw on your front lawn. Juanita had quite a collection of them sitting there unwrapped in the recycle bin.

"Do you ever knock?" Danny asked, surprised to see her in his bedroom.

"No."

"Wasn't the door locked?"

"Nobody round here locks their door. My mom told your mom that, and she thought that was wonderful."

Danny didn't think it was wonderful. He'd lived in East L.A. and several parts of Las Vegas where gunshots were much more common than backfires. He liked having bars on the window and a deadbolt on the door. It made him feel secure.

"How did you find my bedroom?"

"Sense of smell."

"Funny."

Tony pulled back the curtains and, as she did so, Jeffrey jumped into her arms.

"Good girl, good girl . . . don't you worry about a thing, you're going to be OK, you're going to be fine, we're going to look after you."

"She's a he. I mean, he's a he. His name is Jeffrey. And what are you talking about?"

"Read the paper, dude, read the paper."

"Antonia, do you want breakfast?" Danny's mom yelled from the kitchen. Tony carried Jeff to the landing. "That would be lovely, Mrs. Brown," she said.

"What would you like?" Juanita asked.

"Whatever you're having."

"We're having frittata, is that OK?"

Tony's ebullience was given a momentary check. "What's a frittata?" she hissed to Danny.

"It's like an omelet. You'll like it."

"Yes, please," Tony said. And then, walking back to Danny, she said, "Well, what do you think?"

"What do I think about what?" Danny asked.

"The paper! Did you read it?"

Danny looked at the front page of the *Cobalt Daily News*. The headline said PLAN FOR SEWAGE PLANT APPROVED. Danny nodded. She was serious about odor, then, this girl. Maybe she *had* found his room by sniffing him out.

"Well, I guess it's interesting. I don't know if it's worth bursting into someone's house and waking them from a deep sleep just to tell them about it though."

Tony's nose wrinkled up in a way he found very attractive. Unfortunately the wrinkle turned into a frown, which was less becoming. In fact, it was downright intimidating. "I thought you were a different type of person," she said, and snatched the paper back.

"Breakfast, everyone," Juanita called. "Walt, we've got company, so, um, well, we've got company . . ."

"I'll see you downstairs," Tony said and, kidnapping Jeff, marched out of the room.

What's she doing here anyway? Danny thought. Isn't her own house interesting enough for her?

He went to the upstairs bathroom, washed his face, brushed his teeth, and put on his school uniform. His hair was a big black clump that rested on his head like a hat, but it could either rest to the left or the right. Right today, he thought. He combed it to the right. Which because of the mirror meant, of course, left.

When he finally made it to the breakfast table, he'd been given the smallest of four portions of the frittata.

"What a gyp," he muttered.

His mom and Walt were both dressed and ready to go.

"Is there any orange juice?" Danny asked.

"We're all out, darling," his mom said, giving him a smile. Three glasses of orange juice were in front of Juanita, Walt, and Tony.

Grumbling, Danny sat down and started hacking into the frittata with the edge of his fork.

"Your dad was telling me about Bob, that guy we met on the chain gang," Tony said.

"Oh yeah, great guy," Walt said. "You'd like him,

Juanita. He got his PhD while in prison. His degree and his PhD. Can you imagine? He's really Dr. Randall now, if you want to know."

"I was worried when I first heard about this, this chain-gang thing, but they do sound like pretty decent guys on the whole," Juanita said.

"What did he do, anyway?" Tony asked. "I mean, why is he in jail?"

"Probably killed his whole family," Danny muttered.

"No, no, we don't employ anyone like that. It's a minimum-security prison. It's all white-collar stuff. Bob's in for passing bad checks. He wouldn't have gotten so long if it hadn't been across state lines. But he's had a year remitted for good behavior, and he's out in a couple of months."

"Did you ask him about the holes in the fence? That's some prison they've got up there," Danny said.

"As long as they don't make a break for it on my watch . . . Well, Juanita, that was delicious. Let me clear the table," Walt said.

Danny rolled his eyes. The last time Walt had cleared the table was Thanksgiving.

"I'll load the dishwasher, and then we should go," Juanita said.

When they'd both gone to the kitchen, Tony whispered, "I think your dad's nice."

"You don't know anything," Danny said.

"I know more than you. You just arrived yesterday."

"Where from? Vegas, baby. And at least I got a skateboard."

"Rollerblades are cool, skateboards are passé," Tony said.

"Where's my cat? Where's Jeff?" he demanded.

"He's under my chair. Funny name for a cat."

"Not at all. I named him after Jeff Kent."

Tony's face was blank. "Who?"

"The second baseman. I played second base too. You know, Jeff Kent from the Giants? MVP? Kinda scrappy?"

"I don't follow baseball. There's not even a team in Colorado."

"Sure there is, the Rockies."

"Oh," Tony replied, utterly uninterested.

Silence.

Frittata.

That wrinkled-up nose again.

"OK, so what do you like if you don't like baseball?" Danny said, changing tack and allowing her to get in any last jab of annoyance.

Tony smiled, refused the opportunity, and said, "Ever been to a hockey game? The Avalanche are pretty cool."

"Hockey? No. It looks cool, though. I'd like to go sometime, I guess."

"Come with us next time. We get block tickets."

"What, your family?"

"Sure."

"I don't know. Uh, maybe."

Peace had broken out between them, and Tony was impressed that it had been Danny who had made the first move. Maybe she hadn't been wrong about this kid.

"Can you guys walk to school? Is it too far?" Juanita asked, looking in from the kitchen.

Danny sighed. "It's ten minutes to school, Mom . . . Two minutes if you'd let me skateboard there."

"I'm giving your father a ride. You two can come if you want."

"It's OK, Mom."

"I could drive you past the casino. You haven't seen the casino yet."

"I've seen a million casinos," Danny said.

"Yeah, but this is mine. I'm running it. I'm the manager," Juanita said, sounding a little hurt.

Danny knew he'd goofed. "Of course. I'd love to see it. Maybe on Saturday? You could give us the grand tour."

Juanita said OK and she and Walt waved good-bye.

"It's PE today, right?" Danny asked Tony.

"Yeah, and I just know that because it's sunny they're going to make us do it outside," Tony said ominously.

"That's a bad thing?"

"A very bad thing."

She was right. The sun was shining, but a cold polar wind was blowing down the Front Range as if it, too, was on the migration route from Canada to Mexico, like the voleries of geese you could see in the crisp indigo sky above Memorial Park, where PE was, off school grounds.

The girls were playing soccer under Miss Benson and another teacher Danny didn't know. The boys were playing touch football under Mr. Bradley, the gym teacher. And of course, even if they had been playing together he couldn't have talked to Tony anyway. The silence rule apparently still held sway even here, except that when you touch-tackled someone with the ball with two hands you were supposed to say "touch," and the person would stop and the ball would change possession.

Everyone had changed into shorts and sneakers, but apparently there were no facilities for showering, which discouraged you from generating a sweat and making a serious effort. And although you could take your gloves off for PE, it was so cold that no one did.

Despite his height, Danny hadn't been bad at basketball, and if they'd played a proper game of football he felt he could have shown these kids a trick or two.

"Just another twenty minutes to go," Mr. Bradley said in defiance of the general talking rule.

Danny shivered. He had never experienced cold like this. He suspected that this was probably part of the master plan. Make gym so unpopular that eventually it gets removed from the curriculum. More time for the three Rs.

A long lateral came drifting toward him out on the wing.

He tucked the ball under his arm and ran for the improvised goal line, which was really just some orange cones halfway across the park.

Todd, the red-shirt from the day before, was bearing down on him. Danny tried swerving wide, but Todd was coming like a freakin' guided missile.

"Touch," Todd said as his big hands grazed Danny's back.

"No touch!" Danny yelled, and continued sprinting for the orange cones.

"Touch!" Todd insisted, but Danny kept running for the goal. He really wanted this touchdown, and he was close. He could score easily, since all the other kids had stopped moving as soon as Todd had said "touch."

Twenty yards.

Fifteen yards.

Ten.

Kids in his peripheral vision, coming sideways toward him. Todd and that other kid, Charlie.

They weren't going to catch him.

Five yards.

Three.

Falling.

Pain.

Todd and Charlie on top of him.

"Gotcha!" Charlie said.

"This is supposed to be goddamned touch football," Danny said.

"He's talking, sir. He's swearing, sir!" Todd yelled.

Charlie had lifted the ball and was about to run it the other way. Danny grabbed his ankle and pulled him down.

Charlie rolled over and swiped at him. Danny rolled out of the way. Now Hector was there, too.

Coach Bradley blew his whistle and pointed at Danny and Charlie. "You two get back in the school bus. Wait there. Don't speak."

The bus driver opened the doors to let them in.

"Too cold, huh?" the driver said.

"Freezing," Danny said. Charlie didn't speak. He went and sat at the back. Danny sat right next to him. "How the pager work out for ya?" Danny said.

"You think you're so smart. You're not smart," Charlie hissed.

"Your dad drive a bus like this on the *Dr. Quinn* tour?"

"Who told you that?"

"Hey, can I get a discount if I bring my whole family?" Danny said.

"Aren't they all too drunk on your reservation, you Indian?!" Charlie said.

Danny laughed. "'Indian' is not a bad word, you ignorant freako."

Charlie tried to think of something else. "Who are you trying to impress with your Justin Bieber haircut? It's so gay, it's, like, gayer than the Ice Capades."

"Saying something's gay is so gay. Where are you from, the 1980s?"

Charlie shook his head but said nothing.

"Whatsamatter? Not so tough without your shadow, Big Todd, huh?" Danny said, and darted his hand toward Charlie. Charlie backed away, frightened.

"That's what I thought," Danny said with contempt.

They sat in silence while the gym class ended and the ninth grade filed back onto the bus. Charlie squeezed past Danny and went to sit next to Hector.

To get the whole ninth grade onto one bus, some of them had to sit three to a seat. But unfortunately there weren't any pleasant misunderstandings, because girls were on one side, boys on the other.

Danny supposed it was a budgetary thing. Squeeze all the kids into one bus instead of hiring two—a typical stingy move. Three to a seat, but Danny was sitting by himself until Tom plonked himself down next to him. Danny was relieved. He didn't want to become public enemy #1 in his first week. Tom didn't text him on the way back to school, but he seemed to enjoy Danny's company. Sometimes he pointed at things out the window and Danny nodded.

When they got back to CJHCS, Mr. Bradley took Danny and Charlie straight to the principal's office and knocked on the door.

"Come in," Mr. Lebkuchen said.

When the teacher and the two boys entered, Mr. Lebkuchen was in the middle of hanging a framed certificate on the wall.

EXCELLENCE IN SECONDARY TEACHING, the certificate said.

Mr. Lebkuchen turned and stared at the little group. A thin smile passed across his face.

"Mr. Bradley, what can I do for you today?"

"These boys, um, were fighting and talking," Mr. Bradley said, sotto voce.

"Leave us, Mr. Bradley," Mr. Lebkuchen said.

The gym teacher slunk out. Mr. Lebkuchen sat behind his desk.

"It's nothing to do with Charlie. It was my fault," Danny began, but Mr. Lebkuchen put his hand up to stop him.

"I don't even want to know the details. The basic fact remains that you two boys had a problem with each other and instead of taking it to me, you triangulated. Danny, what did I tell you about triangulation?"

"No triangulation."

"No triangulation, *sir*," Mr. Lebkuchen said.

"Sorry, uh, no triangulation, sir."

"Charlie, you should know better. You will have detention today. Forty minutes. I will call your mother and explain why."

"Please don't call my mom," Charlie begged.

"Silence. Danny, since this is your first week, you won't be getting detention. But I won't be so generous next time. Instead, I want you to write me out 'I will not triangulate' a hundred times. I want it by Friday assembly. Lines are frowned upon in other educational systems, but here we learn the old way. Memorization, tables, reading, writing. You will learn not to triangulate, and I will be the one who teaches you. Now, both of you go."

Mr. Lebkuchen had said all this with a calm, soft voice and with what Danny thought was a twinkle in his eye. He hated Mr. Lebkuchen's system and his school, but Danny couldn't quite bring himself to hate the man.

The boys didn't talk on the way back to Miss Benson's

class, but at the door Charlie turned to him and whispered, "You're OK."

Danny was surprised. He offered Charlie his fist.

They fist-bumped.

"You're OK too," Danny said.

"They're going to go after you now, watch out," Charlie whispered, which surprised Danny because "they" implied that Charlie wasn't in charge.

"I'll watch out," Danny said.

They went back to class.

The rest of the day dragged.

They did arithmetic problems on a sheet, which Miss Benson explained from her set script. Then it was reading time again.

Oliver Twist had become nuts. The kid had asked for more gruel and all hell had broken loose. Danny was enjoying it, although he hated the vocab quizzes and the fact that everyone had to read a bit out loud. And if Miss Benson did read magazines under her desk, she wasn't doing it today, for every time Danny tilted his head to the left or right she tapped his desk with a ruler.

This was his second day at CJHCS, and he still wasn't even sure how many kids were in his class, or who they were.

Still, it didn't matter. He was sick of them all anyway, and after lunchtime he found a place by himself on the playground and stared at the mountains. Tom was texting everyone about various theories relating to the death of the universe, but Danny didn't join in.

He actually enjoyed the silence for the rest of the day, and after school Tony found him walking home alone up Alameda.

"Are you going back to your house?" she asked.

"It's either that or back to the Bat Cave, and if I went there I'd blow my secret identity . . . Oops, I've said too much already!" he said.

Tony laughed. "Come with me, then; we're meeting at Tom Sloane's house."

"Who's 'we'?"

"Us. The Watchers. Tom, Cooper, Olivia, me, you. Carol can't come today, I honestly don't know if she's still interested."

Danny was suspicious. "It's not some kind of World of Warcraft thing, is it?"

Tony laughed. "No, no, nothing like that."

"What do you do?"

"Mostly we talk about school, we talk about the system, building the gym . . . Most importantly we collate information on the SSU. But today I'm going to bring up the news that I showed you. I think there's more to it than meets the eye."

Danny didn't fancy spending the afternoon talking about sewage plants with a bunch of geeks, but he didn't want to be completely alone in school and they were *trying* to be his friends. In his precarious state as a new boy and outsider he couldn't afford to alienate everyone, even if their interests didn't exactly intersect with his own.

"OK, I'll come," he said cheerfully.

"Great. We'll have to get the bus. Tom lives in town. We can get the twenty-two on Federal right through Manitou. A buck fifty. You'll need exact change."

Danny had forgotten to take his gloves off and now he did so with glee. He rummaged in his pockets and found half a dozen quarters.

They didn't wait long for the bus, and when it came they were the first passengers. They picked up a couple of others in Manitou, but by the time the bus dropped them at the corner of Kiowa and Williams in Colorado Springs they were the only passengers once again.

"This is us," Tony said.

They got off and walked up a steeply curving road appropriately named Hill Street to Tom's house.

At first the houses were wood, and some were in poor repair and painted odd colors—mustard, cardinal red, sky blue—which in this climate looked gloomy rather than brash, but as the incline increased the houses got bigger and farther apart and the paint jobs became a uniform white. The leaves in the yards disappeared and the wire fences were replaced with high wooden ones.

The hill was steep. A light wind was blowing from the west and snow was falling horizontally from the Front Range.

Tom lived right at the top, opposite something called the Bijou Hill Restaurant. It was a massive house in the

Southern Plantation style. It looked a bit like Monticello or one of those presidential homes, with Greek pillars, a long porch, and a manicured lawn. There were two stories and a huge converted attic with a little turret on one end, which seemed out of place with the rest of the building and reminded Danny of something from *The Munsters* or *The Addams Family*.

"Cool house, eh?" Tony said.

"Yeah. Is Tom well off?"

"Yeah, I think so . . . His dad's a lawyer."

"Really? He told me his dad was in Iraq or something."

"Afghanistan. He's an Army lawyer. JAG reservist. You know he was lieutenant governor, right?"

"Tom's dad was lieutenant governor of Colorado?"

"Yup. Only served half a term, but still . . . Impressed, aren't you?"

"Yeah, a little," Danny said. But he didn't feel impressed, only sad. Tony's father worked at NORAD, Tom's father was a famous politician now serving in Afghanistan, and Danny didn't even know who his dad was.

They rang the doorbell and while they waited Tony said, "Scope the three-sixty."

The view from where they were standing was startling. All of Colorado Springs, the plains to the east, and of course Pikes Peak with layer after layer of mountains behind.

Tom opened the front door. *"Ah, La Grande Armée est complète,"* he said.

"That's kind of a bad analogy, isn't it?" Tony said.

"Yeah, I guess," Tom admitted. "Considering what happened to the Grand Army."

Danny had no idea what they were talking about, and this annoyed him. When you invited people to your home, you didn't try to make them feel uncomfortable.

They went inside.

"You want something to drink?" Tony asked. "Tom makes a famous hot chocolate."

Danny nodded. "Whatever you're having."

"I'm having the hot chocolate. If you're making it, Tom?"

"*Mais oui,*" Tom said.

"Fine by me, then," Danny muttered.

"You take him up," Tom said.

"This way to the attic," Tony said, leading the way.

Inside, the house was a bit of a mess. Books, records, and CDs were everywhere. Antiques and souvenirs from various camping trips or something: shells, signposts, Indian rugs, ceramic jugs, even some firearms. "What is all this stuff?" Danny asked.

"Tom's mom is an antiques dealer. She has a little eBay business. You'd like her . . . Don't know where she is today. She runs the Sunday school at the church. Are you going to join our church, by the way?"

"The faith temple thing?"

"Metropolitan Faith Cathedral."

"Uh, I don't think so."

"Most of the Cobalt Junior High kids go there."

"The second good reason not to go."

A wooden, uncarpeted staircase led to Tom's room, which turned out to be the attic, the one with the turret. It was a big room with two old sofas opposite each other and at right angles to an enormous circular coffee table on which Tom had spread charts, newspapers, pens, pencils, and a laptop.

Tom's clothes were everywhere and the room had a teenage-boy funk.

The posters on the wall were a couple of years out of date and hypergeek: *Iron Man 2*, *Battlestar Galactica*, Arcade Fire, *Star Trek XI*. Hundreds of DVDs, mostly classics and sci-fi classics: *Vertigo*, *The Incredible Shrinking Man*, *Them!*, *Rear Window*, *Casablanca*, *Forbidden Planet*, *A Matter of Life and Death*. The enormous bookcase on the far wall had maybe a thousand books in it. Danny had never seen so many books outside of a library. Who had the time to read all of those? There were also dozens of computers and computer parts all over the room. Old Commodores, Macs and PCs, and new laptops. The bedsheets were black, and next to the bed there was a picture of Tom with his older brother, John, on some fishing trip. Danny liked the room enormously—it was like a villain's lair in a Bond movie.

There were two other kids in the attic: Cooper and Olivia, both of whom were still in their school uniforms. Olivia hadn't even taken her gloves off. Cooper was a skinny boy with wiry red hair and big jug ears that would forever condemn him to the role of comic foil if he ever wanted a career in Hollywood. Olivia was a different kettle of fish entirely. She was obviously Spanish, with black hair cut into an old-fashioned bob, brown eyes, prominent cheekbones, and a rounded chin that reminded Danny of the stern end of his skateboard—high praise indeed. She was shy, and when Danny said hello she only nodded. She was very pretty, though—more so than Tony—more of a real girl, not a tomboy.

Everyone finished saying hi and Cooper said, "Have you seen the camera obscura?"

"The what now?" Danny said.

"No, Cooper, Tom doesn't like us messing with it," Olivia said.

Ignoring her, Cooper pulled shut the heavy curtains, took a lens cap off a box in the ceiling Danny hadn't noticed before, and suddenly the world outside was projected onto the coffee table.

"Wow!" Danny said. But suddenly Cooper heard Tom's footsteps on the stairs and, in a panicky rush, pulled open the curtains and put the lens back on the camera obscura.

Tom appeared with five hot chocolates.

"My speciality. An original Mayan recipe. Actually, the only thing I can make," Tom said.

Danny took a mug and contrived to sit next to Olivia on the two-seater sofa while Tom sat with Cooper and Tony on the three-seater.

After everyone had taken a sip of incredibly good homemade hot chocolate, Tom said, "Everyone, this is

Danny. Danny's from Las Vegas. For those of you who didn't witness it, Danny has already proved a valiant, worthy addition to the Watchers, taking down Todd Gilchrist and absorbing the wrath of Principal Honey Cake."

Does he always talk like this? Danny wanted to ask Tony, but instead he just smiled and looked modest.

"OK, down to business. Charlie attempted to acquire one of our communication devices, but of course I outgeneralled him. I changed the encryption software, and his device became useless. Still, the pagers don't grow on trees. Tony, did you tell him about dues?"

Tony shook her head.

"Danny," Tom continued, "it's twenty bucks to join, and you owe me fifteen for the pager. We'll write off the one you lost."

Danny was surprised by this, but not shocked; he'd seen plenty of rich people in Vegas and a lot of them acted very cheap.

"I don't have thirty bucks on me," he said.

"Thirty-five," Tom said briskly. "But no matter . . . end of the week will be fine. OK, down to business. Cooper, you were talking about architecture?"

"Yes, the plans for the expansion will be put on display at the public library. They won't be secret; neither the SSU nor anyone else has hidden their intentions. Anyone will be able to see them," Cooper said.

Tony's cell phone rang. She let it ring.

"You better get it," Tom said, irritated.

"Hello?" she said.

Someone spoke on the other end and Tony said, "I'm at Tom's house in the Springs."

A pause and then she said, "Tonight? . . . Fine . . . Yeah, OK, I'll be there. Can you pick me up? . . . Thanks."

She hung up and looked at Tom. "I'm sorry, I have to go. Grandpa and Grandma Morris drove down from Denver to see me. I think they're losing their minds. They came down last week."

"We've only just started," Tom protested.

"We haven't even started," Cooper said.

"Dad won't be here for at least fifteen minutes . . . Can't we rush it?"

Tom sighed and shook his head. "All right, we'll do what we can."

"Hey, you couldn't give me a ride back, could you? I'm not sure about these buses and I didn't bring my board," Danny said, unwilling to be left alone with this lot.

"You're going too?" Tom muttered, exasperated.

"Sure, we can give you a ride," Tony said breezily.

"This is a shambles," Cooper complained. "No wonder the SSU is getting bigger and stronger every day and we're getting smaller and weaker."

"*Au contraire.* We're select; they're not. They'll take anyone who'll jump to Charlie's orders," Tom said. "We're exactly the right size for us."

"Can I ask a question?" Danny interjected.

"Sure, we're an open forum here. Anyone can ask anything," Tom said.

"What's the SSU and why are you watching them?"

Cooper laughed and Olivia sniffed. Tom gave them a black look.

"Good question, Danny. We should have explained. They're the Secret Scripture Union. It's actually just the SU—the Scripture Union—but they're in secret, so we call them the SSU."

"Why are they in secret?" Danny asked.

"Another good question . . . Well, we're still a public school, you know. No religion is allowed to be taught or promoted on the premises. The SSU has a secret Bible study group, a secret prayer group, and possibly a covert religious agenda. I formed our team to probe that agenda and keep an eye on them. Hence the Watchers."

"We got the name from *Buffy*," Cooper said.

"They pray and read the Bible . . . That's the big secret?" Danny said, unimpressed.

"Well, no, there's also the covert religious agenda," Tom said.

"Since we're rushing, can I bring up the cat story?" Tony queried.

"In a minute, yes," Tom said. "But Coop, you had some information about Hector Watson?"

"Yeah, apparently he's trying to get a date with Jessica Pereillo," Cooper said.

"I thought it was pertinent information," Tom replied, irritated.

"Who told you he asked her out?" Tony wondered.

"I heard it from Billy Reynolds. Hector was all braggy about it," Cooper said.

"Hector doesn't brag. He's actually an OK guy, if you want to know," Tony said.

"You're friends with that skeevy Hector dude?" Danny asked.

"He's not skeevy, he's OK," Tony said.

"He's the man behind the man," Tom said. "But even so, we'll move on to the security breach. Olivia?"

Olivia cleared her throat and took a piece of paper from her pocket. "They're pretty clueless. They don't have the technology to make a radio descrambler, and they don't know how to do a wireless paging system run on a remote server," Olivia said with satisfaction.

"And that's what you'd need, is it?" Cooper asked quietly.

"Or two cans and a very, very long piece of string," Danny added.

Olivia chuckled with an adorable little laugh.

"Tommy, do you have any cups up there?" a voice yelled from downstairs.

"Dammit, I thought she was at Safeway," Tom said.

"This is some meeting," Cooper said sourly.

"We'll do it at your house, then. I'm sure that will be perfect," Tom said.

"You know we can't with Aunt Lisa always around," Cooper muttered.

"Tommy, do you have any cups?" Tom's mother yelled again.

"No peace at all in here, and we have to come all the way from Cobalt," Cooper said.

"Do something about it, then," Tom snapped.

"Why don't we meet at Starbucks, like I suggested?" Cooper said.

"Zero security at Starbucks. Zero."

"Tom! Cups!"

"I'll take the cups down," Tony said, getting up and grabbing the assorted cups, mugs, and glasses.

"I'll help you," Olivia said.

When they had gone, the mood was even more strained. Finally Cooper cleared his throat and asked Danny, "Listen, er, a couple of us have been wondering if you and Tony are going out?"

"What? Are you kidding? I only just met her."

"Ah, good, good, because I was going to, I was thinking of, well . . ."

"Take it from me, you got no chance with that high-maintenance rich girl," Tom said.

You're one to talk, Danny thought, but said, "She's not that rich. Her dad works at NORAD."

"Everybody that lives in that part of Cobalt is rich," Tom said.

I live in that part of Cobalt, Danny thought. The boys

sat in silence for a minute before Danny said, "Olivia seems nice."

Tom nodded.

Finally Cooper said, "So last night I was on Gears and I was just drifting, chatting, killing people, getting experience—"

Tom began coughing and gasping for air.

"What's happening to you?" Cooper asked with no concern whatsoever.

"I'm feigning an asthma attack," Tom said.

"Why?"

"So you won't tell me any more of your Gears of War story."

Before either of them got really ticked off, the girls came back.

"Tom needs mouth-to-mouth resuscitation," Cooper said to Tony.

"What?" Tony asked.

Tom looked embarrassed. "I'm fine," he said.

"Can I bring up the cat story now?" Tony said.

"What cat story?" Tom asked.

"You'll see," Tony said, and began rummaging in her bag.

The door opened and Mrs. Sloane looked in. She was a striking forty-year-old redhead with green eyes and a pale, nervous face. But then again I'd be nervous too if my spouse was in Afghanistan, Danny thought.

"Hi, kids," she said. "Hey, you're new. Who are you?"

"Danny," Danny said.

"Mom, what is it now?" Tom said with a groan.

"It's about your clothes," Mrs. Sloane said.

"What about them?"

"Your clothes are filthy. They're all wet and covered with mud."

"I know. That's why I put them in the laundry basket."

"What were you doing yesterday?" Mrs. Sloane asked.

"I walked home. Shortcut."

"You know, it took us a year to lobby for a school bus to the Springs, and if you don't ride, they'll cancel it," Mrs. Sloane said.

"Sorry," Tom said, embarrassed.

Mrs. Sloane nodded and left.

"OK, now can I please bring up the cats?" Tony said.

"What about the cats?" Cooper wondered.

"Have a look at this," Tony said, taking out the *Cobalt Daily News*.

It got passed around the circle and Danny finally read the story Tony had been pointing at that morning. It wasn't the one about sewage plants. It was in the bottom left-hand corner of the page, below an advertisement for a gutter-cleaning service:

SECOND COBALT CAT FOUND KILLED
Cobalt animal lovers were urged to keep their pets indoors at night as a second Cobalt-area cat was found eviscerated in the parking lot of the Manitou Road 7-Eleven late last

night. "This may be another coyote attack," said animal welfare officer Kevin Hud. "Or maybe even a mountain lion. If at all possible, keep your pets indoors until spring when other food sources become more plentiful."

Mrs. Marie Craven of 16 Beechfield Road was said to be devastated by the loss of her eight-year-old Persian "Tigerfeet."

"That's the second cat they've found disemboweled. Beechfield Road is the street two over from my house. Something's going on," Tony said when they had all digested the information.

"Like what?" Tom said with a slight eye roll.

"Like a serial cat killer, that's what," Tony insisted.

Tom shook his head. "A serial cat killer? Didn't you read the paper? It was a coyote."

"Or a mountain lion," Cooper said.

"It was a coyote," Olivia insisted.

"It's not a coyote. It's not a mountain lion. A coyote doesn't eat a cat in the parking lot of the 7-Eleven," Tony said.

Tom was clearly bored with this line of inquiry and began drumming his fingers on the coffee table in a fidgety, passive-aggressive kind of way. "Sure it does," he said. "A coyote killed a dog on my granddad's farm. Came right up to the house. Those things are vicious."

"Can we move on to important stuff?" Cooper asked.

"Yes," Tom said. "Now, we need to know where the SSU

is meeting at lunchtime. We know they're meeting inside the school somewhere and—"

"I don't think it was a coyote. A coyote would have killed it and took it deep into the forest," Danny interrupted.

"Thank you," Tony said, feeling validated.

"Maybe it was startled," Tom said. "Come on, people, let's get with the program here."

Tony's phone rang. "Darn it. We have to go," she said.

Danny got up with her. "I should go, too."

"Another productive meeting. And I came all the way in from Manitou," Cooper groaned.

"So you keep telling us," Tom said, irritated.

"Nice meeting you all," Danny said, and went downstairs with Tony.

They waited outside the house where it was dark and cold. Tony had a coat, but Danny was just in his school uniform.

"It's a nice night," Danny said.

It was. The stars were out and there were a dozen planes on big counterclockwise elliptical holding patterns above Denver International.

"Remember what Bob said?" Tony asked.

"What? No."

"About the UFOs? I saw a UFO once, for real," Tony said.

"Yeah?"

"Yeah. A big delta shape, going north along the Front Range. Like a big V with lights on it."

"What do you think that was?"

"I don't know. There's a lot of government stuff going on in Colorado Springs. Probably just a secret plane they haven't told us about yet."

Danny nodded. He liked Tony's sensible attitude about things. Most kids would have said aliens.

A car flashed its lights.

"That's my dad. Come on. God, you're shivering. Are you OK?"

"Yeah, fine. Hey, can I ask you something? What's your second name?"

"Meadows, why?"

"Because you're going to say something like, 'Danny, this is my dad' and then I'll say, 'Hello, Mister uhhh.'"

Tony grinned at him in the dark.

They walked to the car.

"Who's this?" Mr. Meadows asked from the driver's seat.

"Dad, this is Danny Lopez from the family that moved in opposite us. Danny, this is my dad."

Danny stuck his hand through the window. Tony's dad shook it. "Hello, Mr. Meadows," Danny said.

Tony laughed.

"You get in the front, Danny; Antonia, you get in back," Mr. Meadows said.

He was younger than Danny had been expecting—about forty, square-jawed, dark hair, dark eyes. His voice was raspy, as if he yelled a lot in his job.

They drove through Colorado Springs, but when they got

to Manitou, Tony said, "Oh, wait, can we stop at Safeway for a second? Speaking of cats, I need to get some food for Snowflake."

"Just the cat food, nothing else," Mr. Meadows said as they parked in the Safeway lot.

"I have a cat, too," Danny said to make conversation while Tony ran inside.

Mr. Meadows shook his head. "Cats. Who needs 'em? Not anymore. Not since we invented mousetraps. Selfish, dangerous things. The Egyptians worshipped them, thought they were demons from hell. I wanted a dog. Julia said that dogs are for ego cripples. Who even knows what that means?"

Danny gave himself a "foot in the mouth" eye roll, nodded, and said, "Yeah, I guess so . . ."

Tony ran to the car and jumped in. They drove back to Cobalt listening to Christian rock on Q102.7, which Danny knew the demons would be constantly playing for him if he ever got to hell.

When they reached Johnson Close, Mr. Meadows parked and everyone got out.

"Nice meeting you, Danny. Come on in, Tony," Mr. Meadows announced in a voice loud enough to inform the entire cul-de-sac.

"I want to ask Danny a question about the homework," Tony said.

Mr. Meadows grunted something and went inside.

"What question?" Danny wondered.

"There's no question, I just wanted to say thanks for taking the missing cat seriously," she said, taking his hand in hers and interlacing her fingers between his.

"I have a cat myself. I, uh, sorry I didn't notice it this morning," Danny mumbled.

"That's OK."

"So, do you think it's a coyote or a sicko?"

"I don't know. Could be either. It gives me the creeps to think that there's evil like that in the world."

Danny squeezed her hand cautiously. "There is no evil in the world. There's no magic and no evil. If it's not an animal, it's a person; and if it's a person, he's doing it for a reason."

"Yeah. Creepy either way . . . I better go inside," she said.

She let go of his hand and slipped inside the house.

Danny stood there in the Meadowses' driveway for a while. He was grinning, and although it was a brisk, windy night, he didn't really feel that cold at all.

The Executioner's Son

The wind in the fir trees sounded like an ocean to Danny. It woke him. He dressed and went downstairs to the chilly ground floor. He pressed the red button in the hall that ignited the thermostat. The night before, Walt had chopped logs and put kindling and newspapers in the fireplace, but Danny didn't want to light a fire. It seemed . . . what? Primitive. He put the kettle on the stove and made a pot of instant coffee, and when his mother came down he gave it to her. He even made one for Walt, who immediately went to the fireplace, poured kerosene on a scrunched-up newspaper and shoved it under the kindling. He lit a match and the fire caught.

"This reminds me of New Hampshire," he said, rubbing

his hands. "OK, everyone, sit where you are and I'll make breakfast."

"Don't bother, I'm not hungry," Danny said, but after he saw his mother's look he said, "Great, thanks."

"How old is Jeffrey?" Juanita asked Danny.

"Why?" Danny wondered.

"The Sheriff's Department sent us a flyer saying we have to register all our pets," Juanita muttered, looking through the mail.

"And you have to pay a fee, right?" Walt asked.

"Twenty-five dollars," Juanita said.

"Moneymaking scam," Walt said contemptuously.

Danny didn't say anything; he was still thinking of the thirty-five bucks he supposedly owed Tom.

Walt made huevos rancheros, and it wasn't too bad for an Anglo.

But his mom was the real cook.

When they'd finished breakfast it was still only 7:05. Danny got up.

"Where are you going?" his mother asked.

"Payback," he said, pulling on his puffy North Face coat.

He went outside into a frozen world.

No tire tracks or human footprints.

No dogs, cats, or even birds.

This was the opposite of Vegas, where something was always going on.

He broke the virgin snow with the soles of his shoes.

It was only an inch deep, but ice had frozen on top of

the snowfall and it felt like he was walking on a frosted piece of glass. As if he were on the other side of a mirror, like in those books everyone was always trying to get him to read.

The door opened behind him. Walt looked out.

"You can't skateboard on that; you'll break your neck," Walt said.

"I'm not boarding, all right?"

He glared at Walt until he closed the front door again.

Danny composed himself and got back into the groove.

Frozen snow, silent houses, forest, mountain, little entrail-like curls of smoke escaping from the copper chimney tops.

It was a street from a town in a fairy tale.

He went across the cul-de-sac to Tony's house and walked up her drive.

The family drove a black Mercedes SUV. There was a Jesus fish on the back cargo door and predictable bumper stickers: WWJD?, FOCUS ON THE FAMILY, METROPOLITAN FAITH CATHEDRAL—JOIN US!, MCCAIN-PALIN 08.

Danny hesitated at the front door.

He didn't have the moxie that Tony had. He couldn't just walk into someone's house, could he?

Well, she'd done it to him and supposedly that was what this street was all about. An upper-class version of the cup-of-sugar-borrowing ways of the barrio. *Mi casa es su casa.*

He wiped his feet on a mat that said SHALOM, and went inside.

The Christmas tree startled him. It was the middle of

January, and there in the massive, oak-paneled living room was a fully lit-up and decorated Christmas tree.

"Hello?" Danny said.

No answer.

"Hello?" he inquired, a decibel or two louder.

The lights weren't on, and the house was quiet. He was surprised. He'd taken them for early risers. Somehow he thought all religious people were early risers.

All the better to ambush Tony, then.

The living room had a big stone fireplace with family photographs, and there were deer antlers on the wall just like in his house.

There were old books in a locked glass case.

A coffee mug sitting on a glass coffee table.

It felt like a crime scene.

The staircase was a wide mahogany affair that half curved to the upper part of the house. He kicked the remaining snow off his shoes and walked up it. Tony's room was easy to find. It said "Tony" on the door.

Should he knock or just go in and weird her out like she'd weirded him?

He thought about it for a second.

Maybe he should get out of there.

There was a cat at his ankles. White, fluffy, very old, purring. The symmetry of the thing was perfect. Her cat, her room . . . just as she had taken his cat in his room.

"What's your name, kitty?" he asked, bending down, but before the cat could say anything a voice said, "Hold it right there!" in a deep, gravelly, intimidating voice. Danny turned and there was Tony's father standing in his nightgown and pointing a double-barreled shotgun at him.

"I'd be well within my rights to shoot you," Mr. Meadows said.

"Um," Danny replied, terrified.

"At this range, you'd be blown to pieces," Mr. Meadows said quietly.

"Please . . . don't!" Danny begged.

Mr. Meadows bit his lip.

"Have you taken Jesus as your personal savior?" he asked.

Danny wondered what the correct answer was. They didn't go to Mass that often. In fact, they never went. One or two times with his cousins and a couple of occasions on the feast day of Guadalupe, when his mom had been trying for another baby. Danny was pretty sure that Walt was an atheist and one of his grandfathers had been a Cherokee medicine man. Was Jesus his personal savior?

"I think so," Danny said at last.

"You'll have to do better than that," Mr. Meadows said.

"Well, I believe that Jesus existed," Danny said, trying to keep the croak out of his voice.

"It's too late now. Put down the damn cat," Mr. Meadows said.

The cat was snuggled against Danny's chest and hissing at Mr. Meadows. Danny had a fleeting notion that disturbed and intrigued him. He assembled it logically in his head: (1)

Cats were pretty good judges of character. (2) Mr. Meadows was a violent man who hated cats. (3) The coyote going around killing cats wasn't a coyote, but was instead—

It was an interesting concept, and it might be good to think about it when he wasn't about to lose control of his bladder or burst into tears or die a violent death.

"Put down the cat," Mr. Meadows insisted.

"No," Danny said.

Mr. Meadows smiled. "You think I won't shoot you *and* Snowflake? The devil's agent and his familiar?"

"Daddy, what are you doing!" Tony said, opening her bedroom door. Her arms were folded across her chest. She looked furious. She was wearing gray sweats and an iCarly nightgown.

"Caught a burglar red-handed," Mr. Meadows said. "His life is in my hands now."

"Daddy, it's Danny from across the street, and you and I know the gun's only loaded with talcum powder to scare the magpies."

Mr. Meadows's brow furrowed. He gave her a withering look and let the gun point at the floor. "Why did you have to tell him that?" he muttered.

"What were you going to do?" Tony said, standing next to Danny and stroking his back. Mr. Meadows shook his head and looked at his feet. "I don't know, I thought maybe he would embrace the Lord."

"Would that even count . . . a shotgun conversion?" Tony said.

"Of course," Mr. Meadows said.

"Dad, I want you to apologize to Danny right now," Tony said.

"I was well within my rights," Mr. Meadows said.

"Apologize or I'll tell Mom!"

"Tell me what?" Mrs. Meadows said, coming onto the landing. She was a tall, athletic woman with blond hair and a pasty face that within the hour would no doubt acquire the bronzed shade typical of many women Danny had seen in Colorado Springs.

She took one look at the situation and coughed.

And apparently that was enough. "I'm really sorry, I didn't mean to scare you, son," Mr. Meadows said quickly.

"Uh, it's OK. I wasn't scared, not for a second."

Tony and Mrs. Meadows led him downstairs.

"Andrew works at NORAD," Mrs. Meadows explained. "He always thinks we should jump to DEFCON 4 as a first response to anything."

Danny looked at her to see if she was making a joke, but he couldn't tell.

"You want some toast or something, while I get ready?" Tony asked.

But Danny was still shook up and he did not want Tony or any other members of her crazy family to see that. Maybe it was hilarious to them that the gun had been loaded with talcum powder, but Danny had been genuinely afraid.

"You know what, I think I'll wait over at my house. You can come and get me," he said.

Tony appeared twenty minutes later in her uniform, thick winter coat, and a little cream-colored wool hat with tassels running from the ears.

They walked in silence down the hill to school.

At the gate she turned to him and took his hand again. He could feel her cold fingers through the white gloves.

"I'm really sorry," she said.

Danny smiled. "Don't sweat it," he assured her.

It was only a Wednesday, but already it felt like a Friday (a Friday without joy), for it had been a long week.

Miss Benson gave them a combined math and English test and, on the basis of the results, moved Danny to a seat in the right-hand corner of the room, next to the window. Apparently, this was the second-worst position in the class, and the only student behind him was a boy who looked about eleven, with big glasses and a froglike face.

Danny was miles from Tony and Tom in the left-hand corner near the door.

He didn't care too much.

He'd wanted to be away from Miss Benson's desk, and the window was good even though it was snowing.

Snow, he had decided, was a bad thing on the whole.

It made skateboarding tricky and somehow it also slowed everything down. Time already went by slower in Colorado than in Nevada, but here in class things really ground along.

Danny wondered if it was going to be like this until March or April or whenever winter ended round these parts.

Miss Benson read from her prepared script, explaining all the different types of triangles you could get, and Danny listened and read along.

Later they did American geography.

Miss Benson read. The kids read. No one seemed engaged. It was like a school play. A bad, boring school play.

Miss Benson: *What is the capital of Colorado?*

The kids: *Denver.*

Miss Benson: *What is the capital of the United States?*

The kids: *Washington, DC.*

Miss Benson: *What is the longest river in the United States?*

The kids: *The Mississippi-Missouri.*

Everyone dutifully speaking their lines, but no one really there at all.

Danny stared out the window at the big clumsy flakes falling so slowly it made you wonder if gravity had taken the day off.

During a bit on the Hoover Dam, Danny's beeper vibrated in his pocket.

Someone was sending him a text.

In class?

srry abt ths mng - tony

Danny looked at her and saw that she was looking at him. And not only that but Tom, Hector, and Charlie were looking at her looking at him.

What was the matter with her? Did she want to get him into even more hot water?

Danny turned off the beeper and focused on the prepared text.

"Indians were given reservations and food and schools, but many Indians didn't want to live like the white men," Danny read. "The Indians did not embrace the benefits of civilization."

He felt himself blushing. And ticked. In L.A. someone would have kicked up a fuss about a line like that—here everybody just read.

At lunch they had fish. Danny was a little surprised. It didn't occur to him that you could get fish miles from the sea in the middle of the mountains, but of course you could. After lunch he walked on the playground, kicking at snow piles. He could see that Tom and Cooper Reid were trying to text him, but he wasn't that interested and kept the pager turned off.

He was alone by the fence, isolated, when he saw Hector, Todd, and Charlie approaching him. He walked in the direction of Mr. Glass, who was the break teacher, but their plan was well orchestrated. Peggy Carson slipped on the ice near the frozen faucet, fell, hurt herself, and began to yell. While Mr. Glass ran to help, Todd grabbed Danny, pulled his arm behind his back, and dragged him over to the bike sheds.

"Not again," Danny said. "Don't you guys have any originality?"

Todd hadn't hurt him this time, and Danny had a feeling that he had been told not to hurt him.

"You're making a big mistake, Lopez," Charlie said.

"Oh yeah? What's the mistake?"

"Associating with Tom Sloane," Todd said.

"That's a big word for you, well done," Danny replied.

Todd twisted his arm a little harder in response.

"What did they promise you? The tests a day early? An inside track?" Hector asked.

"Nothing like that. Tom's just a hell of a lot sharper than you, that's all," Danny said.

"Sharp? Just because he's class prefect? It doesn't mean anything," Hector said.

"Class what?" Danny wondered.

"Come on, think about it, Lopez. You think he got that because he's a brainiac? It's because his dad's the lieutenant governor. He and Lebkuchen go back. Everybody knows that," Hector went on.

"Yeah, if he's so smart, how come he's in 9B with the rest of us?" Charlie said.

"And Tony? She's only where she is because her dad's on the school board. Tom's crew are all losers," Hector said.

Danny smiled. "I don't get it. You're trying to turn me against Tom and Tony, the only kids who've been half decent to me in the whole school?"

"Join us," Hector said.

Danny looked at the three boys in amazement. This was a sales pitch? They wanted him to leave "Tom's Crew" and join the SSU or whatever they were called?

"What have you got to offer?" Danny asked.

"The real inside track," Hector said.

"What do you mean?" Danny asked.

Hector looked at Charlie and they both looked at Todd. "Give us a minute, will you there, Toddy?" Hector said.

"Sure," Todd said, and walked a little distance away.

"Lebkuchen," Hector said in a whisper.

"The principal?"

"Yeah, Principal Lebkuchen. That big enough for you?"

"How?" Danny asked.

"That's for us to know," Hector said, his eyes narrowing.

"And you to find out," Charlie finished.

"You don't beat a guy up and ask him to join your gang," Danny said, more bemused than anything now.

Hector nodded. Danny had a point. His eyes lost their hostile squint and assumed a more neutral expression. "Look, we're pretty impressed with you," Hector said.

"We've been watching you," Charlie agreed.

"Digging a little. Las Vegas, the casino, your father working up at the prison. It's pretty cool. You seem all right."

Danny was complimented but also spooked.

"So what do you guys do in your group? Isn't it called the Secret Scripture Union or something?" Danny asked, contempt coating every syllable.

"Again, that's for us to know," Charlie said.

"I can guess, though: You sit around and read the Bible and talk about God all the time, is that it?"

"Some of us do," Charlie said defensively.

Danny laughed. "Man, you got me wrong if you think that's my thing."

"Why? What do you want to do?" Hector asked.

"I don't know . . . find out who's been killing cats, for one thing."

Hector and Charlie exchanged another look.

"Where did you hear about that?" Hector asked.

"The newspaper."

"Look, you want an easy life, Lopez?" Charlie asked.

"No, not really," Danny said cheerfully.

"Keep your nose out of other people's business. We run this school. This is our turf. Join us or don't get in our way," Charlie said, and all three of them began walking back to the main playground.

"Jeez, guys, first the threat, now the invitation, now another threat . . . This isn't how you run a gang. I've hung with the East L.A. homeboys; you guys suck. Jesus, you want some tips on intimidation, you come to me."

Charlie and Hector looked annoyed.

"You've been warned," Charlie said, turning around and pointing a finger at him.

"Leave him alone!" Tony said, appearing on the far side of the bike sheds.

"Ah, the Seventh Cavalry, here to save you," Hector said, and winked at Danny as if he knew how wearying it must be to be constantly rescued by a girl.

Danny chest-bumped Hector and got right in his face. "What did you say, holmes?" Danny snarled.

Hector took a step back and lowered his voice. "Look, bro, if you wanna know what's going on, meet me at the Starbucks on South Cascade at four o'clock on Friday," he whispered.

"So you and your pals can jump me again?" Danny said.

"No, just you and me. I'll buy you a caramel frap to show there's no hard feelings. Don't tell Tony or Tom. I'll wait till four thirty and then I'm gone."

Hector sprinted back to the main playground just as Cooper and Tom appeared.

"What was he saying to you?" Tony asked suspiciously.

"Nothing," Danny said.

"He must have said something," Tom insisted.

"The usual threats, no big deal," Danny said.

Tom looked satisfied. "You gotta be more careful; it's a jungle out here," he said.

"Yeah, stick with us, we'll look after you," Tony said cheerfully.

"Sure," Danny said, and walked back with the others to the creepy, silent playground.

Tony had a dance class after school, so Danny walked home by himself, and the evening was long without books, TV, or CDs.

He was so fed up, he actually went out to the Volvo to listen to the radio. The clearest station was the Colorado Springs Focus on the Family Network, but he got bored with the news bulletins about President Obama's Muslim agenda, Communist China's plans to colonize the moon, and how Satan was spreading his influence into every corner of every American home. He was just about to turn it off when one of the DJs mentioned the cat killings, speculating that the local Wiccans were to blame and wondering if a new Salem Witch Trial was what was needed to set the country back on the right track.

Danny turned it off and went to bed.

He left the window open, and by morning the glass of water next to his bed had frozen solid.

His throat was scratchy and he begged his mom to allow him to stay home.

A three-way struggle followed. Walt sided with Danny, and Juanita finally caved. After his parents had left, Danny dug his long board, Black Shadow, from one of the crates, skated downhill to Colorado Springs, found a comic-book shop, bought *Superman: Red Son* by Mark Millar, and caught the bus home.

Skating past the school with his hoodie pulled up and watching the poor saps going to class was delicious.

He read *Superman* all day and ate Ben & Jerry's Peanut Butter Cup.

He finally had some good alone time with Jeff, too. Jeff had explored the outside world and taken against this nightmarish white stuff. Danny's bedroom was his preferred locale, at least during the day.

. . .

The next morning, Danny was "feeling better," and he and Tony walked to school after she had politely inquired about his health.

"I'm doing great," Danny told her.

It was Friday, so there was an outdoor assembly, where Mr. Lebkuchen told the shivering teachers and children about the progress of the gym, the school's latest test scores, and an upcoming visit from the US secretary of education.

No one grabbed him at lunch, and Danny pretended to be fascinated as Olivia, Tom, and Tony texted one another about whether they should go see *The Lion King* when it came to Denver.

Through his mom, of course, Danny had seen every musical that had come to the Glynn casino on the Strip in the last five years, so *The Lion King* was old news.

Hector looked at him a few times during school and Danny nodded. He remembered about their meeting, and he would be there.

After school, Danny ran home, got Sunflower, and skated downhill to the Springs.

Although he got to Starbucks early, Hector was there ahead of him.

He had taken an armchair next to the fireplace in which three huge smoldering gray logs were generating enormous heat.

The Starbucks only had half a dozen other customers, but Hector had kept his word: There was no sign at all of Charlie or Todd.

"Take a seat and I'll get that frap," Hector said.

"You don't need to get me anything."

"My treat," Hector insisted.

He brought the drink and Danny lifted the plastic lid and sipped. It was hot and sweet and good. If it was coffee, it didn't taste like any coffee he'd had before. It was almost as good as Tom's hot chocolate.

Hector looked at Sunflower. "You skateboarded here in this weather? Aren't you freezing?" he asked.

"It was OK," Danny said.

"Colder than normal this time of year. Have you been to the woods yet? I go there all the time, and when you get up to eight thousand feet, it's incredible."

Danny wasn't in the mood for small talk. "So what do you want to tell me?" he asked curtly.

Hector winced. "OK, business is it? I can do business."

"Do it," Danny muttered.

"What do you want to know?"

Hmm. This was Danny's chance to hit him with all the questions he was too embarrassed to ask Tony or Tom.

"OK. Start with the school, the dope on that, and then the SSU—all that stuff."

Hector leaned back in his chair and the leather squeaked beneath him. "You don't even know about the school?"

"Listen, if you're going to be a jerk, I'm out of here," Danny said, getting up.

"Sit down, sit down, sorry. OK, the school, well, it's only been going for two years. It used to be Nikola Tesla

Elementary. Heard of him? Famous scientist, lived around here about a hundred years ago. Did a lot of his experiments on electricity in Colorado Springs. Had a lab up here in Cobalt. He was a pioneer in radio, early TV, electric generation. Some of his ideas even predated Einstein, you know? Never really got the credit he deserved. He's coming back now, though. Heard of the Tesla sports car?"

"Yeah, we got one."

"What?"

"Doesn't matter. Go on."

"Anyway, the school was Tesla Elementary, but it didn't do that well, hard to get good teachers up here. Higher pay in Denver, Boulder . . . It wasn't exactly a failing school, just not a good school. We had all this cool science equipment; most of it's gone now, of course, except for the big Tesla coil in the science lab. Have you seen that? Lebkuchen can't get rid of it because it was a donation from the Ford Foundation or something."

"What's a Tesla coil?"

"You'll see it next week when the classes merg—um, when the, uh, you'll see it next week."

"OK."

"But anyway, if you don't like it here, you can blame your friend Tom for the whole thing."

"Tom?"

"Oh, didn't he tell you?" Hector said with a malicious grin.

"Tell me what?"

"And I suppose Tony didn't tell you about her father, either?"

"What are you talking about?"

"Tom's dad was the lieutenant governor of Colorado."

"Yeah, I knew that. What's that got to do with anything?"

Hector leaned over and, irritatingly, tapped Danny on the arm. "His brother was killed in a car accident three years ago. Tom is devoted to his big brother. He loses it, has a sort of breakdown, runs away from home. Flunks out of school. Runs away again. Tom's dad brings in Lebkuchen as a private tutor and is really impressed by him. Tesla Elementary has recently closed because it's basically crap. Everyone's in a tizzy. All the Cobalt kids are having to get bused into the Springs, so Lebkuchen pitches his whole charter school idea to Tom's father and he goes for it. He's lieutenant governor, which is kind of a joke job, but he does have some influence and so he goes to Tony's dad and Arnie Grainger's mom. You know Arnie in grade eight?"

"No."

"Well, they get half a dozen other parents and they make Jane Close's mom president of the committee. You know Jane? In 8A?"

"No," Danny said, annoyed. "It's only my first week, you know?"

"Sure. Anyway, so the committee lobbies the school board and that's how the whole thing got started. The silence, the DI, the gloves. You can blame your friend Tom for getting the ball rolling."

"Tom doesn't seem to like it," Danny said.

"Doesn't he? His little gang always spying on us, finding ways to flaunt the rules with his pagers . . . Are you kidding me? He laps it up, loves it. Gives him something to do."

Danny wasn't so sure about that. "So what about your 'little group'?" he mocked.

"We're the real rebels. None of our parents is on the school board or the committee."

"But what do you do?"

"Well, it's public school, so there's no school prayer or Bible study or religion or anything like that, and we've found ways around that. We formed a Scripture Union. We've got about a dozen kids. We do read the Bible and we do have prayers, but we also do other stuff too, you know?"

"Like what?"

"We have study circles. Me and Jonah and Tig play WoW every night. We swap novels . . . Tig even got a bottle of whiskey from his uncle. You ever drunk liquor before?"

Danny was confused. It didn't quite gel in his mind. On the one hand, they read the Bible and traditional goody-goody stuff like that, but somehow they had managed to turn this into a radical subversion of the system.

"You're not into the chastity rings and Christian rock crap, are you?"

Hector laughed. "Hell no!"

Danny thought about it for a second. "So, what did

you mean you could deliver Lebkuchen? What does that mean?"

"That I can't tell you. Not until we know we can trust you. Join us and you'll see."

"What if I only pretend to join you, to get the information?" Danny said.

"Go ahead. Join us or pretend to join us. Doesn't matter. Once you start hanging with us, you won't want to be with those losers anymore," Hector said.

Danny looked out the window. The blue sky was gone and clouds had rolled over Pikes Peak from the west. He should probably head back before it started snowing again.

Since time was pressing, he decided to get to the main reason he had come to this rendezvous. "Tell me about the cats," Danny said.

"What cats?" Hector said innocently.

"I saw you looking at Charlie when I brought it up."

Hector shook his head. "I don't think I can do that now."

"Why not?"

"It's a trust thing. Hold on, look, there's April Donovan and Susie McGwire."

Danny recognized two of the girls from 9A. Both had changed out of their school uniforms into what had to be a Colorado version of the mall-rat/valley-girl look he was familiar with in Las Vegas. Short denim skirts, ankle socks, pink sneakers, frilly blouses, fake pearl necklaces, bangles, bracelets, and white-framed sunglasses pitched high in teased, sprayed hair.

Hector's eyes lit up like a lion spotting a baby zebra separated from the herd.

"Let's go over. You've no idea. We'll never get a chance like this in school," he said.

"Are you serious? I'm not going over with you," Danny whispered.

"I'm going for it. Look at the way April's checking us out," Hector replied.

April was the prettier of the two, with dark hair, a pale complexion, and a slightly chubby face. She was wearing red lipstick, and her cheeks were rouged. She looked about nineteen or twenty. Susie was a skinny blonde with a vacant expression and so much perfume that it probably could be considered a weapon of mass destruction.

"No, don't do it," Danny said desperately.

"Hi there!" Hector yelled from where he was standing. The girls giggled and miraculously began walking in their direction.

"Did you say something?" Susie asked.

"You want a coffee?" Hector said.

April's violet eyes fluttered at Danny. "You're the new kid, aren't you?"

"Yeah, Danny Lopez," Danny said. He shook hands with both of them. Hector offered his hand and both ignored him.

"Is that your skateboard?" Susie asked, pointing at Sunflower.

"Yeah," Danny said.

"Ladies, can I interest you in a drink?" Hector said. "Or perhaps a caramel slice?"

April sighed.

"They have very good madeleines. Have you tried those?" Hector continued.

"No," April said coolly.

Hector was foundering badly. "Um, so do you girls like World of Warcraft?" he attempted.

"Come on, April, this kid's a total weirdo," Susie said to her friend.

"Look, at least tell us what we did wrong," Hector said suddenly.

"What do you mean 'we'?" Danny said.

The girls looked embarrassed, but then April decided to rise to the challenge. "You want to know why I think you're, like, super creepy?"

"Uh, yeah," Hector said.

April thought for a moment. "Well. This whole talk, for a start, and those freakos you hang out with and, you know, the whole prison thing, which isn't your fault but even so . . ."

"What if we hung out with you guys," Hector said desperately.

"This conversation is so over. Pretend it's like school. Don't talk to me again," April said, and both girls sat down miles away at a table near the window.

Hector grabbed his jacket and started buttoning it, his face red with shame and consternation.

"I'm getting out of here," he whispered.

"Wait a minute, tell me about the cat killings," Danny said, grabbing Hector by the lapels.

"I gotta go, man, they're laughing."

Danny stood up and grabbed Hector's arm. "No, tell me what you know."

"Why don't you join us, and then you'll know what we know. You've got a cat, right?"

"How did you know that?" Danny wondered suspiciously.

"Hey, you know who could really help get to the bottom of it?"

"Who?" Danny wondered.

"Your friend Bob."

"Bob? I don't know any Bob."

"Sure you do. Bob Randall, Alaskan Bob, the foreman on your dad's work gang. He's an expert. I'll bet he's bursting with ideas."

"What? How the hell do you know about him?"

"Through my dad. Listen, dude, think about joining us; we can do the cat thing, WoW, anything you like, you seem like a pretty cool guy. As a sign of our goodwill—Monday morning, ten fifteen. Remember that."

"Monday what? What are you talking about? How do you know about Bob?" Danny asked, but Hector was already running out of the Starbucks under the giggling gaze of the two 9A girls.

The girls were looking at Danny now. He wished they weren't.

It wasn't that they weren't pretty; they were if you liked tubercular white cheeks, puffy red faces, heavy makeup. But it was more that Danny didn't have that much experience with girls. Not really. In Las Vegas, the girls in his year only went out with older boys, grade 10, grade 11, some even with college kids. They had a haughty disdain for kids their own age, and their *chica latina* intensity was enough to freeze you in your tracks before you even thought of asking them to the movies or the Fat Burger on Las Vegas Boulevard.

Time to head. He picked up Sunflower, put on his beanie, and followed Hector to the door.

"So, what were you hanging with a cheesy dude like Hector Watson for?" April asked when his hand was on the door handle.

"I don't know," Danny said.

"He's in that not-so-secret society," Susie mocked.

"Yeah, I know."

"Stay away from them. They're a bunch of freaks," April muttered.

"Hector's the weirdest. Totally screwed up," Susie added.

"Is he?" Danny said, suddenly interested.

"Oh yeah. Don't you know? His dad works on death row at the Supermax. He's the executioner. The guy that pushes the button to give the lethal injections. Totally creepy, huh?" April said.

"Totally creepy," Danny agreed, and wondered if that was how Hector knew about his father and Bob.

"Tell us about Vegas," one of the girls said, and Danny was about to spin them his Paris Hilton story when he got a peculiar icy feeling on the back of his neck; he turned to look behind him and standing there glaring at him was Tony, who was with her dad. When their eyes met, Tony looked away.

Mr. Meadows had paid and they departed by the east-side door.

Danny followed them to the parking lot.

"Tony!" Danny called.

She ignored him and got inside the Mercedes SUV.

"Tony!" he said again.

Mr. Meadows looked around and recognized him. "You. What are you doing in town?"

"Nothing."

"Hmm, I suppose I should offer you a ride home."

"No. No, thank you. I brought my skateboard."

"Skateboard, eh?" Mr. Meadows muttered as darkly as if Danny had been referring to his portable witchcraft kit.

Danny didn't say anything.

"Well, good-bye, then," Mr. Meadows said, and got into the car.

They drove off along Cascade and turned right on East Colorado Avenue.

A thought occurred to Danny. He got out his pager and texted: **wtf? whts the mattr?**

Thinking of Mr. Meadows, he deleted the "WTF" part and sent the text.

He waited for a minute and then a reply came.

dnt txt me.

He put the pager away and, since there was nothing else to do, he skated home.

Walt had decided to cook again. It was some kind of New England bean thing with odd cuts of meat. His mother pretended to love it, and Danny had to admit that it wasn't bad.

"How was school?" they asked him.

"Great," he told them. He did his homework reading parts of the US Constitution and then wrote some of those lines about triangulation.

After he was finished, he texted Tony again, spelling out every word so she would understand it: **bob from the prison knows something about the cat killings. i could ask walt if we could go see him tomorrow if you want?**

He waited half an hour for a reply, but no reply came. He turned off his light and opened the windows wide to let in the cold air.

He thought about the last two days. Tony's father was obviously a lunatic, and she was pretty difficult herself. Hector was also kind of a weirdo and didn't seem trustworthy either. He was the executioner's son. That couldn't be good for you psychologically. He thought about April and Susie, but the truth was that neither of them really interested him at all.

And even with Jeffrey sleeping at the bottom of his duvet,

he felt lonely. He reached under his bed and got Sunflower. He flipped it deck-side up and hugged it as if it were a stuffed toy.

He put his feet on Jeff's back and shoved the window wider.

That wind again, pushing through the trees like waves on the shore.

He was uneasy.

He didn't feel confident about anything in Cobalt. Not the people, not the weather, not even the icy ground beneath his feet. This was a new game, with new players, and he hadn't figured out any of the rules. He wondered if he ever would, among these big, tall local kids with their happy families and their skiing and their hot chocolate.

He stared out at the black mass of forest. No stars tonight, no moon. Just darkness.

He watched for a long time and then, suddenly, in the trees he saw a tiny light, like a reflective piece of fabric.

He remembered something that either Charlie or Hector or someone had said: *We've been watching you.*

Would they really be out there at this time of night?

Maybe he should shout something. Maybe he should sneak out the front and double back behind them. But what if it was Tony's dad out there with his gun again? Or some other local crazy? He turned on the light and tried to peer through the ambient glow that shone into the trees.

Nothing.

Tomorrow I'll get a powerful flashlight, he thought to himself. He flipped the switch, shut the window, closed the curtains. He fell asleep to the sound of wind blowing and Jeffrey purring peacefully.

TEN

The First Cat

Danny Lopez's window. The light goes off. On again. Off for the final time. And now it's dark. Dark like it was on the ranch.

Stars. Constellations. Orion. The Big Dipper.

He lies down on the pine needles. "Are you curious, Danny Lopez? Do you want to know?"

He pulls up the sleeping bag. He closes his eyes and now he doesn't see the Lopez house or the other houses. Just the belts and the fear.

Get rid of them. Get rid of them. And sure enough, they vanish, eventually.

A dog barking. The rain coming in through the open window. Rain not snow, which means he's dreaming. He is back in the beginning. Crying in the soiled barn light. His father with whiskey on his breath. Horses whinnying and the well rope coming out of the hitching rail. The smell is the sweet-smelling poison they have laid down for the mice.

How the cat got poisoned, no one knows.

He's crying. Bawling his eyes out. "It's your fault!" he's screaming.

"That's enough, pull yourself together!" his father says.

"Leave him alone, he's sensitive. And he's right, you were careless," his mother says.

She contradicting him? It's been going on all day. His father's expression clouds. He slaps her. Suddenly the boy is between them. Everyone's yelling. He gets in the way of a fist. One blow and he's sent flying.

His father's voice: "Oh my God. I'm sorry. I'm sorry. I am so sorry. It will never happen again. You're right. It's crazy out here. We're going crazy. We'll move to the city. And I promise it will never happen again."

They move.

It happens again.

Letter IV

We are lucky, you and I, to live in the mountains. Do you ever
go up there by yourself?

Across the fields. Into the high country. Into the forest.

You can hide there.

See no one. All you hear is the wind and sometimes
voices, campfires on the edge of the wood. Songs that drift
through the trees.

At night, snow. Falling over dry valleys. Black clouds
and that bitter wind from the north. In summer, hard rain
pounding off the baked ground. There's a cave I know about,
and on the walls there are paintings and the ash of fires
from millennia. Or so they say.

Deeper we can go into the wilderness. Through ghost towns
and graveyards. There are wild horses and bears. Muskrat, red
wolf, coyotes.

You and me, Antonia.

No one will see us.

Cars will go by in the darkness, headlights dipped, and they
won't see us. All those drivers sitting ready on the brakes in
case some animal lunges out of the forest into the road in
front of them.

We won't lunge.

We'll hide.

I'll take you with me.

I'll tell you the secrets.

And in the Calvary of noise and wind I'll say words that not a soul can hear but you.

ELEVEN

The Phylogenetic Scale

Saturday. Indigo sky. White surf. Golden sand. Danny was dreaming about the beach at Santa Monica. Bodysurfing with his cousins. Laughing, rolling with the breakers, cradled by the even swell.

"Maybe we should go," a voice said.

"Uh, yeah."

Danny woke but he kept his eyes closed. He knew the score. *She* was in his room again and she'd brought someone with her this time. This outrageous behavior really had to end. Maybe he should tell Walt to buy a shotgun. Walt, though, was some kind of peacenik—opposed to guns. Maybe he should just tell his mother to lock the doors at night.

Two people in his bedroom. Danny was angry, but

underneath the anger there was another current of emotion he was struggling to identify. What was that? Happiness? No, not quite. What then?

Relief.

Yeah, that was it.

He couldn't get really worked up at this repeated home invasion, because if she'd come over to his house, didn't that also mean she'd forgiven him for Starbucks?

"He breathes funny," the stranger said. A boy.

"That's not him making that noise, that's Jeffrey," Tony said.

"Who's Jeffrey?"

"The cat."

"Oh."

Danny now identified a third emotion underneath the anger and the relief.

That emotion was a kind of resentment. He thought, Why should Tony have been ticked off at him anyway? What exactly had he been doing wrong? Talking to two girls from their school? Talking to two girls who were obviously into him. What right did Tony have to be annoyed about that? They weren't boyfriend and girlfriend. They were just neighbors. Not even good neighbors. Tony's dad had tried to kill him, for heaven's sake. That wasn't very friendly.

"Let's wait downstairs, seems a shame to wake him. I could nap on the sofa, I was up late myself."

Danny identified the male voice as Tom's.

He heard them pad out of his room and go downstairs.

He opened his eyes and glared at Jeffrey.

"Fine watch-cat you are. I thought you were a tough street kitty; you've gotten soft."

As if on cue, Jeffrey rolled across the bed, stretching his claws and baring his fanglike yellow chops.

Danny smiled at him and rubbed his belly.

"Sorry, Jeff, I didn't mean it. It just takes a while to get used to a new place."

In Vegas, Jeffrey had brought many dead offerings to the back door of the Lopez house: dormice, field mice, rats, a pigeon, and once, most impressively of all, a rattlesnake. For the first few days in Colorado, Jeffrey had refused to leave the upper floor. The previous night, however, he had proudly brought a dead vole through the newly installed cat flap—something that had horrified Juanita and secretly pleased both Danny and Walt, who'd exchanged a knowing look.

"Tough old geezer," Walt had said, and now Danny repeated it in Jeffrey's ear: "Tough old geezer, ain't ya?"

Danny changed out of his racecar PJs and pulled on blue jeans, his red Converse high-tops, and his Raiders T-shirt.

He went downstairs and affected surprise when he saw Tony and Tom having Frosted Flakes at the breakfast table. Walt was standing there by the kettle with his nightshirt open to the navel, revealing his gray, hairy chest and blotchy corpselike skin.

It was disgusting and embarrassing.

"Morning," Tony said.

"Hi," Danny replied nonchalantly.

"Hey, Danny," Tom said.

"Hey," Danny replied, lifting a finger with rehearsed sangfroid.

"Danny, whatcha want for breakfast? I offered them eggs, but your friends are just having cereal," Walt said.

"Wise choice," Danny muttered.

"What?"

"I'll have cereal, too," Danny said. "Where's Mom?"

"She's sleeping in. I'm bringing her breakfast in bed. End of her first workweek and all that, you know, old chap?"

When there was company around, Walt's nervous tics included a pseudo English or perhaps upper-class Bostonian accent. It was very tedious. Danny was sure that his real father would have been appalled by it.

"You wouldn't mind helping yourself to some Frosted Flakes while I bring this up to her, would you, Danny?"

"Sure," Danny said, and poured the flakes into a bowl.

It was only after he'd eaten several spoonfuls and drank a glass of orange juice that he pretended to become interested in Tom and Tony's appearance in his house.

"So, what brings you two out here? Easy ride for you, Tony, but bit of a drag for you, Tom."

"Easy for me; I've got an electric bike. Ever see one of those? Don't need to wear a helmet or get a license. And besides, I know all the shortcuts."

"Don't tell Walt about that. He's got an electric car; he'll bore you to tears with it," Danny said.

"Electric car? That red thing? Oh God, it's not the Tesla, is it?" Tom said excitedly.

Danny sighed inwardly. He'd be the first to admit that he was geekish, but Tom was some kind of supergeek.

"It is the Tesla," Tony said.

"That is made of awesome!" Tom replied.

"Not to me," Danny muttered.

"Tesla Motors is on fire right now, and we're practically living in Teslaville, and we've got a Tesla coil in our school, so come on! And electric cars are the future," Tom said.

Hector had used that phrase the day before—a Tesla coil.

"What exactly is a Tesla coil?" Danny asked.

"It's a big sort of thing that does stuff," Tony said, which didn't really explain an awful lot.

"You'll see it in science class," Tom said, and looked at them significantly. "Maybe it's time to get down to business?"

"Yeah, why are you guys here?" Danny wondered.

"You haven't heard?" Tony said.

"Heard what?"

"You know Sarah Kolpek, 7A?"

"No."

"She lives on Alameda. About twenty houses from here. They were out for the night, and when they came home they found her cat, Coco, hanging from the tree outside her house," Tony said.

A chill went down Danny's spine. He looked at Jeffrey. Twenty houses from here?

"Hanging?" Danny asked.

"Hanging," Tom said.

For some reason Danny thought of Hector, the son of the state executioner, but Hector had an alibi for at least part of the day, after school.

"What time did it go missing?" he asked.

"No one's sure, but they found it about five this morning on a chestnut tree at the front of the house," Tony said.

"The *front* of the house?" Danny said.

"Yes, what difference does that make?" Tom asked.

"Our killer's getting pretty bold," Danny said. "I take it no one's blaming this on a coyote?"

Tom shook his head and looked embarrassed. "No, I was wrong about that, wasn't I?"

"Not a coyote, not a fox, not a wolf," Tony said.

"So how did you hear about it?" Danny asked.

"I was up at six this morning. I heard the story on the news, texted Tom, told him what you told me last night, and he came right over," Tony muttered.

Danny was confused. "Wait a minute. What did I tell you last night?"

"That your friend Bob Randall was an expert and he could break open the whole cat-killing case for us."

Danny nodded. "Oh yeah, that. I forgot about that. Yeah, he's got a PhD in criminal psych."

"Can we go see him today?" Tony said anxiously.

"I'd like to talk to this guy, too," Tom said, and he was fidgeting and drumming his fingers, which Danny knew would eventually drive him up the wall.

"Uh, I don't think so. It's a Saturday. It is a Saturday, right?"

"Yes," Tony said impatiently.

"No . . . maybe after school on Monday or something," Danny said.

Tony pulled open the living room curtains, flooding the room with light and making Danny wince. "No," she announced. "We have to do it today. Something's changed. Something's happened. 'Bold,' you said. Yes, he's gotten bolder and the interval between the killings has dropped. First weeks, now days," Tony said forcefully.

"This Bob sounds like a pretty interesting dude," Tom said.

Danny shook his head. It would mean asking Walt to take them, and the last thing he wanted to do was involve Walt.

"It's a Saturday. I don't think we can go to the prison on a Saturday," Danny said.

"All we can do is ask. When your parents come down, we'll ask them. They can only say no."

Danny nodded reluctantly. "OK, we'll see. Look, I need to take a shower."

"I'll say," Tony said, and winked to show that she was only kidding.

After finishing his cereal, Danny went into the bathroom to have a shower. When he came out, having changed into jeans and a gray hoodie, everyone was eating some kind of cake.

"Sit down," Juanita said. "Look what Walt got us."

"Have some cake," Walt said.

Danny shook his head. "I just brushed my teeth," he said, but he sat at the table anyway.

"What's the occasion?" Danny asked, staring at a large carrot cake.

"Your mother's first full week at her new job. Some of my chaps made it for her," Walt said.

Danny regarded the carrot cake with suspicion. "This was made by convicts?"

Walt shook his head. "We don't call them that. They're really a very nice bunch of people," Walt said.

"Did you check if there were any poisoners in there?" Danny asked.

Tom paled and looked suspiciously at the bit of cake, frozen on the fork in front of him.

Tony laughed and swallowed the big piece in her mouth. "Actually, that's why we came over here," she said.

"Oh?" Walt said.

"Yes, Danny tells us that your foreman, Bob Randall, is an expert in criminal psychology, and we were wondering if he had any insight into the cat killings that have been going on around here."

"What cat killings?" Juanita asked.

"You want to go and see Bob?" Walt asked.

"This morning, if possible," Tom said.

"Hmm, I don't know," Walt said, looking at Juanita. "We promised that we'd take a trip up to the casino."

Danny's mother put down her fork. "What cat killings?"

Tony filled her in and explained that they wanted to look into it because nobody else was taking it seriously.

"What about the local police?" Juanita asked.

Tony scoffed. "Sarah Kolpek's mother told my mother that Sheriff Rossi thinks it was some kind of freak accident."

"You told your mother to call Sarah's mother without consulting me? I mean . . . us?" Tom said, clearly miffed and looking at Danny for support.

"*Could* it have been a freak accident?" Juanita asked.

Tony shrugged. "I guess . . . maybe . . . I don't know. That's why we need to talk to Bob. Danny says he's the big expert."

Juanita looked at the three kids and suppressed a tight smile. It was certainly rather morbid that they were taking an interest in a cat that had died, and it was definitely strange that they wanted to interview a prisoner, but Danny didn't make friends that easily and these children seemed to be his friends. And they weren't "the bad crowd"—quite the reverse. Tony was intelligent, polite, nice. And Tom, although a little odder, was the same.

"I want you to call up your parents and get permission, and if they say it's OK, then we'll all go. What do you think, Walt?" Juanita said.

Walt shook his head. "Honey, I know you had your heart set on showing us the casino."

"We can do both. Ask your parents if it's OK and we'll do both!" Juanita said brightly.

"Great," Tony said.

"Yeah, sure," Tom said.

Tom called his mother, who didn't appear to mind at all and merely asked if it was some kind of school project for Mr. Lebkuchen, to which Tom replied that it wasn't—not really.

Tony got out her cell phone and fake-dialed her home. Not in a million years would her father let her visit a casino, never mind a federal prison, but her imaginary father was a man cut from a different cloth.

"Dad . . . yeah, it's me. Listen, Danny's mom wants to know if it's OK to drive out to Correctional Institution Road? . . . No! Don't be silly. The minimum-security prison next to the Supermax . . . Oh, there's some kind of psychology expert there we want to talk to about the cat killings . . . I will . . . Thank you, Papa. Oh, and can we visit Danny's mom's casino? . . . Thanks, Dad."

She hung up.

Danny had seen through the lie immediately, and he marveled at her. On the surface Tony was a bubbly, typically extroverted teenager, but Tony's icebergian depths were a lot more interesting—she'd probably (to extend the analogy) quite enjoy ramming into a passenger ship in the dead of night just to see what happened. And now that he was in the psych biz Danny had a go at summing up everyone else's personality, too. Tom seemed a pretty well-adjusted kid—a little fidgety, a little geeky, but doing OK considering his dad was off at war and his brother had died. Walt also had a few nervous tics: He sang to himself with distressing regularity, and that Englishy accent was worse than Madonna's during her London years. Juanita was a hardworking, fairly typical Latina mother, and if there was a mystical Cherokee side to her, Danny never saw it.

That's everyone, Danny thought, and then shook his head.

No, not quite everyone. What about me?

While the others talked and finished their cake, Danny did something he rarely did, which was to turn his external sensors on himself.

What kind of a person is Danny Lopez? he asked. An only child who dug skateboarding and, until his laptop vanished into some UPS black hole, Halo 3 and YouTube. Shy? Introverted? Yeah, those were good words. He was also a bit of a dreamer, too: that day he'd tried to hitch to Chicago to see his father, getting Jeffrey from the Tropicana Wash and—

He looked up.

Everyone was staring at him.

"Well?" Tom said impatiently.

"Well what?"

"Are you ready to go?"

"Sure."

In ten minutes they were in the car. Predictably, Walt wanted them to split into two groups so he could show Tom the Tesla, but Juanita sensibly insisted that they all take the Volvo instead. Walt huffed a little in the front passenger's seat, which made Danny oddly pleased. He did not want to sit in the middle between Tony and Tom, though, and he didn't want either of his "guests" to be forced into the middle, so they pulled out the third-row seat and Danny sat behind everyone.

Juanita turned on the radio but all they could get was Focus on the Family again, and Pastor Ted Swanson's local phone-in program, which was all "Gay soldiers are terrorizing their colleagues at Fort Carson" and "Mexicans in Colorado Springs worship the Devil," so she turned it off.

They drove through the Ute Reservation, which to Danny's eyes didn't look that different from any other part of Colorado. The houses that he caught glimpses of between the trees were the same ranch-style homes as those in Colorado Springs. He didn't know what he'd been expecting, but it certainly wasn't like the pueblos he'd visited in New Mexico, with big communal buildings and a very distinct look.

"Where's the actual Reservation itself?" he asked his mother.

"This is it. It's all around you," she replied.

The casino was also something of a letdown.

The exterior looked like a Motel 6, and a small simple neon sign declared, THE GLYNN CASINO AT THE UTE AND CHEROKEE NATIONS FAMILY RESORT, which wasn't the most memorable name he'd ever seen. Doubtless, with time people would just call it the Glynn. Inside, it reminded

Danny not of the new complexes on the southern part of the Strip but rather of the older casinos in downtown Las Vegas like the Golden Nugget—but admittedly a Golden Nugget without the cigarette-stained carpet or plaster-cracked walls, because everything, of course, was brand-new. Rows of slots, blackjack tables covered with tarp, roulette wheels, a sports book. There were bars, a restaurant, even a kids' play area. There were no windows but a lot of flashing lights and big extractor fans to suck out the cigarette smoke. Smoking was banned in bars in Colorado, but this was an Indian nation and thus exempted from the rule.

"So this is a casino?" Tony said with wide-eyed wonder.

"You never been in one before?" Tom scoffed.

"Have you?" Tony asked.

"Well, no, actually not really," Tom admitted.

"What do you think?" Juanita asked.

"Wow, it's really cool," Danny said. "And you're running the whole thing, huh?"

Juanita glowed with pride. "The whole kit and caboodle. Of course, we still have so much to do—so much, you've no idea—but I think we'll open on time."

They took a tour and as Juanita was explaining how the various games of chance worked to Tom and Tony, Danny was looking at the rows of slot machines and imagined the grim-faced retirees with their buckets of change sitting in front of them, putting in quarter after quarter of their savings, day after day, month after month, until one day it would all be gone.

"Listen, can I meet you guys back at the car? I'm feeling a bit funny," Danny said.

Walt nodded. "We were climbing the whole time, we're up at nine thousand feet now."

"That must be it," Danny said.

"Are you OK?" Juanita asked.

Danny nodded and slipped away from the others. The sun was out now and it was into the forties. He sat on the curb by the car in the massive, empty parking lot.

"Help you, son?" a man asked.

Danny looked up into the face of a security guard. A lean, dark-skinned man in his sixties, with a short gray ponytail. Bit of a beaky nose and dark eyes. Obviously a Native American. He was carrying a walkie-talkie.

"I'm just waiting for my mom," Danny said, and then he added: "She's the manager here. Juanita Brown."

The man nodded. "Mind if I sit?" he asked after a long pause.

"Help yourself."

The security guard sat down next to Danny on the curb. The effort made his lungs give off a rattly, wheezing sound, and Danny wondered if he'd be able to get back up again. "Thought you might be one of those protestors," the security guard said when his breath was back.

"Protestors? What do you mean?"

"Oh, we've had a few protestors from town, about the casino. It was bad about six months ago—people chaining themselves to bulldozers, that kind of thing. Church folk.

Stopped now mostly. Mr. Glynn told us to make some donations to the right people. We did it, and it stopped."

"Focus on the Family, the Metropolitan Faith Cathedral thingy . . . those people?"

"Yes. And we had the Tesla folks, too. Did one of his big scientific experiments up here. Radio or radar or something. From here to his lab in Cobalt, where that school is now. There was only a shack left here, but those folks said we should preserve it as a national monument. Preserve the hut! Ha!"

"Did you preserve it?"

"Of course not. This is our land, Tesla had no business being here in the first place."

"You're a member of the uh, the Ute tribe?"

"Cherokee Nation. Dan Flight of Eagles," the man said, offering Danny his hand. Danny shook it. "Hey, my name's Danny, too. And you know, technically I'm Cherokee as well—at least part Cherokee, I guess."

The security guard nodded, looked at him closely. "You either is or you ain't," he said.

Danny nodded shamefacedly and stared at his shoelaces, then at the pristine concrete of the parking lot stretched in front of him. Man and boy lapsed into a long silence.

Juanita and the others came back from their tour. The security guard got sprightly to his feet and gave Juanita a little nod.

"How was it?" Danny asked.

"Good. Everyone's hungry now. Are you feeling any better?"

"Fine," Danny said.

They did McDonald's drive-through for lunch and as she was sucking down a strawberry milkshake, Tony whispered to Danny in the backseat, "A casino, a prison, and McDonald's in one morning—this is, like, the greatest day ever. Don't ever mention this to my dad."

The prison was not what Tony, Juanita, or Tom had been expecting. Juanita was clearly relieved, but Danny could tell that both Tom and Tony were disappointed. Peach tree groves, allotment gardens, and a series of mobile homes with wire mesh over the plastic windows was not anyone's idea of a prison—especially since to get here, they'd had to drive past the heavily armored Supermax ADX.

"There are holes in the fence!" Tom said.

Danny nodded. Great big holes that no one seemed to have any interest in repairing. Any of the prisoners could get out anytime they wanted if they put a little effort into it. Danny speculated that since most of them were nearly finished with their sentences, no one felt the need.

Juanita pulled up to the gate and Walt leaned across her to talk to the guard sitting in the little booth. It was one of the guards Walt knew from chain-gang duty.

"Hey, Trey!" Walt said.

"Mr. Brown, what are you doing out here on a Saturday? There's not a work detail going out today that I don't know about, is there?"

Danny was taken aback; people rarely called Walt mister anything. And certainly not people in uniform.

Walt laughed. "No, no work detail. Just thought I'd show my family around if that's OK, and I wanted to talk to Bob Randall if he's here? . . . Wait a minute, 'course he's here. Where else is he gonna be?"

Trey laughed and opened the barrier, and they drove into the prison.

Bob was working in a garden, brushing snow off little bushy things that had been wrapped in plastic bags. He was in jeans and an orange T-shirt and he was wearing a Rockies beanie cap. Houdini the cat was sunning itself next to him.

"That's Bob over there," Walt said, pointing him out.

"He's not exactly Hannibal Lecter, is he?" Tom muttered sarcastically.

Walt introduced everyone, and Bob wiped his hand on his shirt and shook hands, giving Tony and Juanita little bows and saying, "Pleased to make your acquaintance, ma'am," like an old-timey character from a Western.

They met Houdini. Houdini was clearly not impressed by any of them, for as soon as they tried to pet him he ran off and hid under a wheelbarrow.

"How do you like my vines?" Bob asked, pointing at the stubby bushes.

"Grapevines?" Walt asked. "You can grow grapes in Colorado?"

"Yeah, we get good quick frosts here and a lot of August heat; they make a nice Malbec-style red if you blend it with some of the grapes from around Trinidad. We sell six crates a year, makes a little money for the facility."

"Oh, that's a wonderful idea," Juanita said.

"Bob's too modest to say it, but I'll bet the idea was his," Walt said.

Bob grinned and nodded. "I just hope they keep it up after I leave; none of my colleagues seems that interested, and these little guys take a lot of work."

They talked grapes and wine and other subjects Danny couldn't care less about before Bob finally came to it. "So what brings you folks out here today?"

Everyone turned to Danny. His face glowed.

"Uh, well, we thought that maybe you could, uh, you know, 'cause you're sort of an expert, not an expert because you're in here, Walt says you have a PhD, you know, that's why," he began before Tony interrupted.

"Someone's been killing cats in Cobalt and we wondered if you'd help us catch him," she said.

Bob rubbed his chin.

"Well," he said. "I'll see what I can do."

They repaired to Bob's trailer. As Danny recalled, it was a little cramped, but it wasn't that bad: toilet, shower, window with a grill over it, a desk, a bookcase stuffed full of books. There were only two chairs though, so Danny, Tom, and Tony sat on Bob's bed while Walt and Juanita sat in the chairs and Bob stood. He liked to stand, he claimed.

Behind Bob on the wall there was a painting of guys walking through the snow. It seemed an odd thing to have on your wall. If it had been Danny in prison in landlocked Colorado, he'd have a Pacific Ocean scene on his wall, not snow. If you wanted snow, you could look at Pikes Peak any day of the year.

"Check this out," Tom whispered, taking a huge book from under his butt called *The Encyclopedia of Serial Killers* and thumbing through the index. "Let's flick to the Ls and see if Lebkuchen is in here," Tom joked.

"Put that down," Danny whispered.

Bob also appeared to collect little painted postcards from Europe and North America: the Eiffel Tower painted in an Art Deco style, Big Ben done like a watercolor, a cathedral in Barcelona in a surrealist style, the Empire State Building also in Art Deco.

"Those are nice postcards," Danny said.

"I collect 'em. When someone gets out of here and they say they're going anywhere near any of the places on the postcards, I ask them if they'll mail one to me. So far I've gotten back New York, Paris, Barcelona, Los Angeles. Harder to get the European ones, because of parole and stuff like that. Makes me think of the outside world."

Danny didn't reply. Tom was fidgeting like mad and, worse, Tony was half reclining against the wall and the back of her hand was suddenly resting against Danny's thigh. Danny wondered if she knew that this was taking place or if she hadn't noticed. Danny certainly was aware of it, and he was finding it very hard to concentrate.

"And I like this big picture," Juanita said.

Bob grinned. "Pieter Bruegel the Elder, 1565. Lovely,

isn't it? *Hunters in the Snow*. I came across it in a book and fell in love with it. The details are incredible. Kids pulling sleds, people making fires, the men with their dogs . . . oh, it's wonderful. It's like a whole universe in there. When I get out, I'm going to go to Vienna and see the real thing."

"I love the Dutch masters," Walt said.

Danny groaned. Walt could go on about art for hours, but somehow sensing this, Tony said, "So let me tell you what we know about the cats . . ."

She told them about the three cats they knew about that had been killed, all of them in Cobalt, two supposedly by a coyote and the third in what the sheriff thought was "some kind of freak accident."

"That seems reasonable, a coyote and an accident," Bob said.

"Well, the one in the parking lot had its guts pulled out and the cat was just lying there; it hadn't been eaten or anything," Tony said.

"Except that its heart was missing," Tom added.

Bob shook his head. "Coyote could have been disturbed before eating the rest of the kill."

"That's what they said in the paper," Danny admitted.

"And then this last one could have been an accident," Bob continued, rubbing his red goatee.

"Hanging from a tree?" Tony said.

"Hanging by what?" Bob asked.

"I don't know, does it matter?" Tony asked.

"Yes, it matters. Hanging by a wire, rope, piece of string . . . they're all different. And these other cats, were they displayed or just left there?" Bob asked.

"What do you mean 'displayed'?" Walt asked.

"Ritually displayed, in a certain shape or pointing in a certain direction. You need to know these things. You need to do a lot of legwork."

"What sort of legwork?" Tom asked.

"Well, if you're convinced it's somebody, not *something*, I can help you with a profile, but you guys are going to have to do the research. How long were the cats missing first? Did the people who lost the cats have yards, fences? Where did these cats come from? How were they taken? Were the houses broken into? Geographically, where were the houses located? Is there a pattern to the geography? What type of cats were taken? Are there similarities between the breeds? Where were the bodies found? The same place? Different places? Is there a link between the places? What was the condition of the bodies? Did the Sheriff's Department take photographs of the finds? . . . I mean, do you have any of those answers?"

Tony looked at Danny. Danny looked at Tom. Tom shrugged.

"No, we don't," Danny said.

Bob sighed. "Well, I don't know why you'd want me to take this seriously when you're obviously not taking it very seriously."

"Hey, they're just kids, you know?" Walt said defensively.

Bob's eyes flashed angrily. "Who do you think has been killing the cats?"

"What do you mean?" Danny asked.

"Kids. Kids are doing it," Bob said.

Silence filled the room for an uncomfortable couple of seconds.

"How do you know that?" Danny wondered.

"Serial killers start young, and they start with animals. It's called zoo sadism. Almost never do they begin with human beings. They begin with insects or arachnids: wasps, spiders, flies, ants . . . Then when the thrill of killing those creatures fades, they move up the phylogenetic scale. Perhaps mice, rats. Then they move higher, perhaps to squirrels, possum, and maybe even house cats. What we're looking at here is a serial killer in the third stage of his progression."

"What's the fourth stage?" Juanita asked, shocked.

"Once you've moved on to mammals, there is nowhere else to go but humans. People," Bob said dispassionately.

"So if he's not caught, he'll get bored with cats and start killing people?" Tony asked.

Bob shook his head. "No, I don't mean that at all. He'll probably stop. Most nascent serial killers, most animal abusers, never cross that species hurdle. Ninety percent of animal abusers wouldn't dream of killing a person, but there is that chance."

"You said 'he.' Couldn't it be a girl, too?" Tony said.

Bob nodded. "You know what? It probably is a fox or a coyote, but if it's a person, yes, it could be a girl. Though that also is unlikely, since the vast majority of serial killers and nascent serial killers are male. What I'll need is more information before I can say anything with any degree of certainty."

"What about a team of killers?" Tony asked.

"Could be, especially with kids, but again most serial killers are loners—in case the other guy turns you in. The chronology might be interesting, too. Was it related to any particular time of year? Christmas Day, New Year's Day? And what were the intervals? Are they getting shorter, longer?"

Tony's hand had moved to her own lap and Danny could focus properly again, but Tom's fidgeting was increasing and Danny had the feeling that he was becoming less interested in all of this. The visit to the prison had been something of a letdown and he hadn't seemed that engaged in what Bob had to say. Danny wondered if he had only gotten involved in all of this because Tony felt that it was important. Could Tom have a crush on Tony? Was that why he had come here?

They thanked Bob for his time and on the ride back to Cobalt Danny thought about the back of Tony's hand against his thigh. He'd kissed a girl before. Two. He'd even had a sort of girlfriend for a week, Syria Hughes, but it turned out that she'd only been seeing him to make Adrian Ortega jealous. And he'd gotten to second base with an older girl on Ponson Street in East L.A., but with Tony it felt different. There was a spark there.

Tony was special. He could see that. Tom could probably see that, too.

They drove into Colorado Springs and dropped off Tom and then headed back to Cobalt. Tony waved good-bye and Danny went inside and helped his mother unpack some more of their boxes.

It was a Saturday, so they had hamburgers for dinner. And since the cable still hadn't been connected, instead of watching TV they played Scrabble, which Walt won by more than fifty points.

It started snowing at nine, and Juanita sent Danny outside to close the garage doors. He had just turned the key in the lock when he noticed Tony's front door open. And who should walk out of Tony's house but none other than Hector Watson. Mr. Frappuccino. Mr. Monday Morning, 10:15. Danny turned off the garage light and slipped into the shadows. He was surprised to see Mr. Meadows shake Hector warmly by the hand and was even more surprised when Tony appeared behind Mr. Meadows wearing a dress. Hector said something that made Tony and Mr. Meadows laugh. Finally Mr. Meadows and Hector got into the Mercedes and drove off.

Tony waved and closed the front door.

"So, you had Hector over for dinner," Danny said petulantly to himself. "And it looks like you all had a great time. I guess you don't care that there's a lunatic out there, breaking into people's yards, killing their cats!"

He stood there watching the snow fall and turn weirdly

orange under the halogen streetlamps. He shivered. There was something about this stupid town. Something he didn't like but that he couldn't quite put his finger on. What was it? The smallness? The fact that everyone knew everyone else? Or was it just the people themselves? At least in Vegas people told you they were out to get you. Here they stabbed you in the back.

Danny went back inside. He turned on the TV, but without cable all he was looking at was static: gray and black dots vaporizing on the screen.

He went upstairs and got his skateboard out from under his bed. He skated on the hardwood landing back and forth, back and forth while Jeffrey watched him glassily every time he passed the bedroom door.

He finally came down for supper. Juanita had placed Oreos and a glass of milk on the living room table.

He could only manage one cookie. He was very tired and already the wind in the trees had begun to work its soporific magic.

He went up to bed. Jeffrey curled up next to him on the duvet.

"Cat killers," he said. "Don't you worry, Jeff. Whether it's a coyote or a kid, we'll keep you safe, old buddy."

Jeffrey blinked his green cat eyes in slow, measured indifference.

TWELVE

Monday Morning, 10:15

A noise before the dawn. Danny bolted out of bed and shouted "Aha!" pointing his finger at Tony, Tom, or whoever else she'd brought with her in this latest bedroom invasion.

There was no one there.

Jeffrey wasn't there either.

He looked at the clock. The luminous hands of SpongeBob SquarePants were pointing at the five and the two. He squinted a little and saw that it was ten past five.

It was Monday morning.

Sunday had been a total bust.

Tony hadn't come round to see him.

Tom hadn't texted him.

He'd skated to the Cobalt Sheriff's Department, but

their office had been closed. Everything in Cobalt turned out to be closed on Sundays. The 7-Eleven, the Safeway, the Laundromat, the hardware store, the sorry excuse for a strip mall on Manitou Springs Road. Everything except the two Pentecostal churches, which were packed—at least, they appeared to be from the number of cars in the parking lots.

The sun had come out and Danny had skated around aimlessly.

He'd seen Cooper drive past with his mom and he'd waved to him, but Cooper had frowned like he knew Danny from somewhere but couldn't quite figure out where.

Danny skated home and sat there all day with no books or TV or computer.

And now it was Monday.

Monday morning, eleven minutes past five.

And something had woken him.

"Jeff?" he said. But Jeff wasn't there.

He went to the window and stared out at the blackness. Some of that void was mountain and some forest, but it was impossible to tell which was which.

Danny slapped his forehead. "And I forgot that stupid flashlight again!" he muttered, and then forgave himself, because unless they'd gone into Colorado Springs there was nowhere to buy the flashlight anyway.

"Jeff?" he tried one more time.

He hadn't gone out there, had he?

Danny stared into the nothingness.

He couldn't see his hand in front of his face. If it hadn't been for SpongeBob's hands there would be no—

Wait a minute. Wait a minute, what the hell was that?

Out there in the woods, that little bobbing rectangle. There, just for a moment at the edge of his vision and then gone. And there again. And gone again.

Danny knew exactly what it was. It was the fluorescent patch on a pear of sneakers. There was nothing animal, vegetable, or mineral about it; it was a person. Someone was definitely out there.

His first instinct was to call out "I can see you!" but he thought better of it immediately.

He fumbled for his jeans and pulled them over his pajama bottoms, shoved on sneakers and a sweater, and grabbed his new ski coat before realizing that it was covered in fluorescent patches, too.

He got his leather jacket instead and opened the bedroom door.

Down the hallway he could hear Walt snoring loudly.

Maybe he should wake him and his mom? No, they'd do more harm than good.

He jogged down the stairs, went to the back door, picked the key from the hook, turned it in the lock. The large yard at the rear of the house had a wooden fence around it with a gate in the fence that led directly to the forest.

He had never gone through the gate; no one had.

He looked into the garden. About an inch of snow had fallen—not too bad. He walked across the garden and came to the gate. It was chilly, and although his breath wasn't freezing on his face like earlier, twenty minutes outside without a hat wouldn't be pleasant.

He fumbled at the gate for a second, found an iron latch, lifted it, and pushed hard. The gate opened easily and swung out on well-oiled hinges into the forest.

Danny's eyes were becoming accustomed to the dark. There were streetlights in the cul-de-sac, and between the clouds, stars from trillions of miles away were scattering a few random photons here and there.

The fluorescent patches were about thirty yards to the north in the woods. It looked like they were roughly behind Tony's house.

Danny walked toward the light, stepping over fallen trees and split branches.

He was afraid but not *that* afraid, and he wasn't entirely sure that he wasn't still in bed dreaming all this.

He stepped over a fallen log and waded through a two-inch layer of pine needles.

When he got to within fifteen or twenty yards of Tony's house he discovered that the person (if it had been a person) was no longer visible.

An owl hooted and Danny bumped into a tree, causing snow to drift down from the upper branches like powdered sugar onto a churro.

His teeth began to chatter and he shoved his hands deep into his pockets.

The fluorescent patches had vanished, but he hadn't heard

anyone running away. Maybe he'd been seeing things? Or perhaps it was a—

A noise came from behind him and he turned and got his arm up just in time as something came crashing down on top of him.

He crumpled like a rag doll and his face hit the snow.

He flinched and curled himself into a ball, expecting more blows, but nothing came. He opened one eye and then another.

There was no one there.

Next to him was a broken tree branch.

Could it have just snapped and fallen?

He got to his feet, wiped the snow from his jacket, and looked around him. It was dark, but there was not even a hint of motion and no sound of running.

He walked through the woods to where he thought the person had been, right behind Tony's house. If that *was* the cat killer, perhaps Snowflake, Tony's cat, was going to be his next target.

But then again maybe it was just a homeless person, or a bear.

No, bears did not wear sneakers.

Danny pulled himself up onto the fence and gazed into Tony's backyard. A swing set covered with snow, no tracks in the fresh powder.

He looked back into the woods.

"Hello?" he said.

Silence.

He stood there.

Was someone watching him or not? How could you tell?

"I'm not afraid of you!" he said.

He stood there for a while longer and then went home.

Walt and Juanita were making breakfast.

"What were you doing outside?" Walt asked.

"I thought I saw someone. I went to check it out," Danny said.

"Oh my God, are you crazy? Why did you do that?" Juanita said. Then to Walt, "I knew we shouldn't have taken the kids to that prison. Filling their heads with crazy stories. What was I thinking?" She seemed freaked, so Danny decided not to tell her that the person had maybe tried to hit him.

"It might have been a bear, son. They have bears all over this place," Walt said.

"A bear!" Juanita looked at Walt. "I know your views, but if bears are starting to come up to the house, maybe we should get a gun?"

Danny went upstairs.

When he got out of the shower, he rummaged in his school blazer, found Tom's pager, and sent a text to Tony.

myb hv sn ct kllr! or myb hmless dude.

He waited for a reply, but none came.

He put on the rest of his school uniform.

While they were all eating breakfast there was a knock at the front door. Walt opened it to Tony's father, who looked upset.

Mr. Meadows muttered something to Walt. Walt shook his head. Mr. Meadows then pointed at Danny and Walt shook his head again. Mr. Meadows nodded, pointed his finger at Danny, and tried to come inside the house. Walt put his hand up to stop him. Mr. Meadows fumed for a second and then turned on his heel and walked off.

Walt came back to the breakfast table and sat down.

"What was that all about?" Juanita asked.

Walt sighed. "He thinks he saw Danny creeping around outside their daughter Antonia's window this morning. He was pretty angry."

"What?" Danny said, aghast.

"Don't worry about it, son. I took care of it," Walt said.

Juanita looked furious. "Did you tell him about the bear?"

"He thinks I was spying on his daughter?" Danny said.

"Look, he wasn't talking a lot of sense. He says you came into their house the other day, too," Walt said.

"Jesus!" Danny muttered.

"Danny?" his mom asked.

"What?"

"Did you go inside their house?"

Danny's cheeks were burning with outrage. "Are you kidding me? She's been in *here* three times!"

Juanita reached across the table and tried to take Danny's hand. "It's different for a girl, Danny. You can't just go into a girl's room, and you can't go outside her window, either."

Danny stood up, knocking over his orange juice. "I

wasn't spying on anybody! What's the matter with you people?"

"Sit down, Danny, I told him you weren't outside. No point in mentioning the bears or anything else," Walt said.

Danny looked incredulously at the pair of them. Were they nuts? What was it that made adults unable to listen?

He seethed for a second and then grabbed his binder and coat.

"I'm off to school," he said.

When he got outside, he saw Tony in the back of her father's Mercedes, driving out of the cul-de-sac. She saw him, but she didn't wave back when he gave her a little half wave from the hip. Maybe she didn't see the wave or maybe she thought he really was a creepo hanging around outside her bedroom window at five in the morning in freezing temperatures.

"Hell with her," Danny said.

He went inside again, got Sunflower, and strapped it to his backpack. If Tony wasn't going to walk with him, he could freewheel to school from the top of the hill.

He skated along Johnson Close, pulling on his ridiculous white gloves as he did so.

There was a blue sky, it was cold, and he was still hatless.

At the junction of Manitou and Alameda he saw Charlie and Hector waiting under one of those electric heaters the county had installed at the bus stops. If you stood directly underneath one, the temperature was a balmy ten degrees above freezing; a few feet to the left and it was close to and often under zero. But CJHCS was only seven blocks away. Were they lazy or just really cold?

"Hi," Hector called out.

"Hey, we've been waiting for you!" Charlie added.

"Oh my God, you're going to mug me at the bottom of my own street? You guys are lame," Danny said.

Hector shook his head. "We only want to talk to you."

"We want to share with you what we've got, and you can share with us what you've got," Charlie said civilly.

Danny skidded to a halt. Charlie had a sneering, condescending look on his face and Hector looked tired and a little frazzled.

"I don't know what you're talking about," Danny said. "Share what?"

"The cat killings," Charlie said. "Hec says you went to see Bob Randall over at the prison. He gave you a profile of the guy who's been killing cats, right?"

Danny said nothing.

"Well, after Bible study on Sunday we talked to Sheriff Rossi about Sarah Kolpek's cat," Hector said.

"We can share with you what we've got and you can share with us what you've got. How does that sound?" Charlie said again.

"I don't think so," Danny said.

Hector took Charlie to one side and whispered something to him.

"Look," Hector said. "We got off on the wrong foot. All we want to know is what your friend Bob told you."

"He's not my friend," Danny said, unwilling to be associated with his father's criminal pals.

Todd came running up Alameda and joined them. His hair was unkempt and he was out of breath and attempting to tie his tie.

"Where have you been?" Charlie asked.

"I had things to do," Todd said.

Danny looked at Todd. He knew nothing about him. Where he was from, what his parents did. Zero. He looked as if he might be one of those "troubled kids" Mr. Lebkuchen was always talking about who'd been turned around by Direct Instruction and the silent system. As Todd tried again to tie his tie Danny noticed that his fingernails were dirty. He, at least, would benefit from wearing gloves to school.

"Let me help you with that," Hector said, and everyone stopped talking while Hector tied Todd's tie.

"Let's go to school. Walk with us, Danny," Charlie said.

"OK," Danny replied.

"He joined us?" Todd asked when they got moving. His face was pale and he had dark eyes that radiated a sort of animal intelligence.

"Not yet. We were asking Danny what his friend Bob Randall told him about the cat killer," Hector said.

Todd flinched and said nothing.

"So what do you know?" Charlie asked.

"You go first," Danny said.

Hector shrugged. "OK. Sheriff Rossi said that Sarah's

cat was strung up by a clothesline tied to the tree. Sarah's mom said that the cat was really old. So that rules out an accident. How could it have gotten up there, and how did it get the clothesline around its neck? It doesn't make sense. Someone did it. Someone grabbed the cat and hung it."

"Who would do a thing like that?" Todd wondered.

"I don't know," Hector said, "but Danny does, don't you, Danny? Your turn."

"I didn't agree to anything. I'm outta here, guys," Danny said with a grin.

"You little punk!" Hector said. "You're making a mistake. You're committing social suicide hanging with them. You should be with us. That Tom Sloane is a total freak, Cooper is a weirdo, Tony's probably a lesbo, and I hate to tell you this but if you're hanging out with them, you're going to be in the weirdo camp too, pal."

Danny was suddenly angry. "What did you say about Tony?"

Hector smiled. "I said she's probably a lesbo."

"What the hell were you doing at her house on Saturday night?" Danny asked.

"Having dinner," Hector said with evident satisfaction. He had found the chink in Danny's armor and he was going to exploit it for all it was worth. "Tony and I were finalists for the YCCY Award last year, and Mr. Meadows knows my dad. Didn't Tony tell you? I go over there sometimes. She comes to my house."

"What's the YCCY?" Danny couldn't help himself asking.

"Young Christian Coloradan of the Year. Oh yeah, we go way back. Old friends from kindergarten."

"Some friend, the way you talk about her . . ."

"What's the matter? Are you in love with her or something?" Charlie mocked.

"His freako friend is," Hector sneered.

Danny couldn't think of anything to say except what the girls had said to him in the Colorado Springs Starbucks. "Yeah, well, April Donovan says it's you that's the total weirdo."

Hector frowned. "How's that?"

"She says that your dad's the executioner on death row and he pushes the button and he kills people and everybody hates him and you're completely screwed up because of it. Hannibal-style," Danny said.

"April Donovan said that?"

"Yeah, pal, she did."

"Oh man, that's so wrong. My dad works on death row, but it's the doctors who administer the lethal injection. But so what if he did? It'd be a cool job. I'm not screwed up. That's so funny that she said that," Hector replied quickly.

"He told you," Charlie said.

"Yeah," Todd added.

"*Niños blancos* . . . see you guys," Danny muttered. He bomb-dropped onto his board and began kicking away from them.

"Remember, ten fifteen this morning, you'll see who's running the school and it's not Tom and his loser circle! And hey, we're giving you that for nothing," Hector shouted after him.

"Thanks," Danny said, and kicked hard all the way to school.

An hour and a bit later Danny was sitting at the window seat in the corner, watching the clock while Miss Benson read through the new heading on her teacher book. Clock-watching was a normal part of Danny's school day, but as the minute hand marched around to 10:13 he grew especially engaged.

Was something really going to happen?

He looked at Hector and Charlie.

What were they planning?

For a moment he worried about a Columbine-style thing. Littleton wasn't too far away . . . but then, to his surprise, at exactly 10:15 Mr. Lebkuchen knocked on the door and entered.

Everyone stood. Mr. Lebkuchen motioned them to sit. He smiled at the kids and then turned to Miss Benson, announcing in a quiet voice, "Miss Benson, I'm afraid I'm going to have to ask you to pack up your things."

Miss Benson's glassy eyes became even more opaque. "I'm sorry?" she said.

"We should discuss it outside," Mr. Lebkuchen said.

"Discuss what outside?" Miss Benson wondered.

"I'm sorry to say that we are terminating your contract."

"What? Why?"

"Wouldn't you rather talk in my office?" Mr. Lebkuchen asked.

"Like hell I would. I've been with this school from the beginning. And you're telling me this now in front of my own class? What is this crap?"

Mr. Lebkuchen tucked his arms behind his back and interlaced his fingers—rather like an angry baseball manager who doesn't want to get into a shoving match with an ump, Danny thought.

Mr. Lebkuchen pointed at a boy named James Nguyen.

"James, you're running the class for the time being. Danny, please get Miss Benson's bag and coat. Miss Benson, please come with me."

Mr. Lebkuchen walked out of the classroom and Miss Benson had no choice but to follow him. Danny grabbed her coat and followed them outside as James began reading the teacher's portion of the lesson.

Danny followed Mr. Lebkuchen and Miss Benson to the principal's office. He handed Miss Benson her stuff.

"Thank you, Danny. Now, go back to your class. There's a good lad," Mr. Lebkuchen said.

Danny saw that there were tears in Miss Benson's eyes and her bottom lip was trembling. Mr. Lebkuchen, by contrast, was completely emotionless.

"Run along, Danny," Mr. Lebkuchen said, closing the office door.

Danny thought about going back to class, but his natural curiosity kept him outside the door.

"What is all this?" Miss Benson demanded angrily.

"Well, if you must know, you've been triangulating, Miss Benson."

"Triangulating?"

"In violation of your contract, you and Miss Indurian wrote an article for the *Journal of Secondary Education* criticizing the school and its methods."

"That was two months ago."

"It was only brought to my attention recently. You are dismissed, Miss Benson. Now, please take your remaining things and leave. Miss Bailey will have a check for you in her office. I think you will find that we've been quite generous, considering your blatant breach of contract."

"You're firing me?" Miss Benson was still not able to quite take it in.

"I am dismissing you and Miss Indurian. I shall teach both classes until we find suitable replacements."

"This is a violation of the Constitution. I have a right to free speech. I'm going to talk to a lawyer," Miss Benson muttered.

"We are represented by Hart and McConnell. I will look forward to hearing from your attorney. Now, please go, Miss Benson, and do see Miss Bailey on the way out for your severance."

"I'll see her, all right!" Miss Benson yelled.

The office door burst open and Miss Benson came out.

She looked at Danny, stopped short, and smiled. Her hair was dangling over her face in little nooses and her eyes had swollen and her cheeks were red. It made her look younger, Danny thought, like she was yet another student Mr. Lebkuchen had to punish for their wayward antics.

"And please, Miss Benson, no shouting. Remember, we have a silence policy," Mr. Lebkuchen said from inside his office.

Miss Benson waved at Danny to go back to class and then, in a brief but passionate and expletive-filled tirade, informed Mr. Lebkuchen what he could do with his silence policy and where he could put it—a place, Danny thought, that few people except perhaps Mr. Lebkuchen's mother had ever seen.

Danny ran back to class and took his seat about a minute before Mr. Lebkuchen came in and picked up the Direct Instruction manual and continued where James had left off. He didn't even need to ask a student where in the reading they were because along the side of the page it listed what must be read at what time and how long each exercise had to take.

Danny followed along in his book, but soon became aware that he was being stared at. He looked up into Charlie and Hector's grinning faces. Hector winked at him and Danny nodded.

"*Yes. I'm impressed,*" he mouthed, and all three of them returned to their books before Mr. Lebkuchen could catch them looking at each other.

When class was over, Mr. Lebkuchen thanked them for their attention, apologized for the disruption, and informed them that from this afternoon and until two new teachers were hired they would be meeting in the old physics room and merging their class with 9A.

"I know what you're thinking," Mr. Lebkuchen said.

I doubt that, Danny thought, staring at Tony's bra strap, which was showing through her shirt.

"You're thinking why can't we just have substitute teachers, like in other schools?" Mr. Lebkuchen said. "Well, this is a special school and it needs special teachers. On top of my other duties I will be teaching both classes. Fear not, children! Your learning will not suffer and with a little bit of luck we will have you back in your seats before the month is out. I will be giving you all a note to take home to your parents, explaining this situation. An unfortunate situation, with Open Night looming so closely. Now, off with you. Class is dismissed. Danny Brown, I'd like you to remain seated."

When all the other kids had filed out—some, including Tony, giving him concerned looks—Mr. Lebkuchen summoned Danny to the seat directly in front of Miss Benson's desk.

When Danny sat, Mr. Lebkuchen smiled at him and shook his head.

"You have fallen in with a bad crowd, Danny. Could you turn out your pockets, please?"

Danny wondered if he could try Miss Benson's Constitutional or profanity-based arguments, but neither was quite his style. Still, for a second he tried to remember the lyrics to Jay-Z's "99 Problems," which went something like: "My glove compartment is closed, so you're going to need a warrant for that."

"Don't you need a warrant or something?" he said.

Mr. Lebkuchen laughed. "No. Of course not. Now, let me see what you've got in there."

Danny turned out his pockets, putting a pencil, coins, a five-dollar bill, a stick of Wrigley's and, finally, Tom's pager on the desk in front of him. Mr. Lebkuchen lifted the gum and the pager. He examined them for a brief moment and sighed.

"The gum is not permitted, and this is a device for sending text messages in contravention of the school rules, if I am not mistaken," Mr. Lebkuchen said.

Danny nodded.

"Who gave you this?" Mr. Lebkuchen asked.

"I don't remember," Danny said.

"Detention every day for the rest of the week will help you recall, perhaps," he said.

"I doubt it," Danny said.

"Morning and afternoon detention. And all of next week, too," Mr. Lebkuchen said.

Danny said nothing, but an unfortunate sniffle escaped his nostrils and Mr. Lebkuchen bit his lip.

"Are you OK?" he asked.

"Yes. I'm fine," Danny replied.

Mr. Lebkuchen took off his glasses and cleaned them with a handkerchief. He smiled at Danny and looked out the window. "It's snowing," he said.

Danny nodded.

"I suppose you don't know Hokusai?" Mr. Lebkuchen asked.

Danny shook his head.

"Or Basho?"

"No."

"One was an artist, the other a poet. Japanese. Both of them in their different media gave snow a lightness, an elegance, a crisp beauty, an almost magical quality that we don't really see in Western art. Yes, I know one immediately thinks of Robert Frost, but even Frost's snow was a harsh, heavy New England snow. Claustrophobic, dense, icy . . . and Colorado snow, as you've seen, can be even heavier."

"Uh, yeah," Danny said.

"You might find this interesting, Danny: The state religion of Japan is Shinto. Shinto is the worship of nature. Nature is imbued with what we would call the Holy Spirit, or what the Native Americans called the Great Spirit," Mr. Lebkuchen said, giving him a significant look.

Danny saw the opening but didn't take the bait. He wasn't going to talk about his Indian background with this skeevy character. He nodded but said nothing.

"I suppose Okinawa doesn't have the fascination for you or many other people that it would obviously have for me. Do you know *Stairway to Heaven*?" Mr. Lebkuchen asked after a pause.

"The song?" Danny asked incredulously.

"There's a song? No. I'm talking about the film."

"Don't know the film," Danny said.

Mr. Lebkuchen blinked, as if remembering something. "Oh, all right. Um, do you like science fiction, then?"

"Sure," Danny said.

"Did you ever see *The Incredible Shrinking Man*?"

Danny had seen that one, on a particularly dreary evening a couple of years ago. He hadn't thought much of it. It was in black-and-white.

"Yeah," he said.

Mr. Lebkuchen smiled. "You see, that's what I'm trying to say. At the end of *The Incredible Shrinking Man* he realizes that as long as God can see him, it doesn't matter how small he is. God sees everything and shines through everything. Even snow."

Mr. Lebkuchen frowned. "I suppose I shouldn't be talking about God in a public school. Well, I am. And I know about that Scripture club of theirs and frankly I wish it didn't have to be a secret, but that's not the law—at the moment."

Mr. Lebkuchen's clear blue eyes were boring into him.

Danny wondered if Mr. Lebkuchen was probing his defenses or perhaps, more charitably, maybe he was just trying to connect? But Hokusai? *The Incredible Shrinking Man*? That was the best he could do to try to reach a fourteen-year-old kid?

"Oh, I agree with you," Danny said, deciding to play along. "My mom does, too. 'Without God, there can't really be any kind of meaningful education at all,' she says.

She's Catholic. Very devout. I'm not as serious as her, but I pray every day."

Mr. Lebkuchen smiled. "Good. Good. I knew that. I had a feeling that you did. I'm a good judge of character. And I had a feeling about you."

Danny sniffed and tried not to look guilty.

"You're young and life is short. That's why I'm tolerant of things in this school. The secret societies, the rule violations . . . But there are limits and limits are very important, don't you think?"

"Yes."

"The history of Western civilization has been a struggle between liberalism and conservatism. Neither is right, of course. Sometimes we need more liberty, other times we need to pull back on the reins. Do you see what I'm saying? It's a balance."

"I think so," Danny said.

Mr. Lebkuchen smiled. The interview was terminated, but Danny saw a little opening: "Sir, that Japanese poet who wrote about the snow, you wouldn't have a copy of him, would you?"

Mr. Lebkuchen's smile widened. "I'll see what I can do," he said.

THIRTEEN

A Message from Indrid Cold

Silence. Silence in the corridor. Silence in the classes. Silence so deep they could hear Canada geese honking in Bear Creek Park. Silence, Danny realized, had many layers and textures. Not all of them were unpleasant. If you grew up in Vegas you lived in a world that was 24/7, 365. If you wanted to go to the movies or go bowling at three in the morning, you could.

Here you were limited.

And as Principal Lebkuchen had tried to explain, sometimes it was good to have limits. Complete freedom was no freedom at all.

Danny thought about this over lunch.

He sat by himself.

He didn't want another dressing-down from Tom about another lost pager.

He ate and enjoyed the food and listened to the layers of nothingness.

To his own breath.

He closed his eyes and breathed.

The silence of a roomful of people was very different from the silence of a wood or a bedroom.

It was—

A sneeze was coming on.

He reached into his blazer pocket for a tissue.

There was something in the pocket. A note.

He sneezed and looked at the note. It had been printed in Times New Roman in italic on a flat piece of card. It said:

Physics class. Lunchtime. Come alone.
It will be worth your while. —Indrid Cold

He looked around the canteen. Indrid Cold was obviously a pseudonym, but Danny guessed the person might be watching him right now. He nodded.

I assume you'll arrange for the physics classroom door to be unlocked, Mr. Cold? he thought to himself on his way over.

The door was unlocked. Danny turned the handle and went inside.

"Hello?" Danny said.

No answer.

"Hello?" he tried again.

Again no answer.

Danny sat in one of the chairs. The physics classroom was a large room with a hardwood floor, gas taps for Bunsen burners, wide windows, and a gigantic machine at the back of the room, covered in a gray tarpaulin sheet with interesting-looking wires protruding from the bottom. This, Danny assumed, was the famous Tesla coil.

He was keen to get a look at it, but this was probably not the best time.

"Hello?" Danny tried again.

He sat back in his chair.

He liked this room better than any other class in the school. It was not only bigger and airier but it had more light, an interesting smell, and a tremendous view of Pikes Peak and the whole of the Front Range.

Danny drummed his fingers on the desk and let five minutes go by.

He walked to the back of the classroom and looked under the tarp at the Tesla coil.

He froze when he heard footsteps outside, but it was just someone walking by.

He went to the window and watched the poor suckers stuck outside on this freezing January day.

"Hello? Is there anybody here?" he tried again.

He sat back down in one of the desk-chairs.

He yawned.

He watched the clouds advance north from New Mexico over the high desert.

He put his hands on the desk and rested his chin on them.

He yawned again.

He closed his eyes.

He thought about his mom. She worked hard. Too hard. He thought about Walt. Walt would be OK if he wasn't such a jerk about everything. Why couldn't he just leave things alone? He thought about Jeffrey. What a cat. The cat of cats. The king of the Tropicana Wash. Cats were good pets, he thought. You could bend the will of a dog, but a cat chose to be with you of its volition.

His thoughts became less focused.

He was drifting.

Falling.

Falling for a long time.

Into blackness.

Into the pit.

He landed with a thud.

He couldn't breathe.

The air was thick.

He was afraid.

First there was nothing and then the wolves came with yellow eyes and skinny legs and long tongues. Their ribs shimmering in the light, their bodies mincing and trailing after the feet of the alpha dog. They trotted and sniffed the air.

They smelled him.

"Ahhh, we caught one," the alpha bitch snarled, and they all advanced.

"No!" Danny screamed.

He breathed cold clear air.

He filled his lungs with it.

He opened his eyes.

An oxygen mask. Two firemen standing over him. The classroom filled with people.

"He'll be all right, mild gas asphyxiation. It could have been serious," one firefighter said.

"We'll take him to the hospital anyway," the other replied.

"No, no hospitals, just take me home," Danny protested.

Mr. Lebkuchen and Cooper Reid rode with him in the ambulance. Mr. Lebkuchen held Danny's hand. Danny was fully conscious and utterly embarrassed.

He heard Mr. Lebkuchen explain the situation to the ER nurse.

"We were meeting in a different class after lunch. Danny's new, so he must have gone there early to find it. Unfortunately someone had left the door open and Danny went inside. He must have knocked against one of the gas taps for the Bunsen burner. Young Cooper Reid found him slumped on the floor. He ran to get the rest of the class and they tried to revive him before I called 911."

They kept him for observation overnight.

His mother cried.

Even Walt looked upset.

At midnight he begged his mom to let him go home.

He got out of the hospital nightgown and changed back into his school clothes.

Just as he'd been expecting, the note in his blazer pocket was no longer there.

"What an unlucky accident," his mom said in the front seat. "But it could have been so much worse."

An accident.

Was it an accident? Had there been a note at all?

Danny didn't know. He was confused, embarrassed, and he resolved to say nothing more about it until he had everything clearer in his head.

Letter V

You are a special person, Antonia. I can tell that. I think
that if I opened myself up to you, you would understand. You
would look through the surface to the real me.

I would tell you things about me and you would
understand.

I like to sleep outside at night. Even in the winter. Did you
know that?

Supposedly our nomadic ancestors in Africa lived outside
for a million years. We lay under the stars and watched the
Milky Way.

I like to lie in my zero-rated sleeping bag and bivouac bag.

I'm never cold or wet.

I like to think about you in your house.

I wonder what you're doing there.

Someday I will come in and you will welcome me.

I know that.

I just know it.

PART TWO

In the Shadow of the Coil

FOURTEEN

Camera Obscura

Danny fired up Internet Explorer and clicked on Google.

"Tesla built his own camera obscura, and he had one of the first working concepts for a television but he got no credit for it, just as he got no credit for any of his other inventions," Cooper was saying.

"Pull the lens cover off. No, not that way! You'll break it! Gently," Tom said.

The conversation continued, but Danny wasn't listening.

He still didn't have his computer or Internet at home so he was using one of Tom's many laptops while Tom and Cooper fiddled with Tom's camera obscura.

In a lot of ways these kids are OK dudes, Danny thought. Tom had not kicked up a fuss about the second missing pager in light of Danny's near asphyxiation. And Cooper had not lorded it over him for maybe saving his life.

And Danny knew that it was better to have friends who were geeks than not to have friends at all.

He Googled the words "Indrid Cold."

There were over two hundred thousand results, including a couple of rock bands, a bank robber, a painter, and a performance artist. Indrid Cold was also the pseudonym of various hoaxers and imposters from the nineteenth century onward.

"What are you reading over there?" Tom asked.

"Uh, nothing really," Danny said.

"Put that away; we're nearly ready."

Danny sighed. A hoaxer and an imposter. That figured. He closed the laptop.

"So what is this camera thing anyway?" he asked.

"Ta-da!" Tom said.

The mountain wind blowing through oak trees. The mountain wind blowing through wide boulevards in a shadow world. People going about their business, unobserved, unaware that they were characters in a silent film. Not self-conscious but real, better than actors could ever be. The camera projecting the whole of the visible world in a rich shade of January blue on Tom's faded mahogany table. Danny had seen projected films before, but this was more compelling. This wasn't like a movie, for these were actual people living out their actual lives. Everyone was moving, going somewhere else. Undergraduates riding bicycles to the Colorado College campus. Kids walking home from school.

A group of soldier recruits from Fort Carson quick-marching in tight formation and a band of Olympians from the US Olympic Training Center on Willamette Avenue running a circuit of Colorado Springs at a ridiculously fast pace.

Danny watched, entranced as they entered one side of the camera obscura's viewfinder and exited through the other. He still didn't quite understand how the device operated, but according to Tom this entire attic room was the camera box and the oak table was the screen, but if that were true it meant they were *in* the camera right now. Which was really weird.

"This is awesome," Danny said.

"Yes it is, isn't it?" Tom said proudly. "I got the idea from this old movie called *A Matter of Life and Death*. The old doc looks at the whole world through his camera obscura."

"We still have to get down to business," Cooper said.

"What business?" Danny muttered.

"Come on, drink up your chocolate and we shall begin," Tom insisted.

It was a meeting of the Watchers in Tom's room. Cooper, Olivia, and Tom were there, but not Tony. It was disappointing because Danny thought that Tony was going to come and finally he'd get a chance to talk to her.

It had been a frustrating day.

His first day back after "the accident."

Tony had smiled at him politely, but she hadn't spoken to him, hadn't texted him, and that morning she'd gotten a ride to school.

To add insult to injury, he'd seen her, through the science classroom window, walking home with Hector.

He'd wanted to talk to her. To tell her what had really happened in the science classroom (something he had told no one) and to run by her an idea he had for maybe catching the cat killer. But she, apparently, was still miffed at him.

Olivia cleared her throat and Danny looked at her.

She really was very pretty. No comparison between her and Tony. A 10 versus an 8. "We don't know how they knew about Miss Benson's dismissal; it is possible that Mr. Lebkuchen attends or even runs the meetings of the SSU, in which case he is in breach of Colorado law and could be reported," Olivia was saying with her most serious face. How could you not like that face? There was an elfin Taylor Swift quality to it.

And yet . . .

She bored him.

They all bored him.

"Nice bit of blackmail," Cooper was saying.

Tom was rolling a twenty-sided die and making notes.

"We don't really know anything," Olivia replied dismissively. "Guesses ain't facts."

"The SSU thinks it runs the school, but we have to show them that we can't be pushed around," Tom said, tapping the table in one of his less annoying fidgets.

"We really should put someone inside the SSU as a mole; it's the only way to know for sure," Olivia said, and put her binder back in her backpack.

Tom was nodding sagely and making notes. "Yup, you might be right about that. We should know what they're doing. Let's discuss it next time. It's a good plan. One we have to move on quickly. In case everyone's forgotten, it's the ninth-grade parents' night tonight. And I've got a big part."

Everyone groaned. No one had forgotten that at seven P.M. they'd have to put their uniforms back on and return to school. Near the start of each term Mr. Lebkuchen invited the parents to watch how a typical class worked and ask questions about Direct Instruction. Tonight was 9B's turn.

"What's your part?" Cooper asked.

"I've been picked as usher by Mr. Lebkuchen, but it's not because I asked for the job or anything," Tom said.

What was it Hector had said?

"Wait, aren't you class prefect, too?" Danny asked a little suspiciously.

"God, who told you that?" Tom muttered. "Yeah, I am. I'm supposed to represent the class at ceremonies and intermural events. It's a total scam. I probably only got it because of my dad—Lebkuchen's very transparent like that. Still, it's going to be good on my résumé. We're not all destined to go to Colorado State."

Danny was surprised to hear Tom say this. He never boasted that his dad had been lieutenant governor of Colorado, never really mentioned his dad at all.

"When's your dad coming back from Afghanistan?" Danny asked.

"March," Tom said without much excitement. "OK. We gotta move along, people. Let me see. The SSU. The camera obscura, we did that. OK, item three, the cat killings. Any ideas, anyone? Danny said he thought there might be someone creeping around outside his house."

Tom looked at Danny and Danny knew Tom wanted him to elaborate, but he said nothing.

"I've got something," Olivia said.

"You do?" Tom responded, a little surprised.

"I've made a map of Cobalt, showing where the cats have gone missing and where the dead cats have been found." She spread the map on the oak table.

"This is great. Good work, Olivia," Tom said.

"I helped!" Cooper protested.

"If you look at where the cats were found, it gives us no information. They were just dumped, abandoned perhaps, but where they were taken is interesting," Olivia continued. Danny looked at her and admired the dimpled hollows of her cheeks. Definitely attractive. He liked the red lips and green eyes.

"Where they were taken?" Danny found himself saying. "There's a clue in the map?"

Before Olivia could answer, Tom's mother yelled that the second batch of hot chocolate was ready.

"Your mom makes great hot chocolate," Danny said.

"My mom?! It's *my* recipe. I melt real Guatemalan chocolate with full cream, a hint of brown sugar, and a secret ingredient."

When everyone had gotten their hot chocolate from downstairs, Tom said, "So, there's a clue in the map?"

"Yes," Olivia replied.

Danny looked at the map of Cobalt more carefully. It was a small town. Just a dozen streets, a school, the small strip mall—all of it like an island of civilization in the primeval forest.

"You see," Olivia began, "the first three cats were taken from these houses. Now, if you look on the map, these houses form the cardinal points of a pentangle."

"What's a pentangle?" Tom asked.

"Exactly the same thing as a pentagram. It's a mystical symbol, looks like this," Olivia replied, drawing a dotted line between the points of a five-pointed star.

"Oh yeah, one of those. I knew that," Tom said. "But couldn't you basically form any shape at all using those three points?"

"Yes, but I think it's a pentangle," Olivia said.

"Those are the cats we know about; there could be others that didn't get reported or whose owners don't know they're missing," Tom suggested.

"In a small place like Cobalt, that's pretty unlikely," Olivia insisted. "Anyway, it's what's at the center of the pentangle that's exciting."

"What is at the center?" Danny asked.

"Look! Open your eyes!" Olivia said.

"Our school!" Danny said.

Tom nodded. "Hmm, yes, I see that. You might have

something here. Maybe we should take this to your friend Bob. What do you think, Danny?"

"Maybe," Danny said.

Tom pressed forward. "OK, now what about the chronology? Danny's expert witness told us to be aware of the chronology. Anyone working on that?"

Nobody was.

"Coop, what about you? Something in my bones tells me that things are coming to a head. That last incident with the tree, I think that represents a significant raising of the stakes. Danny and I will do some snooping on the ground. We'll try the Sheriff's Department, and if we finally get a day that isn't absolutely freezing, we can check out the scene of the crime. Or, rather, scenes of the crimes," Tom said.

Danny nodded vaguely.

"OK, then. Food for thought. I know a lot of us have things to do, me especially," Tom muttered, which meant that he was closing the meeting.

On the way out, Danny went to the bathroom.

He peed in the toilet and was dabbing water on his face when he noticed that the sliding door of the little mirrored cupboard above the sink was open. He slid it open a little more and discovered an amazing pharmacopoeia of pills that Tom's mother kept there. Ambien, Valium, uppers, downers, mellowers, antihistamines, potpourris, assorted herbs, St. John's wort, gingerroot, codeine—the poor woman must be going out of her mind worrying about her husband. If things ever got really really stressful, this would be a good place to come and steal some meds . . .

"Bye," Danny muttered and tried to catch Olivia's eye to see if she wanted him to walk her home, but she was looking elsewhere.

On his skateboard ride back to Cobalt, Danny thought about one thing Tom had said: "Things are coming to a head." He too felt that things were moving faster now. The dismissal of the teachers, the cat hanging from the tree. Perhaps it was all linked.

The cold wind on Colorado Avenue blew the cobwebs from Danny's head and the molasses from his limbs. That room of Tom's . . . He'd felt like a sleepwalker in there, watching the shadow world unfold before his eyes. But out here on Sunflower, he was cold, alive, feeling every bump on the ground, every gradient on the blacktop.

After the big hill out of Manitou, Danny stopped at the gates of CJHCS. He looked at his watch. It was 5:15. He couldn't believe that they'd have to come back here in less than two hours. He felt drawn by the school and looked at it through the wire mesh fence for a moment. Mr. Lebkuchen's car was in the parking lot. An old beat-up tan Sierra four-door sedan.

Danny checked his watch again. It said 5:20. Time to move or he might as well just stay there.

He skated up Alameda, and on the level mesa that made up the upper part of the town of Cobalt, he found himself skating the map that Olivia had shown them.

The map of Cobalt with the cat killings on it.

The first house he came to was 16 Beechfield Road. A lady named Mrs. Craven. Beechfield was the oldest street in the town. Small ranch-style houses with gables and steep roofs and chain fences. Number 16 was no different from the others. Painted white, empty flowerpots, leaves in the yard. Single-story and, yes, it backed onto the woods. An eight-year-old Persian called Tigerfeet had been taken from here.

The second point of the pentagram was on Mott Street. Number 11. Mrs. Pigeon's tabby called Spartacus. Danny skated there, and that was also a single-story ranch-style house. A newer house with an ornamental fountain in the front yard. It didn't appear to have a backyard at all; the house just stopped and the forest began.

The last house on the pentagram so far was 9 Douglas Street, Sarah Kolpek's house.

He skated there.

A two-story wooden cabin-style home, kids' toys in a small yard, and that cat-hanging chestnut tree. Part of the clothesline the cat had apparently been hanged with was still there. Danny shivered. Why hadn't someone cut it down?

He stood there. He was starting to feel a little weirded out. Who hangs a cat from a tree? It was gruesome and cruel.

"What do you want?" a voice said. A girl was walking toward him. Older girl, college age, wearing a black sweater and furry boots. Her orange hair was tied up in a black bandanna. She looked pissed.

"What do you want?" she repeated.

"I don't know," Danny said truthfully.

"Get lost," the girl said.

"I was just looking," Danny said.

The girl crossed her arms. "Taking pictures for your blog or for YouTube, I suppose. You kids are sick. If my dad sees you, he'll come out with the baseball bat. Now scram!"

"Other kids have been here?" Danny asked.

"Yeah, now beat it!"

"Wait a second, how many kids?"

"Three altogether. Now, listen to me, kid, you better—"

"Boys? Tall blond one, a kind of darker one, and a pale one with glasses?" Danny asked.

"Yeah."

Hector, Charlie, and Todd.

"Are they with you?" the girl asked angrily.

"No. They're not with me. They were taking photographs?"

"Yes, they oughtta be ashamed of themselves. Same with you; you're all little creeps," the girl said.

Danny shook his head, kicked up his skateboard, and held it vertically in the tips of his fingers. "I'm here because I was worried," he said.

The girl's face softened. "Sarah's fine. She's doing better anyway. Better than yesterday."

"I wasn't worried about her. What I mean is, I *am* worried about her; she goes to my school and I'm glad she's doing better, but the thing is . . . My name is Danny Lopez, by the way. She knows me a little bit . . . The thing is, I have a cat and I'm worried that whoever did this is going to come for my cat next."

The girl's eyes widened. "*Whoever* did it?"

"Yeah."

"Sheriff Rossi says it was a freak accident," she said, but he could tell in her eyes that she didn't believe that for a second.

"It wasn't an accident, was it?" she said. She bit her lip, unfolded her arms, and offered her hand. "I'm Claire, Sarah's sister."

Danny shook her hand.

"You have a cat, too?" she asked skeptically.

"Yes."

"What's her name?"

"It's a he. Jeffrey."

"Hmm."

She looked at him for a second and then nodded to herself. "OK. Dad's home, so we'll have to go quietly. Follow me."

She led him around the side of the house, past an old lawn mower and stacks of chopped wood for the stove.

She put her finger to her lips as she went past one window. "Sarah's room," she whispered.

Danny trod carefully.

When they got to the backyard, Claire led him to the fence at the rear of the house. "Look at this," she said, pointing to where two of the fence slats had been broken at the top. "That's where they climbed over. I think they tried the gate first. Normally the gate's unlocked, but I came back from CU for a few days to get my laundry done and I always lock the gate because of bears."

Danny looked at the broken fence and nodded.

"Why 'they'?"

"I don't know, I just have a feeling that this was more than a two-man operation," Claire said. "At least one of them was a kid, to get through the dog flap, and they knew they couldn't get back over the fence with Coco. Then someone saw them or they panicked and they grabbed the clothesline and hung poor Coco from the tree."

"Did you tell the sheriff this?"

"I told my mom and she told him. He didn't seem interested. Sheriff Rossi's a bit out of it. Have you ever met him? He's been sheriff of Cobalt County since the sixties or something. God knows what he'd be like in a real emergency, like a mass breakout from any one of the dozen penitentiaries in his jurisdiction."

"Thanks for showing me this."

"What are you going to do with it?"

Danny promised to make sure his own backyard fence was in good working order.

As he was about to get on his board he said, "And tell Sarah that I'm really sorry and tell her that there are some of us who are trying to figure out a way to catch this guy."

When he got home it was nearly 6:15.

He started to get changed out of his school uniform, but Juanita told him that he might as well just leave it on because they were leaving for the school open house in half an hour.

He had oxtail soup for dinner and his mom gave him the bone, which was his favorite bit. After dinner he went outside to the cul-de-sac to goof around on his board.

He did a few simple verts and a 360.

"Look at you!" Tony said from across the street.

"Hey," he said shyly.

"I texted you."

"Did you? I didn't check. I actually thought you weren't speaking to me," Danny said.

Tony laughed. "I wasn't speaking to you for a bit. I thought you were spying on me."

"I wasn't."

"Yeah, I know you weren't."

Danny put his hands in the pockets of his school blazer.

"You didn't try and kill yourself because of me, did you?" Tony asked.

"Are you mental? That was . . . I got this . . . That was an accident," Danny muttered.

"Well, I'm glad you're alive."

"Me too. You didn't come to the meeting."

Tony shrugged. "I might be getting too old for that stuff," she said.

"I saw you with Hector."

"So what? He's a friend from church. My dad likes him. We're all going to *The Lion King* together for church. Hey, you like *The Lion King*?"

Danny shook his head. "Not particularly."

Tony smiled. "So what did you crazy kids in the Watchers talk about?"

"I don't know, I wasn't really listening to much of it, but the stuff about the cats seems spot-on. We're the nexus. It's all happening in Cobalt. Olivia drew a map. And I went over to Sarah's house and I met her sister."

"What did *she* say?"

"She thinks someone came over the back fence. Your pal Hector was lurking around there too and she told him to buzz off. And I think I have a theory about what he's going to do next. I was thinking about it before I even talked to her."

"What?"

"Well, I think the cat killer is using the woods to move around town."

"Yeah, so?"

"Well, I think he's been prowling around the backs of the houses on our street. If your dad really did see someone—"

"What do you mean 'if'? He saw someone, I just don't think it was you."

"I saw someone too, but I don't know who. It could have been your father, actually, if he was lurking out there at the same time . . ."

"What are you talking about? Why would my dad be *lurking* around our own house?" Tony asked sharply.

"Well, you know he says he 'hates cats.' He told me that."

"You think my dad's the cat killer? Are you crazy? Are you trying to be funny? Bob said it was a kid."

"Bob said it was *probably* a kid."

Tony shook her head and glared at him. "You really know how to blow it, Lopez, don't you? You know what, I'll see you later," she said, and marched back to her own house.

FIFTEEN

Parents' Night

She did see him later. Thirty-five minutes later, in the science classroom of CJHCS.

Snow was falling outside.

Big downy flakes, drifting down out of the dark.

"To my students, welcome, welcome, welcome," Mr. Lebkuchen said to the thirty kids of the joint ninth-grade class sitting there in their brushed wool blazers, crisp black pants or skirts, and washed white gloves.

"And to their parents, an even more emphatic welcome," he said to the fifty or so parents jammed on the sides and around the back of the classrom. "I apologize for the lack of space. Once that monstrosity is removed, we will have more room in here," Mr. Lebkuchen said, pointing to the massive Tesla coil still covered with gray tarp. "Of course, this cramming is only a temporary arrangement until we find two new teachers to replace those we unfortunately lost."

"Yeah, why did you lose them?" one of the parents asked.

"We will have a question-and-answer session later. I hope you will keep all your questions until then, but let me just say that unfortunately our two dismissees were not up to the high standards I expect from teachers under my employ. However, the hiring process has commenced and it will be terminated in the coming weeks with, I hope, two brilliant new teachers joining our school."

Mr. Lebkuchen adjusted his glasses and continued.

"Now, what I'd like to show you all first is how a typical lesson operates in the Direct Instruction system, and then we will have some refreshments that our student Tom Sloane has prepared in the teachers' lounge. And that will be the opportunity for you to ask about any aspect of the school or your student's progress or the school's progress. Just no questions about the Oprah Network, please. We're still in talks with Oprah's producers and I don't know if an interview is going to come off or not," Mr. Lebkuchen said with a little laugh.

He was dressed in a light cream suit with a checked waistcoat and blue tie. He looked cheerful and happy. It was the first time Danny had heard about the Oprah business, but if billionaire casino mogul Steve Glynn was one of the school's trustees, then why not have another billionaire involved, too?

Mr. Lebkuchen sat. "OK, everyone, open your geography books to page fourteen, South America," he said.

They spent the next forty-five minutes going over the countries, capitals, principal rivers, and mountain ranges of South America.

Occasionally Danny glanced back at his mom. She was wearing a brown Sunday Mass dress and looked really nice with her hair done up in a bun. And of course Walt was there beside her, ten years older if he was a day, and dressed in a gray suit and tie just like a real person or something. All the parents were there. Hector's mom and dad, Charlie's folks, Tom's mother, and there was no mistaking Todd's father—the giant guy in the corner whose head was nearly touching the ceiling.

Danny caught the eye of Tony's father and quickly returned to his book.

The lesson continued.

Danny wondered if anyone would see through all of this Direct Instruction stuff. Mr. Lebkuchen reading out loud, the kids reading out loud, everyone following along with the lesson that had been laid out in the book and repeating it all several times: *"Bogotá is the capital of Colombia, Caracas is the capital of Venezuela, Quito is the capital . . ."*

To Danny it was a bit like learning lines in a play. You memorized the stuff for the weekly test and it hung around in your short-term memory until the test was over, but then, surely, you quickly forgot it.

I wonder what everyone else is making of this crap? he

asked himself and allowed himself another quick glance around the room.

But of course Danny couldn't know anyone else's thoughts, which was a shame because one mind in particular would have interested him.

A mind that was consumed by images of blood and violence and that was thinking right then that the room had an electric smell.

An electric smell he did not like.

Electricity had robbed the world of darkness, of stars, of constellations.

How much more beautiful the world, lit only by fire. How pleasant it would have been to have lived then. To go there. That world of pilgrims and penitents arrayed with garlands and crowns of violets. How different from this place.

A world of fewer people.

Not everyone jammed together like sardines. So close, so near, all of them breathing my air, breathing my air . . .

Breathing.

Breathing.

Breathing.

Calm down. It's OK. It's OK. Close your eyes. Close your eyes and when you open them they will be gone. It will be all right.

Soon you will be standing under the moon.

Watching the blood drip from your hands.

If I were the cat and the cat were me, he'd do the same thing.

Look at you, Danny Lopez, look at you trying to trap me.

What are you? You're nothing. You are too naive and too slow and too clumsy.

You're like a cat. Soon to be dying. Soon to be dead.

And yes I know that you have been walking the route.

And yes I know that the net is closing.

How can you hope to compete with me?

All it means is that things will have to be accelerated. Two more cats to complete the pentagram, and then a child.

Sit tight, Danny. Do you feel that breeze on the back of your neck? That's me. Whispering my songs of death. Will you be the first one, Danny boy? You're shivering. Why are you doing that? Are you reading thoughts? Or are you merely cold?

Can you read malice?

Well, read this: Embrace thy father, kiss thy mother, drink thy fill of the cool night air. Thy days on this world have been reduced by the thousand and the ten thousand.

For I am coming.

I am coming.

SIXTEEN

Detention

"How come you don't walk to school with Tony anymore?" Juanita asked Danny at the breakfast table.

He sipped his orange juice and thought about his answer. There were a lot of lies and untold truths to navigate before he could reply. He didn't want to tell his mom that he and Tony had fallen out or that her father still thought he was a pervert or that he thought her father might be the cat killer or that he had to leave early for school because he had morning and evening detention for a few more days.

"I'd just rather skate," he said.

"That's a pity. You two haven't had a fight or anything, have you?" Juanita asked.

"No. Nothing like that. It's been so cold, she'd rather

have her dad give her a ride and, to tell the truth, I prefer to skate," Danny said.

"Your mother's going the wrong way, but I can give you a ride in the T if you'd like," Walt said. "You've barely been in it, and we only get it for another few weeks."

"Nah, I don't think so," Danny said.

"Manners, please, Danny," said Juanita.

"No. Thank. You," Danny said.

"Bob and I were talking, and he was wondering if you had cracked that disappearing-cat case yet," Walt said, turning the pages of the *Denver Post*.

Danny sighed heavily. "The cats didn't disappear. We know where the cats are. They're all dead," he said with withering sarcasm.

"Daniel, watch yourself," Juanita said.

"Hmm," Danny muttered.

"The cats are *all* dead?" Walt asked, irritating Danny with his lack of attention.

"Yup."

"Ooh, sorry to hear that." Walt grimaced, then finished the last of his cornflakes. Unlike Danny and Juanita he tilted the bowl away from him to get the last of the sugary milk into his spoon. Danny watched him with fascination. Is that how you learned to eat cereal back East? Is that how old-money New England types ate cereal? He suddenly wondered what the hell this guy was doing in their house. Living with them, eating with them. There were back doors to Walt, back doors and secrets. If the first two cats hadn't been killed long before they'd moved to Colorado, he'd have put Walt close to the top of his list of suspects.

"I like that Bob person," Juanita said. "It's a real shame he's in prison. What's he in for again?"

"Check fraud. White-collar stuff. He's a model prisoner. I'm pretty sure he's going to make his parole in March. Certainly I'll give him a great report. There but for the grace of God and all that stuff. Although . . . ," Walt said, but his voice trailed off into silence.

Danny's eye caught the blank TV screen gathering dust on its IKEA TV stand. "Hey, when are we supposed to get cable? It's going to be two weeks on Saturday and we still don't have cable or wireless Internet. And where's our stuff? Have they lost our stuff?"

"I checked up on that," Juanita said. "Our boxes are in Denver; we should get them in a couple of days. Cable guy's coming on Sunday."

"When I was growing up, we didn't have TV or computers; we read books, you know?" Walt said.

"Yeah, that was like a hundred years ago. Things are different now," Danny muttered.

Juanita put down her spoon. She gave Danny a look that meant *This is your final warning, young man.*

"Walt, what do you mean by 'although'?" she asked to change the subject. "You said Bob's a good guy, *although . . .*"

Walt sipped his coffee and shook his head.

"What?" Juanita persisted.

Walt frowned. "I was trying not to say anything in front of the boy. He likes Bob, and this was told to me in confidence."

Juanita realized her mistake, but there was no going back now. Danny would worry away at it until it came out. "What were you told?" she said.

"OK, but this stays at this table," he said. He looked at Juanita, who nodded, and at Danny, who gave him a "whatever" shrug.

"You know Freddie Sessions?" Walt asked Danny.

"No."

"The big guy with the handlebar mustache?"

"No."

"All right, well, anyway, I was talking to Freddie—Bob wasn't with us yesterday because he was working on his parole application—and Freddie's just chewing the fat, you know, and we're talking about Bob's board meeting and Freddie says it's a good thing the juvie record's sealed. And I'm saying what juvie record? And Freddie says oh Bob had this bad juvie record in Alaska. He was up in Fairbanks. That was meth central even back then; anyway he did some pretty bad things."

"What things?" Danny asked, interested now.

"Well, uh, don't get too angry. He was just a kid . . ."

"What things?" Danny insisted.

"Well, some boys took a girl's dog . . . a neighbor of theirs . . . Bob was part of the group. They tied it to some railway lines . . . Nasty business. It was big news up there.

Reward money came in from California. They caught the kids. Bob was only fourteen, but he was the oldest, so they reckoned he was the ringleader."

"Bob tortured and killed a dog?" Danny asked, aghast.

"Well, yeah, I guess," Walt said.

Juanita was also horrified. "I don't want you to see him anymore, Danny. Walt, I don't want Danny or the other kids going to that prison. I don't know what I was thinking. I made a serious mistake."

Walt nodded. "I should have kept my mouth shut."

"No, I'm glad you told me. I made a mistake," Juanita insisted.

"But please don't say anything. Freddie told me this in confidence. No one's supposed to know about it, not even the parole board."

"I won't say anything. Who am I going to talk to anyway around here?" Juanita said.

Neither Danny nor Walt picked up on the loneliness in that remark.

Danny got up from the table, grabbed Sunflower, his heaviest coat, a beanie, and black fleece gloves to go on over his white gloves.

He went out and tested the air. It was so cold that morning that it stung his face but not so cold that it froze his tongue. He could skate. He went back inside and got his iPod and selected his '70s playlist.

He got lucky and the iPod picked Boston, Led Zep, Floyd, and Aerosmith for the ride downhill to school.

He thought about what Walt had said about Bob Randall. It kind of all made sense.

His mom and Walt couldn't put two and two together, but he could.

Bob tells them the cat killer is a kid to throw them off the scent and he goes out at night through the holes in the prison fence. What didn't make sense was the motive. Why was Bob doing it? Was the compulsion to torture animals so strong that he'd risk his parole for it?

Danny raced down the hill and skidded to a beautiful halt in front of the school gates. He was the first one there of course, before the teachers even, and he took the opportunity to skate across the playground all the way to the school entrance. He put Sunflower in his locker and walked to his detention classroom. Danny felt that he practically lived in the science classroom now. Twenty minutes before school, his classes there all day, twenty minutes after school . . . and he'd had to come back for parents' night.

It sucked.

"Sit," Mr. Lebkuchen said without looking up. He was doing paperwork—pink forms and blue forms that were clearly very complicated.

Danny sat.

"Read pages thirteen to seventeen in Scott, quietly. I'll give you a pop quiz at the end."

Danny opened his geography textbook. It was a chapter on glacial landforms. It was an odd book, and Scott kept saying things like "Drumlins are a common feature of glacial deposits, though they could also have been formed in a global flood such as has been mentioned in numerous sources including the book of Genesis."

When he was on page sixteen, which explained that all of Long Island was a glacial deposit or possibly one of the sandbanks that Noah's Ark had rested upon, Mr. Lebkuchen finished his paperwork and sighed heavily. Danny looked up.

"Words, words, words. You know why people quit teaching? So much paperwork. More paperwork than teaching time. I protect my teachers from most of it, but it's hard."

"Yes, sir," Danny said.

Mr. Lebkuchen took off his glasses and pinched his nose where they'd been resting. "How are you holding up, Danny?" he asked

"Fine."

"You're a good kid and you come from good people. Other people would have tried to sue us over that gas tap incident. Although you shouldn't have been in there in the first place."

"No, sir."

"How does this compare to your other schools?"

"Uh, fine."

"What do you like about it?"

"You learn more and, um, I like the uniforms. You don't have to worry about what you're going to wear," Danny lied.

Mr. Lebkuchen smiled. "Oh, I'm so glad to hear you say that. That's been one of my theories. Kids are resistant to the uniforms, but secretly it relieves them of so much stress."

"Yes, yes, it does," Danny said.

Mr. Lebkuchen's grin widened. Danny's arrow had hit its mark as he knew it would. In many ways, grown-ups were a lot more predictable than kids. Mr. Lebkuchen brought his fingertips together and then tapped them on the table as if he were playing a piano. He of course was also wearing the school's standard white gloves, and today he had on a dark blue suit, with a green waistcoat, watch fob, and a checked bow tie. He looked like a children's TV presenter from one of the wackier cable channels.

"And I also like the environment. The quiet is good for study and learning," Danny continued.

Mr. Lebkuchen nodded and looked at the clock. "We have a couple of minutes to kill. Do you want that quiz or would you rather just talk?"

"We could talk if you want."

"Good. So, you're liking it here?"

"It's OK."

Mr. Lebkuchen smiled and put his glasses back on. "Las Vegas must have been exciting. How did you like it there? Is that where your mother and father met?" he asked.

"My parents? Um, you don't want to hear that story," Danny said.

"Excuse me?"

"I mean, do I have to tell you?"

"Daniel, you don't *have* to tell me. I'm just curious."

"OK, they both worked at the casino. Mr. Glynn's casino on the Strip. Do you know it?"

"I know Glynn, but I've never been inside a casino, not even when I lived in New York, though some of the people at Teachers College went to Atlantic City every weekend," Mr. Lebkuchen said.

"Well, it's a big, newish casino on the Strip, near the Bellagio. Walt, that's my stepdad, he had kind of drifted for a while, I guess. I don't really know what he did. He worked a few places and got into casinos. He was a lead dealer, which is a pretty responsible job, but then he got this job escorting whales around."

"Whales?"

"Yes, fat cats, wealthy gamblers. Walt has this New England accent and he's from like *Mayflower* settlers and stuff. He can kind of talk a bit like a butler or something. People think it's classy. Anyway that was his job. Seeing the whales around, making sure everything was comped, giving them a good time. But of course he blew that gig. They fired him because he was always too concerned for the whales' well-being. Like, he was always telling the whales not to gamble so much and to go to bed early, that kind of thing. My mom was the one who actually fired him . . . I don't really know how they ended up falling in love in all that stuff."

"And you never really knew your real father?" Mr. Lebkuchen asked.

"No."

"My father died when I was young, so we're both a little bit in the same boat," Mr. Lebkuchen said. "Let me ask you something. If someone was making a film about your life, who would you get to play you?"

Danny shrugged. "They wouldn't want to make a film about my life. It's not interesting."

"Of course it is!"

"No, it isn't. And I'm not a good character for a movie. Everybody in the movies is all big and loud. You never see movies about people who just mind their own business. You know? Unless they're funny or something, and I'm not funny."

Mr. Lebkuchen seemed moved. He cleared his throat. "You're our newest student and you'll be leaving us in June. We'll hardly get a chance to mold you at all."

"Well, at least I'll know the capitals and rivers in South America," Danny said.

Mr. Lebkuchen nodded. "Yes." And again his face assumed a faraway, melancholic expression.

"Would you be interested in there being a tenth grade here? It's an idea I'm batting around."

"That'd be awesome," Danny lied through gritted teeth.

The man and the boy looked at each other.

There seemed to be a connection between them. Something that could not really be expressed in words. Something that was unsaid in a building full of unsaid things.

Mr. Lebkuchen leaned forward and his voice dropped

several decibels. "Can I tell you something? A sort of secret?"

"Well, I don't know," Danny replied warily.

Mr. Lebkuchen folded his hands in front of himself, interlinking those gloved fingers again.

"I am not a well man, Danny. You—you don't need to know the details, but every day for me is especially precious."

"You're dying?"

"Doctors tell me there's a fifty-fifty chance I'll live for another five years and about a five percent chance that I could live for another ten years. And you know, ten years is a long time when you think about it."

"What's the matter with you?"

Mr. Lebkuchen sighed. "I won't freak you out with the boring oncological details. I probably shouldn't have said anything. I just thought . . ."

Outside they could hear kids beginning to arrive on the playground.

Mr. Lebkuchen cleared his throat. "Let's keep that between ourselves, if you don't mind," he said.

"Sure," Danny said.

"You know what? You can forget about the afternoon detention from now on, but I still want you to come in the mornings. I'm enjoying these little chats and I have a sneaking suspicion that you're enjoying them, too."

"Uh, yeah," Danny lied again.

"You go outside and join your friends and I'll see you

later, and remember . . ." Mr. Lebkuchen put his finger to his lips and Danny nodded.

"Oh and before you go, here's that book of poems you wanted," Mr. Lebkuchen said, handing Danny *The Narrow Road to the Deep North* by Basho.

"Oh gee, thanks," Danny said, and went outside.

Interesting developments.

Mr. Lebkuchen had given him a book and had trusted him with two interesting pieces of information: first that he was probably running some kind of illegal Bible-study group within the school and second that he had some kind of terminal disease. This was not the sort of information you gave to a teenage boy—certainly not a misfit newly arrived from Vegas. But Danny knew he was not going to do anything with it. He wasn't going to blab—not to Tom and his little group of Watchers, nor to his mom, and probably not even to Tony. Principal Lebkuchen was one of those rare adults who put their faith in children, and Danny liked that. He couldn't bring himself to like the man, but he liked that.

He saw Tom and Cooper on the playground discreetly text-talking. They were probably having an argument about realism in *The Matrix*.

Danny would have groaned if he had been allowed to groan.

Instead, he avoided them.

Avoided everyone.

Didn't speak.

Said his lines in class.

Ate his lunch.

Mr. Lebkuchen didn't look at him, didn't give him special treatment, corrected him severely when he veered off script in the DI literature book.

He clock-watched until three thirty, and because he no longer had afternoon detention he raced outside to intercept Tony on her walk home, but she'd already gone on with a group of other kids, including Charlie and Hector. They were all going downhill in the direction of Manitou Springs. "Tony!" he wanted to yell, but he was way too self-conscious.

They were a good bit ahead, and Tony was laughing at something Hector had said.

Suddenly it seemed the most important thing in the world to Danny that he talk to her. He'd have to risk a shortcut. He started running across the frozen pond.

In some dark recess of his brain, he knew the ice was going to crack.

Perhaps he wanted it to crack.

In either case, crack it did.

A huge fissure splitting between his legs.

He'd seen a film once where a boy fell into a frozen lake and a current took him up under a clear piece of ice. Everyone tried to break through the ice, but it was too thick and they'd watched, horrified, as he'd drowned in front of them.

That film had freaked him out for weeks, and now it all came racing back.

"Help me!" Danny screamed. "Help me!"

Tony and her friends stopped to look at him. The crack was widening. His backpack would sink him straight to the bottom, he thought, so he took if off and yelled again.

"I don't really swim!" he called out.

Tony walked across the frozen pond toward him.

"No, go back! Call the cops, you'll go under too!"

But she kept walking until she was a few feet from him.

"Are you trying to be funny?" she said.

Danny shook his head, terrified.

"It's grass under here," she said. "This is Cobalt Common."

"Grass? It's not a pond?"

"No," she muttered, and walked back over to Charlie and Hector.

Swallowing his embarrassment, Danny picked up his backpack and ran to catch up with her.

"Drift, small guy," Hector said, like he'd heard someone say in a movie.

Danny laughed at him. "You wanna take me on? Without Todd? I don't think so," Danny said, hoping the bravado would cover his embarrassment. "Tony, I gotta talk to you."

"She doesn't want to talk to you," Hector insisted.

"I can tell him myself," Tony said, furiously removing Hector's arm, which had somehow crept up onto her shoulder.

"I just need one minute. It's important," Danny said.

"OK, one minute," Tony replied.

"In private," Danny insisted.

Tony walked him to a massive pine tree that looked like it had been at the corner of Manitou and Alameda for a thousand years.

"What?" she said when they were out of earshot.

"First of all, thanks for saving my life. Never wanted to die plunging into grass," Danny said.

Tony laughed and, seizing the moment, Danny said, "I was wrong about your dad. He's got no motive. Unless he's crazy. And you would know if he was crazy, right? Although the BTK killer's family didn't know he was a serial killer . . . Still, that's not really relevant here," Danny said.

Tony's hands were on her hips. "This is your apology?"

"No. No, it's not. I'm sorry. I was wrong about your dad. Probably. Anyway, I think I know who the real killer is."

"Who?"

"Bob Randall."

"Who's that?"

"Bob. Bob from the prison."

"What?"

"My dad's friend . . . I mean, Walt's friend . . . another convict told him that Bob has a teenage record of animal abuse. He tortured dogs and cats. It's him, I know it."

"How?"

"Think about it: the holes in the fence. He comes through the holes, kills the cats, sneaks back into prison. It's perfect. He has the perfect alibi. He's locked up in prison!" Danny said breathlessly.

"Why would he do a thing like that?"

"He can't help himself."

"But he helped us."

"No. He didn't. He was just trying to throw us off the scent. Remember that picture in his room? *Hunters in the Snow*? That's him, a hunter in the snow . . . literally. It all fits!"

Tony's nose wrinkled up in that way Danny found almost maddeningly attractive. She thought for a moment. "You may have something here," she said finally.

"I do have something! Do you think we should take it to Tom and the others?"

"Maybe. Hmm . . . I kind of wasn't speaking to you and I was avoiding them," Tony muttered.

"Is everything OK over there?" Hector called.

"Yeah, fine," Tony said.

"One thing puzzles me, though," Danny said.

"What?" Tony asked. Her eyes twinkled in the winter sun. She was beautiful. How could he have even thought that Olivia was the better-looking of the two girls? He must have been crazy.

Tony poked him in the ribs.

"What?" he said.

"You were saying that one thing puzzled you . . ."

"Oh yeah. How does he know what houses to break into? There's what, five hundred houses in Cobalt? How many people have cats? You can't just go around breaking into houses, you know, at random. Especially if you're like Cinderella and you have to get back into jail by dawn."

Tony shook her head. "I've already figured that one out. The um, the rules of the town . . . What are those things called? The something laws?"

"The bylaws?" Danny suggested.

"Yes, the bylaws of Cobalt say that all pets apart from tropical fish need to be licensed with the Sheriff's Department. So to find out who has a pet, all you have to do is check the licenses."

"Yes, you're right! My mom got a notice about that the day we moved in. Walt was complaining about it. Said it was a moneymaking scam. And all the Sheriff's Department employees could see it, couldn't they?"

"All the county employees, but Bob could have hacked the password. He's pretty smart, right?"

"Yeah."

"And remember that thing you said the other day?"

"What thing?"

"About using the woods to scout our street. He'd know where we live; he'd know that *we* have cats."

"Yes."

"Which means that you should keep Jeffrey indoors and I should keep Snowflake indoors, because we might be next on the list."

She shivered. Danny knew it was an opening.

"Hey, you wanna walk home with me?"

"I can't. I'm going over to Hector's house. It's a church thing. Sorry. I'd like to, but I can't."

"I don't trust him. Sarah Kolpek's sister saw him and

Charlie and Todd hanging around outside her house," Danny said.

"Not everybody can be the killer, Danny," Tony said with a touch of frustration.

"I saw this movie on TV once and this guy got killed on a train and everybody did it. You know the big reveal scene at the end? Well, it was everybody—they were all in on it. And I saw this other movie where this guy comes to this town and the whole town is in a conspiracy to kill him."

"Is that what you think? You think we're all in a conspiracy? Really, Danny, I thought you were taking this seriously."

Her nose was doing that wrinkling thing again, but he didn't have to bear it for too long because almost immediately she turned on her heel, walked over to Hector and Charlie, and began heading back downhill toward Manitou.

Danny watched her for a while before finally unstrapping Sunflower and kicking in the other direction.

After five minutes of cold wind and rough gradient he was actually relieved to encounter his father's work gang laying blacktop on the new casino road.

"Hello, Danny," Walt said.

The half dozen men and Vern, the guard with the shotgun, all said hi.

"Cold today, huh?" Bob said, coming over.

"Yeah," Danny said.

"So how's your case coming along? I asked your dad and he didn't seem to know."

Danny looked Bob square in the face. "Why do you think it's a kid doing it? Why not an adult who used to torture animals as a kid and he's just returned to his old ways?" he said bitterly.

Bob stroked his goatee and looked at his fellow convicts. He took off his hat. "So, somebody's been talking, then, have they?" he said.

"I've seen the holes in the fence," Danny said.

Bob nodded. "Elks did that three months ago. Hasn't been repaired. No one's seen the need. We're all short-timers. No one would risk their parole for a quick excursion around the countryside."

"Unless you were crazy, right?" Danny said.

"Yeah, unless you were crazy," Bob replied.

"Do you have access to a computer?" Danny asked.

Bob nodded. "Why?"

"Well, the cat killer's hacked the Cobalt Sheriff's Department's pet registry system to figure out who owns a cat; that's how he knows what houses to break into. He's crazy, but he's not stupid."

Bob nodded at Danny. "You figured that out by yourself?"

"Pretty much."

They stood and looked at each other for a moment before Bob said, "It's not me. I was a mixed-up kid. I don't even know that boy anymore."

Danny nodded. There was a fundamental difference between someone like Principal Lebkuchen and someone like Bob or Walt. Mr. Lebkuchen conveyed vulnerability and trust; Bob projected a tough, bristling, defensive posture that no doubt had been exacerbated by his years in federal prison.

Danny swallowed and decided to go on the offensive. "I think I know how I'm going to catch the killer. I'm working on a plan," he said.

"Oh, really?" Bob replied, looking surprised.

"Yeah. It's still coming together, but I think it'll work. This guy's gotta be stopped. It may only be cats, but he's really hurting people."

Bob nodded. "I suppose you've found a pattern in what he's doing and you're going to leap one step ahead?"

"Something like that."

"Just watch out he doesn't leap two places," Bob said.

Danny felt a chill go down his spine. "I'll be careful," he said.

"Be better than careful," Bob said. "Be smart."

Bob blinked slowly at Danny and then walked back to Walt.

Danny threw his board on the ground and skated home.

SEVENTEEN

The Apex of the Pentangle

Danny'd had his dinner, finished his geography homework, and was thinking about turning in early when he got the text:

dnny, cm schl nw. emrgncy.

The text wasn't signed so he couldn't tell if it was from Tom or Tony or Olivia or Cooper. But it didn't matter. "I gotta go out," he said.

"It's almost nine o'clock," Juanita replied from the living room.

"Just for a bit. It's supposed to snow tomorrow and I want to get some skateboarding in," Danny replied.

"Wrap up well," Juanita said. "And don't be too long."

The streets were icy and for a second Danny thought about walking, but he reckoned that he and Sunflower could handle it. He grabbed a black ski mask, his beanie, ski gloves, and his thick black North Face jacket.

He kicked hard, and on Alameda he was soon hitting twenty-five miles per hour easily.

He was doing close to thirty when he jump-braked and almost spilled outside the school.

The sheriff's car was parked outside—a big black Escalade with COBALT COMMUNITY SHERIFF'S DEPARTMENT written on the side.

The cops had set up spotlights and there was a crowd.

Everyone was there.

Tom, Olivia, Cooper, Tony, Hector, Todd, Charlie, Susie, April. A dozen other kids from various grades. Quite a few adults, too: the sheriff, his deputy, parents, teachers, and a distraught-looking Mr. Lebkuchen.

Everyone was gathered near the school entrance in a semicircle around *something*.

Danny flipped his board, caught it, and walked across the playground.

He pushed to the front.

A competent police official would have moved the crowd back farther or gotten them off the school playground completely, because this was definitely a crime scene.

A cat was hanging from the school flagpole. A silvery gray cat, which had been strangled on the pull rope.

It had been disemboweled and its internal organs laid out beneath it. Tiny kidneys, lungs . . . something that might have been a liver. The person who had killed it had drawn a pentangle in chalk on the playground surface, using the organs as cardinal points of the star.

There was a curious hush, punctuated by people whispering into cell phones.

"Danny, is that you?" Tony said, coming up beside him.

He took off his ski mask.

"The cat's named Whiskers. It belongs to Jessie Walker," Tony said.

"Don't know her."

"Year below us—that big tall redheaded girl."

"She live in Cobalt?"

"Yeah, Point Avenue."

"When did the cat go missing?" he asked. It was a crucial question. If it had been the day before, Bob could have stored it somewhere and somehow got to CJHCS from the prison, put it on "display," and then raced back. But if it had gone missing that day, Bob's opportunity window would have been very tight.

"I don't know," Tony said.

Tom pushed in beside Danny. He seemed excited. "Last time they saw him was this morning. He's moving faster now, isn't he?"

Danny nodded. "He is."

"Two days between kills," Tom whispered.

"No one's going to say that this is a freak accident, that's for sure," Tony muttered.

They lingered for a while but it was cold.

And they had seen enough.

"Let's get out of here," Danny said to Tony.

They walked home together up the hill.

They didn't talk.

Water vapor from their breaths condensed and froze on their ski masks in the subzero cold.

At the cul-de-sac he turned to look at her. "I'm sorry I hurt your feelings," he muttered.

"It's OK," she said. She looked at him. "This is scary, isn't it?"

"Yeah."

"At church they're always telling us to be on the lookout for the devil and stuff, but you think it's just, uh, you know . . ."

"Theoretical?"

"Yeah."

They walked across Johnson Close to her front door.

"You know, I kind of miss it when you would come into our house in the mornings," Danny said.

Tony nodded. "Me too," she said.

She stepped onto her porch, grabbed the handle of her front door, turned, and looked at him.

Danny held her gaze.

She smiled, leaned forward, kissed him on the lips, and then went inside.

Danny stood there for a while, dazed.

Finally he walked across the street to his own house.

He felt confused, elated, exhausted.

He said good night to his mother and went to bed.

It was snowing, and high up on the mountain he could see a 4x4 or a rescue vehicle on the Pikes Peak road, its lights making a descending arc through the blue dark. The car descended and then all was black on the mountain. No moon, no stars, and the silence like a frozen fermata between violent acts.

Letter VI

Have you ever seen anything die? An ant, an insect, a grandparent perhaps?

A cat?

Maybe you've just looked at old photographs.

Those people frozen in sepia.

What happened to them?

They're all gone. Dead. As if they never were. Shadows on an old photograph.

We'll be like them soon.

A fading memory. This little moment of our lives a speck of nothingness in an ocean of nothingness. Such is the fate of individuals, peoples, and even planets. In a few billion years the sun will expand and the earth will be vaporized by its corona, and a billion years after that, will anyone remember the earth at all? Or will it be reduced to rumor, a couple of legends in that black, still, empty ocean of deep space?

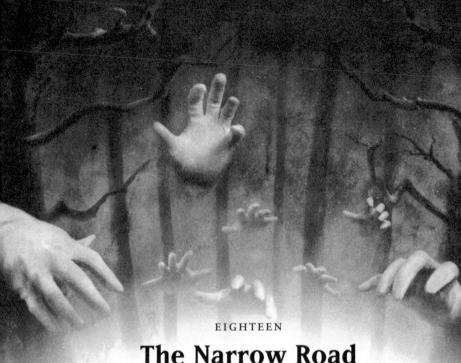

EIGHTEEN

The Narrow Road
to the Deep North

The mood was somber the next morning on the playground at the front of the school. All traces of the incident had been eradicated, but even though the physical evidence had gone, everyone knew that this was still the actual space where an animal had been killed, in—at the very least—some twisted act of cruelty and probably in some kind of evil satanic ritual.

The *Cobalt Daily News* that had thumped against everyone's front door had carried the headline SATAN COMES TO COBALT, and on the first page Pastor Younger of the Metropolitan Faith Cathedral had called for an immediate return to Christian values and a suspension of the practice of letting soldiers from Fort Carson be buried under the Wiccan Pentagram alongside those buried under the Star of David, Christian Cross, and Muslim Crescent.

Mr. Lebkuchen, however, did not look panicked.

He was standing silently, calmly, on an upturned plastic box, wearing a blue suit but no coat, hat, or scarf. The pupils and staff were arrayed before him in their respective classes. Since Danny's homeroom teacher was Mr. Lebkuchen himself, his joint class was at the very front of the assembly. It gave him a great perspective on Mr. Lebkuchen's pale skin, which was starting to turn red in the biting wind coming down from the Arctic.

Uncomfortable seconds passed while Mr. Lebkuchen sought the right thing to say.

Danny shoved his hands deeper into the pockets of his jacket.

He was standing between Tom and Tony. Tony was placid and stoic; Tom was fidgeting like crazy and swaying slightly from having to stand so long.

The only sound was the wind and a murmuring from the school gates, where a reporter from the *Colorado Springs Gazette* was testing his tape recorder mike so he could catch Mr. Lebkuchen's response to the previous night's grizzly events.

Tony's teeth started chattering.

Tom was stamping his feet.

"'It is not right that in the house of the muses there be

lament,'" Lebkuchen began suddenly in a commanding voice. And then, weirdly, he smiled. A big, genuine grin that Danny didn't understand at all.

"What did he say?" Tom whispered, but before Danny could tell him that he didn't have a clue, Mr. Lebkuchen continued: "Someone was clearly targeting our school. No doubt they were looking for headlines. But they will not get the kind of publicity they are seeking. The instruments of darkness will not destroy what we have so painstakingly constructed here. They will not sabotage what we have built in this community. For this was not just an attack on a defenseless member of God's creation. This was an attack on Cobalt itself, on you and me, and of course on our precious school."

Mr. Lebkuchen's face had an ecstatic quality to it, a wildness that Danny did not like. It made him nervous, and he hoped Lebkuchen wasn't going to make them sing or anything.

"When this school opened originally some thirty years ago, it had the name of a man who mocked God. Naturally, a school built on such a rocky foundation faltered and the Cobalt Tesla Elementary dwindled year after year and finally failed. But our school was built up from the community. Our charter school belongs to the community, and those outsiders will not destroy it. They will not sabotage our school; they will not destroy it, because they have already been beaten. They have already lost and we have already won," Lebkuchen said, his voice rising in a note of triumph.

What is he talking about? Danny wondered to himself.

"After last night's vicious attack on our school, I was in despair," Mr. Lebkuchen continued. "I thought of what we had made here. I thought of what we had lost. Two years ago this place was an empty shell. Look what we have done in so short a time. And now this? All this negative publicity, just when we were on the verge of becoming noticed nationally. Oh, I lamented and I despaired. And then I realized that these thoughts were selfish. I thought about the poor girl Jessie Walker who lost her pet while she and her family were out having fun at the movies, and I prayed, I prayed for her and for her family and I put my trust in God. I put my trust in God and I laid down by the Rivers of Babylon and I wept. And let me tell you, children, I am not someone who believes, as some do, that the age of miracles is past. Oh no. Satan's power is strong, as we have seen, but the power of the Lord is stronger by far. I went to sleep last night and this morning I was awakened by a phone call.

"I picked up the phone and it was Sheriff Rossi. He told me that they had caught the man who had done this terrible crime. They had caught him and he was already in custody. He was a—I am sorry to use these words, children, but I feel I must let you know the truth—crack cocaine addict from Colorado Springs. He had taken drugs and he was high on crack cocaine and methamphetamines. He had been speeding on I-70. He attempted to escape from the police, but thanks to the brave efforts of the men and women in our law-enforcement community he was pulled over near Castle

Rock and arrested. The police found . . ." Mr. Lebkuchen's voice faltered for a moment. "Sheriff Rossi told me that as well as drugs the State Police found Satanist paraphernalia in his car. Taken into police custody and prompted about the Satanic outrage on our school, he confessed to killing Jessie Walker's cat last night and said that he had been prompted to do it by fellow Satanists over the Internet.

"Students, teachers, and ancillary workers of CJHCS, I cannot tell you how relieved I am that we can put these tragic events behind us. We can put them behind us and move on to a new tomorrow. Yes. A new tomorrow. And so, as I said at the beginning of my remarks, 'it is not right that in the house of the muses there be lament.'"

Mr. Lebkuchen coughed and grinned again.

"There will be no lament! We will take today off and resume classes on Monday, as if these terrible events had never occurred."

A murmuring went through the assembly.

"Yes, you heard me correctly. Today will be a holiday! We are in the process of calling your parents right now, and school buses are being laid on to take you home!"

Mr. Lebkuchen nodded to a teacher named Mr. Scott, who began dividing the kids up into those who could walk home and those who needed a bus. Everyone else began talking, and in the spirit of the holiday Mr. Lebkuchen did not instruct anyone to stop them.

"Oh my goodness, that's so awesome. I was almost going to cancel Denver tonight," Tony said to Danny excitedly.

Danny was still trying to take everything in. They had caught the cat killer? They had a holiday?

"What?" he replied.

"I said it's great news! Now we can go to Denver."

"Denver?"

"Are you listening to me? I said I was almost gonna cancel Denver tonight," Tony repeated.

Danny looked clueless, so Tony further explained, "Denver. *The Lion King*. Remember?"

"Oh yeah. Why did you want to cancel?"

"I was almost going to cancel because of the guy you saw, and I didn't want to leave Snowflake in the house by himself." She coughed, hesitated, and went on. "You know, Dad said that there are still some seats left. Do you want to come? You have to have a suit and tie. We all sort of have to dress up."

Danny did not have a suit and tie and Juanita hadn't had time to drag him to Mass, otherwise he would have had to get one.

"Uh, no thanks, not exactly my scene," Danny said with a distaste that was maybe laid on a little too thick.

His reply was not the answer Tony had been expecting. She shook her head. "You know what your problem is, Danny Lopez?"

"I'd love you to tell me," Danny said.

"You're way too cool for school. You know? You're stuck here with us in Colorado. You're not in Las Vegas anymore. You should join in once in a while."

I joined your stupid group, I go to your stupid meetings, Danny thought, but before he could say anything Tom punched him quite hard on the shoulder. "We got him," Tom said, grinning. "We got him."

"Well, *we* didn't," Danny said.

"Sure we did. We kept the screws on tight. And we got him. Look, you guys wanna come? I'm going to talk to the reporter, I'll hit him with my theory about the pentagram and all that."

"Olivia's theory," Danny said.

"Oh yeah, 'course," Tom mumbled.

"No, you go," Tony said.

"OK," Tom said, and walked off.

Students Danny had never heard talking before were saying hi and chatting and laughing. Everyone's mood was relaxed, relieved, festive, like they'd just been released from ninety days in solitary.

Hector walked over to them. "Hey, Danny. Look, I'm sorry, Tony, I don't think I can come. My mom's been feeling sick this morning and with Dad in Portland, I'm kind of the man of the house," he said.

"You can't come?" Tony said, disappointed.

"No, I don't think I can," Hector said.

"Oh, well, I'm sorry about that," Tony replied.

"I'll still pay for my ticket. The church won't lose any money," Hector said.

"Oh, don't worry about it, I'm just sorry you're going to miss out."

Hector offered Danny his hand. "Hey, man, no hard feelings, OK?"

Hard feelings about what? Danny wondered, shaking his hand.

"Yeah, that's the spirit," Hector replied cheerfully. "Well, I gotta go, guys. See you Monday."

"I better get my board," Danny said, and began making his way through the throng of kids heading for the school buses.

He went to his locker, got his skateboard and, as a gesture of defiance, laid it on the floor and skated the corridor.

"Danny Lopez?" a voice said.

"Dammit!" he muttered, turned, and of course it was Mr. Lebkuchen.

"And where do you think you're going, young man?" Mr. Lebkuchen asked.

"Home," Danny said.

Mr. Lebkuchen shook his head. "You still have detention, young man. Did you forget about that?"

"Detention?" Danny said, but something was happening to Mr. Lebkuchen's face.

It was turning red.

He was suppressing a laugh.

"Ha-ha, don't look so worried. I'm joking! I'm joking. Of course you can go home with everyone else. Have a great weekend. You'll have to make up the detention on Monday morning, though. And no skateboarding on school grounds!"

"Yes sir," Danny said, not at all amused by Mr. Lebkuchen's attempt at humor but relieved to have gotten off so lightly.

"What did you think of Basho?" Mr. Lebkuchen asked.

"Oh, I've been saving it," Danny said.

"Excellent. Got me through some hard times when I was younger—not just the poems, but nature itself. Our Americans aren't bad either; you should try Thoreau. In fact, I might put him on the curriculum. Have you read Thoreau?"

"Not really, no."

"Well, OK, we'll see. All right, off you go, have a good weekend."

"I will, sir."

When Danny got outside, Tony was chatting with a girl he didn't know.

"Excuse me," Danny said to the girls and then, turning to Tony, "Can I talk to you for a second?"

"Sure," Tony said happily.

He led her to the overhang at the bike sheds.

"What is it?" Tony asked.

"I don't know about all this. It doesn't feel right. This guy they caught, the whole thing . . . it's too easy," Danny said.

"He was a druggie. Druggies do stupid things."

Danny shook his head. "There's more to it than that."

"Like what?"

"Like . . . I don't know. Lebkuchen told me he was dying,

for one thing. Does that seem weird to you?" Danny asked, immediately feeling bad about betraying the poor man's trust.

"He said that?"

"Yeah."

"Lebkuchen's dying?"

"Yeah."

Tony looked very dubious. "Of what?"

"Cancer, it sounds like."

"Why did he tell you?"

"Because he likes me. You know what? I shouldn't have said anything. What a jerk I am."

"We go to the same dentist. I've seen him close-up in the waiting room. He seems fine," Tony protested.

"Yeah, well, that's what he said."

"Are you sure he wasn't kidding?"

"Pretty sure."

"I hope it's nothing contagious. Anyway, what's that got to do with anything?"

Danny shook his head. "I don't know."

"Tony! Tony!" someone called from across the playground.

"I have to go," Tony said. "You'll think about the show?"

"Sure."

"Bye."

"Bye."

Tony walked off and Danny carried Sunflower across the yard. As he reached the school gates Charlie intercepted him. He also was grinning and happy. Clearly the cat thing had been hanging over everyone like a bad spell. "Dan the man," Charlie said.

"Hey," Danny said suspiciously.

"You want to come to *The Lion King*? We've got three extra concessions. Todd can't go now; obviously Jessie's not going; and last night Hector tells me he can't come, so we've got the tickets," Charlie said. "Whaddya say?"

"I don't have a suit . . . and really, I just don't want to go."

"Bygones be bygones. Come on, dude. You want laughs? It's got laughs. You want excitement? It's got excitement. You want aloof, interplanetary robot sex? Well, it doesn't have that, actually, but it's pretty good. I saw it on Broadway."

Danny smiled in a way that he hoped was friendly. "Thanks for the offer, Charlie. Can I get a rain check? Another time, maybe the movies or something, I really would like to."

"OK, man, I guess I'll see you Monday, OK?"

"OK," Danny said, and kicked his board hard to get away from all the good-natured people being nice to him.

He was a good ten meters away before he stopped and skated back to Charlie.

"What did you say about Hector?" Danny asked.

"Hector says he can't come," Charlie said.

"No. You said he told you last night he couldn't come," Danny said.

Charlie shrugged. "Yeah, he did. Why?"

"He told Tony his mom got sick this morning."

"Oh yeah? Well, she's eight months pregnant. Maybe she got sick last night and this morning. I don't know. Look, you wanna come? We've got the whole theater. Have you been to Denver yet?"

"No. And thanks, but no."

"OK. Give me a call if you change your mind. Have you got a pen? Wait, you're just opposite Tony's house? If you change your mind, tell her dad; he's in charge."

"I will, thanks," Danny said.

Charlie went over to some of the other kids to try to sell them tickets, and Danny really could have escaped this time but by then Tom was done with the reporter at the gate. He grabbed Danny's arm in that annoying, pawing way of his. "I think I'm going to be in the paper—probably guaranteed it when I told him I was Tom Sloane, *the* Tom Sloane, the governor's son. Gives them an angle. Didn't mention you or Olivia, though. Forgot, sorry," he said.

You're not the governor's son, you're the lieutenant governor's son—the *ex*–lieutenant governor's son, Danny thought, but kept these reflections to himself.

"So what are you going to do for the rest of the day?" Tom said, grinning.

"I don't know, go home, skateboard, I don't know."

"You skateboard? Really? Oh yeah, 'course you do. Hey, you should take up snowboarding," Tom said.

"Everybody says that."

"You should."

"Yeah. Maybe. Look, I better go. See ya Monday."

But both boys just stood there. Both knew there was something more to say. Finally Danny shook his head slowly and muttered, "I don't know."

"What?" Tom asked.

"I just don't know," Danny said. "Does this make any sense to you?"

"What? The cat killer?"

"Yeah. The cat killer. A crack addict? Are you kidding me?"

Tom shrugged. "What's wrong with that?"

"How did he hack the database? How did he know who had a cat? A crack addict's not hacking a database."

"He got help on the Internet. Lebkuchen said that."

"No, no, that doesn't work for me. And anyway, it's more than that. You're bound to have played Dungeons and Dragons, right?" Danny said.

Tom's cheeks colored. "Uh, not really, just a little bit, I guess. Just a little. I had this twelfth-level Cleric once, could raise the dead, that was pretty cool . . . and of course in Expedition to the Barrier Peaks—"

"OK," Danny interrupted. "So you remember the alignments? Good/Evil, Lawful/Chaotic?"

"Yes," Tom admitted.

"A crack addict is someone who's Chaotic Evil, crazy, off the wall, totally out for themselves. This was not the crime of a crack addict. The person who did all these killings was smart—very smart—cool under pressure . . . in other words, Lawful Evil."

"What are you saying? You think they got the wrong guy? He just confessed for no reason?" Tom asked, squinting into the sun and doing his little fidgety dance.

"People confess to things they didn't do all the time," Danny said.

"Do they?"

"Sure."

Tom nodded, unconvinced.

"Maybe I'm crazy," Danny said.

"No 'maybe' about it." Tom laughed.

"OK, bro, I guess I should go," Danny said, and offered Tom his hand. Tom shook it.

"See you Monday?" Tom said.

Danny nodded. "Sure," he replied.

Danny gave him a wave, bomb-dropped onto his board, waved to Tony, and skated home.

He found the key under the mat and opened the front door.

"Hello? Hello?" he called out, but of course no one was there.

Even Jeffrey didn't come to say hi.

He made himself a PB&J, got some Coke from the fridge, and sat in front of the blank TV for a while. The sandwich was bad. The jelly was plum and the peanut butter was some kind of crazy organic kind that wasn't terrific-tasting.

He tried to get a picture on the TV by sticking a metal coat hanger in the back of it to use as an aerial, but the only channel that would come in featured a blurry woman selling a kitchen whisk with a demented level of enthusiasm.

He turned off the TV, went upstairs, and found Jeffrey.

"Well, you're safe. You don't know what's been going on, do you? We might even unlock the cat flap now. Would you like that?" Danny asked.

Jeffrey purred, closed his eyes and, after ten minutes of Danny's petting, fell asleep.

"I remember when you used to be a bad-ass cat," Danny said, and went back downstairs. He was bored. No TV. No radio. He was sick of everything on his iPod. And they didn't even have books except for that book Mr. Lebkuchen had loaned him. He rummaged in his backpack and pulled it out. *The Narrow Road to the Deep North*, it was called. He read a poem.

Cold night: the wild duck
sick, falls from the sky
and sleeps awhile.

The poems weren't really his thing, but they were kind of cool. He flipped over the book and read the author information on the back.

Danny closed the book and stared at the cover, which looked remarkably like the view of Pikes Peak out the living room window. A snowy mountain, a forest, an empty road. Basho was a guy who lived in ancient Japan, traveling around and seeing things. He sounded a bit like a wandering samurai in a manga, which was made of awesome if you thought about it.

Danny put the book on the coffee table.

"That's what I need. A quest. A mission," he said aloud.

An idea was brewing in his mind.

He went back upstairs and got changed into his jeans, fleece sweater, and Converse sneakers. He pulled on his North Face jacket, grabbed Sunflower, and went outside. He skated in the cul-de-sac for a minute or two, hoping that Tony would appear. Not so much as a curtain twitch, so he skated down Alameda and found himself kicking in the direction of the new casino road to Walt's road crew.

The road was very nearly finished.

Only a couple of hundred yards to go. What would happen to Walt then? Would they have other jobs for the prisoners to do around town, or would Walt become a bum again, hanging around the house all the time? That prospect was grim; the dude would only get himself into mischief.

"Hey, son," Walt said.

"Hey, boy," some of the other prisoners called out.

"Is it OK if I talk to Bob for a minute?" Danny asked Vern.

Vern shrugged. "You have to ask Walt," he said.

Danny was a little taken aback by this casting of his lame-ass stepdad as some kind of authority figure.

"Can I talk to Bob?" Danny asked.

"'Course you can," Walt said.

Danny flipped Sunflower, caught it in his fingertips, put it under his arm, and walked over to Bob, who was supervising a machine that was pulverizing gravel. Bob turned off the earth flattener and offered Danny his hand. Danny looked at it for a second and then shook it.

"They caught the cat killer," Danny said.

"Oh yeah?" Bob replied in his Alaskan drawl.

"Yeah, last night he killed another cat at our school and then supposedly they caught him speeding on I-70. It was a crack addict."

"That's good news. Good news about catching this guy, not about the cat," Bob said.

Danny shook his head. "I guess, but . . ." His voice trailed off.

"But what?"

"These killings were so well planned, it just doesn't seem like the actions of someone on crack or meth."

Bob shrugged. "Well, it's true that most criminals are pretty stupid, but sometimes you'd be surprised."

"To find out who owns cats in Cobalt, you'd have to hack into the town database. And then you'd have to stalk the houses and make sure no one's home. You gotta have patience for that kind of thing."

Bob grew thoughtful. "Maybe you don't need patience. Maybe you make sure they're not at home, somehow."

"Jessie and her family were at the movies. How could he make her go to the movies?"

"What if he sent them free tickets to the movies that can only be used at a certain time? That would be the smart thing to do. He pays cash, then he fakes up some letter saying they've been given the tickets through a special offer, a free gift, a competition, something like that?"

"Yes!" Danny said excitedly.

"It would be an easy thing to check. Though it probably won't come to anything; they've probably got the right guy. Ninety percent of criminal cases end in a confession or a guilty plea," Bob said, but Danny was already on Sunflower, skating back toward Cobalt.

In the back pocket of his jeans he found the list of addresses of everyone whose cat had been abducted.

There was no one home at Mrs. Pigeon's house, but on Beechfield Road, he found Mrs. Craven, who had lost her Persian cat Tigerfeet supposedly to the coyote.

He rang her doorbell and when she answered it he recognized her as one of the lunch ladies at CJHCS.

She recognized him too, but of course they had never spoken.

"Hi," he said. "I'm Danny Lopez, grade nine."

"Hello, Danny, I know you," she said.

Danny had thought about beating around the bush or inventing some lie, but instead he decided to come right out with it: "Mrs. Craven, the night your cat went missing, when they thought it was the coyote, were you at home?"

"Why do you want to know?" she asked suspiciously.

"We're doing a project on it at school, sort of a special homework."

Mrs. Craven shook her head. "That's an odd subject for

homework, but then . . ." Her voice trailed off a moment, but then she concluded the thought: "It's an odd school."

"Were you at home?" Danny persisted.

"No. I wasn't. I got a voucher for a free meal at that new restaurant. A brasserie, they call it. Les Deux Magots on Center Street in the Springs. Well, it's not that new anymore, but it's new to me. I'm so sorry that I went now. If I'd been home . . ."

Danny had heard all he needed to. He said good-bye to Mrs. Craven and rushed away.

Danny's cell phone had died days earlier, so five minutes later he found himself at a pay phone outside the Cobalt 7-Eleven.

He put in fifty cents and Information gave him the number of Les Deux Magots. After a couple of flunkies he got the manager.

"If I wanted to get a voucher for a meal as a present for someone, would I need a credit card or could I pay cash?" he asked.

"You could pay cash if you come in," the restaurant manager replied.

The cat killer wasn't stupid enough to have used a credit card, so he must have gone there in person and paid cash, Danny thought.

His next question was obvious. "Do you sell a lot of gift vouchers?"

"Yes, it's a popular gift," the manager said.

"About how many a month?" Danny asked.

"I don't know, twenty or thirty. Why do you want to know?"

"Thank you," Danny said, and hung up.

Twenty or thirty a month. That was too many for him to work with. If it had been half a dozen he could maybe have gotten a description of who'd bought one, but twenty or thirty? Unlikely. Still, it was excellent data.

"OK, work to do," he said, and jumped on Sunflower again. He kicked hard to Douglas Street, walked past that awful chestnut tree, and knocked on the door of number 9.

A girl with brown hair and green eyes in a CJHCS uniform answered the door. Sarah Kolpek.

"Hi, I'm Danny Lopez. I'm in grade nine. I was talking to your sister about Coco," he said.

"I know you. I've seen you around. You're Tom Sloane's friend."

"Yeah."

"What do you want?"

"Well, I wanted to talk to you. I don't know if they caught the right guy who's been going around killing cats."

"What are you talking about?" Sarah said. "Nobody killed Coco. Coco's death was just an accident. A freak accident was what the sheriff said."

Danny nodded.

Sarah's sister, Claire, knew, but Sarah did not.

There was absolutely no point trying to convince her otherwise. "Yeah, I forgot. But listen, I just wanted to know how come you guys were out that night? Where were you?"

Sarah shook her head. "What difference does that make?"

"It might be important," Danny insisted.

"Uh, yeah, we were out. How did you know that? We were at *The Lion King* in Denver."

"*The Lion King*? And your tickets, lemme guess . . . You got free tickets, right?"

Sarah nodded. "Yeah, apparently the theater pulled our name out of the phonebook, totally at random, like a lottery or something. We got tickets for the whole family. We were pretty excited . . ."

Her lips continued to move. She was still talking, but Danny no longer heard what she was saying.

Free tickets to the movies.

Free tickets to a restaurant.

Free tickets to *The Lion King* in Denver.

That's how he got them out of the house.

He knew what houses had cats and he knew when the owners wouldn't be home.

"Do you mind if I take a look at the dog flap for a sec? Your sister said the only way the intruder could have gotten into the house was through the dog flap."

"It wasn't an intruder. It was an accident," Sarah said, but Danny had already pulled the screen door back and was examining the flap in the lower part of the front door.

It was about fifteen inches across.

It would be tough for a kid to squeeze through that.

For a grown-up it would be very difficult.

He got to his feet.

"I'm sorry about your cat, Sarah, I really am," he said.

"It's OK. Dad says we can get a new one from the shelter," she muttered without enthusiasm.

Danny nodded, walked down her path, laid down Sunflower, and skated back to Alameda.

And now he knew.

This was no crazed crack addict. This was someone who was intelligent. This was someone who planned each cat killing like a military operation and, what's more, this was someone who was patient enough to wait until a cat came outside or who was small enough to squeeze through a dog flap.

Three of the four cats had belonged to people who were connected with Danny's school. Probably the fourth was too.

Danny kicked hard to the casino road crew.

He knew.

He *knew*.

The wind was cold.

The mountain was like the painting on the cover of his Basho book.

Snow was beginning to fall.

He thought of the poems and the poet, the wandering samurai, traveling through ancient Japan.

I'm like him.

Investigating.

Seeing things that others don't.

And this is Japan.

That is, Japan before the A-bombs hit.

This is Japan before the nightmare goes down.

"Hey, I forgot to ask: Why aren't you at school today?" Walt wondered as Danny skidded to a halt in front of the road crew.

Danny ignored him and walked straight over to Bob.

Bob turned off his machine and took his mufflers off.

"Hello again," Bob said.

"They got the wrong guy," Danny said. "It's a kid, it's a kid at my school. And he's going to strike again tonight. And I know where and I know when and I'm gonna catch him in the act."

NINETEEN

Hunters in the Snow

After Danny had explained his plan, Bob shook his head slowly from side to side. His long red hippie hair, straggly goatee, and pinched figure-eight face made him seem more like a puppeteer on *Sesame Street* than a convict working on a chain gang. He lacked gravitas and, as if to compensate, he drew himself up to his full height, which was well over six feet.

"Well?" Danny asked.

"I don't think I can do that, son," he said. "I think I'm going to have to tell your dad."

"You can't break a promise."

"I didn't promise you anything," Bob said.

"There was a . . . um . . . what do you call those things?" Danny tried.

"Tacit understanding of confidentiality?" Bob suggested.

"Yes, exactly. And you'll be breaking your word."

Bob smiled. Danny wondered how old he was. He thought thirty, maybe thirty-three? It was hard to tell. Too old for pinkie swears. Danny was too old for pinkie swears.

"Look, I want you to promise that you won't say anything," Danny said.

"If you're right, this is a potentially dangerous situation, Danny. You should contact the Sheriff's Department," Bob insisted.

"What good will that do? They already think they caught the right guy."

"The FBI, then," Bob said.

"As if the FBI is going to get involved in a catnapping case. Come on, Bob. You and I both know they'll laugh me off the phone line."

"Maybe, maybe not."

"And besides, nothing's going to happen. I'm just going to stake out her house and no one's going to come by, and if they *do* come by and steal her cat while she's up at *The Lion King*, all I'll do is take some vid of them with my Handycam."

One of the guys working on the road crew grunted. Bob looked at Walt, who couldn't care less that he wasn't working, but Bob figured his fellow prisoners might start to get resentful if he was doing less than his fair share.

"Son, I'd better get back to work, but I've got a compromise," Bob said. "Why don't you do this stakeout plan from the comfort of your own bedroom? You say you can see the back of your house from Tony's?"

"Yes," Danny lied.

"OK. Go to your bedroom, turn off your light, and watch Tony's house from there. If you see anything out of the ordinary, call the cops. OK? Stake out the house from your room."

"OK. And you won't tell anyone what I'm going to do?"

"If you promise me that you won't leave the house under any circumstances."

Danny nodded. "I promise."

"Don't lie to me. You'll stay inside? You won't try to be a hero?"

"I'll do it that way if you'll keep this to yourself."

Bob grinned. "It's a deal, then."

"I gotta go," Danny said.

"OK," Bob said. "I got to get back to work."

Danny looked at him.

"What?" Bob said.

There'd been something bothering Danny. He needed to know. He bit his tongue. Then unbit it. "Why'd you kill that dog?" he asked.

Bob lost his smile and looked at the ground. "I don't know, son. It was a mean thing to do, that's for sure."

"I don't believe you. You know why you did it. You've got a PhD in this stuff."

"Yeah, I've read hundreds of cases. I've read about practically every serial killer that ever was, and I don't know why any of them did it. Who knows why anybody does anything?"

"I'm not asking about them, I'm asking about you."

"Well, it wasn't to show off . . . I don't think so, anyway . . . I don't know. And it wasn't out of malice . . . And I didn't even know the girl who owned it."

"Did you enjoy it?"

Bob shook his head. "No, I didn't enjoy it."

"So why did you do it?"

Bob stroked his goatee. "I guess so I could prove to myself that I was still alive. Does that make any sense? I was a nobody, in a nowhere place. Someone who had fallen through the cracks. I needed to show myself that I was alive and I could only do that by taking a life."

"I don't get it," Danny said.

"Me neither. Maybe that's why I've been looking for answers all these years. We want to understand ourselves. At the Oracle in Delphi there was a sign above the entrance that said 'Know Thyself.' That's what I've been trying to do."

Me too, Danny thought.

"I'm sorry, Danny. I gotta go back to work."

"OK. And don't worry about me, I'll be careful."

"Be better than careful, Danny. Be smart."

Danny said good-bye to Walt and was about to go home when Walt actually came up with a good suggestion for once. "You should go through the clear-cut and find your mother," he said. "It's almost five o'clock, you can get a ride home with her."

"Go to the casino?"

"Sure."

It was a decent idea, but Danny couldn't help but roll his eyes and say "Thanks, Walt" with a sarcastic edge.

He walked to the end of the unfinished road and sure enough the casino parking lot was only a short hike through what used to be forest but was now a muddy, pothole-filled wasteland that resembled a World War I battlefield. Of course, when Walt's crew got here the potholes would be filled in, the site leveled, tarmac poured, white lines painted, and anyone who wanted to could drive to a brand-new Indian casino.

Twenty minutes to Colorado Springs, five to Manitou Springs, two to Cobalt.

With some difficulty Danny avoided the potholes and the mud and climbed over a three-foot wall to the casino parking lot.

There were half a dozen cars and Juanita's XC90 in a space by itself near the entrance.

Danny had a spare car key on his key ring but he decided to go inside and find his mother. He'd gotten only ten feet through the entrance of the casino before the security guard he'd talked to a few days earlier intercepted him.

"Kids aren't allow—oh, it's you. Are you looking for Mrs. Brown?"

"Mom. Yeah."

"I'll take you to her office."

"She has an office?"

"Of course."

Dan Flight of Eagles led him through a door marked NO ENTRY into the administrative center of the casino. Danny had been to the Eye in the Sky Room once at the Glynn Casino, where the Glynn's one thousand surveillance cameras were monitored by a group of professional observers watching 24/7 for cheating by players and spectators and also by dealers and pit bosses.

This admin area, of course, wasn't as huge, so it was even more of a surprise to see that his mother's office was so big that it had two leather sofas and its own bathroom.

His mother, however, was not inside, so the guard called her over the walkie-talkie.

"Danny's here? Tell him to wait. I'll be there in five," Juanita said.

"She says to wait," the guard said.

"Yeah, I heard. I'm not deaf," Danny replied.

The guard looked at him and frowned. Danny saw the look and said, "What?"

The guard shook his head. "You are young."

"That's what everybody says, but I'm not a kid, I'm practically a grown-up."

"Then perhaps you should act like one," Dan Flight of Eagles said.

"Is that what a good Cherokee would do?" Danny snapped.

The guard smiled and shook his head. "Where does your anger come from?" he asked.

"My anger? I'm not angry about anything, bro. I got everything I want, apart from cable," Danny said.

"Can I tell you a story?" Dan Flight of Eagles said.

"As long as it's not the one about the three bears. I heard that one already," Danny said.

"When I was your age, I got a job at a bakery in Colorado Springs. In the bakery itself. The back room, where it was a hundred and twenty degrees. I had to take the baked goods out of the oven and bring them on trays to the front of the shop. I hated that job. The owner, Mr. Farley, used to call me Tonto. I hated him. So you know what I did? I used to spit on my hand and smear it on the bread and the muffins, so when all those white people ate an expensive muffin they were eating my spit. And you know what that made me?"

"Yeah, a freakin' sociopath," Danny said.

"A coward. It made me a coward. The customers weren't the enemy. Mr. Farley wasn't even the enemy. It was me. I was the one I had to deal with. You understand?"

Danny nodded. "I think so," he said.

Juanita arrived and embarrassingly kissed Danny on both cheeks.

"Mrs. Brown," Dan Flight of Eagles said. And with a look at Danny, he excused himself.

"Are you OK?" Juanita asked.

"Yeah, school got canceled. They found the guy who's been killing cats, and your buddy there, Chief Little Feather, thinks I'm a chicken and not Cherokee enough."

"What? He said that?"

"No. No, he didn't. All the rest is true though."

"They canceled school?"

"Yup. Celebration, I guess. They caught that dude who killed the girl's cat."

"Really? Well, that is good news. He is obviously a very crazy person who needs help."

"Yeah, I guess so. What about your day?"

"It's been a day," Juanita said. She looked harassed, tired. She had black rings under her eyes and her face had a gray tinge.

"Everything all right?" Danny asked.

"Oh yeah, everything's fine, really . . . just having a few problems with the plumbing. I don't know why you can't get a decent plumber in this state. In Las Vegas you can put a call in at midnight and a plumber will be there in fifteen minutes. Remember when we lived in that apartment building on Bellaqua and the washer under the sink came off?"

"Yeah. I remember. Walt said he could fix it, but of course he couldn't. We all could have drowned in there."

"That guy came in five minutes. I can't get the plumbers here to show up for their appointment on time. It's so crazy. You waste so much of your day getting people to do their jobs properly."

"Sorry to hear that," Danny said, and gave his mother an uncharacteristic kiss on the cheek, which cheered her up.

She smiled at him. "Hey, your little friend Tony was looking for you. She left a message. She said it was important."

"For me? How did she get your number?"

"Oh, I swapped numbers with her mother. You wanna call her back? You can use my phone."

"Sure. I'll talk to her. Thanks. Hey, Mom? Walt said you could give me a ride home. Is that OK? If not, it's easy to skate."

"I can give you a ride. In about twenty minutes?"

"That's fine."

"I'm going out for a bit; I'll give you some privacy to talk to your friend," she said, and her face had assumed a knowing expression that Danny didn't like at all.

"I don't need privacy, we're just talking about boring stuff, you can stay," Danny said, but Juanita just grinned and exited.

"Hmm," Danny said, annoyed. He touched his mother's iPhone's Contacts icon and scanned through the list until he found "Meadows." He touched the screen and the number dialed. He wondered if this was Tony's phone or the house phone and, if it was the house phone, was he going to have to talk to her father? He had a brief episode of panic but after eight or nine rings Tony's voice came on: "Hi, I can't get to the phone right now. Unlike you losers, I have a life. But if you leave your name and number and you're very, very lucky, I might get back to you."

"It's Danny. Mom said there was something you wanted to talk to me about. I guess I'll talk to you another time," he said, and hung up.

He guessed everyone must have already left for *The Lion*

King in Denver. They were always telling people not to bring their phones to theaters, so she'd probably left hers at home. He went back into the main menu and touched the green Phone icon and then pressed the icon for Juanita's voice mail. She seemed to get a lot of messages on a standard day, but finally he found two from Meadows.

He played the first message: "Hi, Danny, it's me. Listen, it's not too late to change your mind. Give me a call before five if you do. And you know what? If you're worried about my dad, don't be. He can't even come tonight. He's gotta go on up to Fort Collins instead, so think about it, OK?"

The second message was a little more interesting: "Danny, it's me, Tony. I was thinking about what you were saying earlier, so I did a little investigating on my own. You'd be proud of me, I was just like Lois Lane—you know, intrepid reporting, not like that clown flying around the world saving people. Anyway, yeah, I did some digging and I got some good stuff. Don't want to say over the phone, so you should come by Saturday if you want. You're intrigued, I can tell. Anyway the upshot is that you were right. Yeah, you heard me. You were right. Drop in before we go if you can, otherwise I'll see you tomorrow. Talk to you later. Bye."

Danny hung up and went to find his mother.

"Mom, can we go home now? I want to try and talk to Tony before she leaves for Denver," he said.

"Is there anything the matter?"

"No. Nothing. I just wanna talk to her."

When they got home it was nearly six o'clock and Tony's

house was empty. The lights were off, the doors locked, the cat flap swinging in the breeze.

The cat flap. Dog flap, really.

Flaps. Plural.

One at the front of the Meadows house and one at the back.

Big enough for a kid to fit through?

Hmm.

Danny looked at the sky. It was dark, and thick clouds were blotting out the moon and stars.

With a guaranteed-empty house and the moon concealed, this was a perfect night to break in . . . Whatever Tony's information had been was going to have to wait.

The night felt right.

He crossed the cul-de-sac and ate dinner with his mother and Walt. It was spaghetti, and Danny made a point to say how delicious it was. He complimented Walt on his sauce and he cleared the table and loaded the dishwasher.

Then he went outside and hung up a sheet next to the garage light.

He skated around the cul-de-sac to check that everything was normal.

Everything was normal.

"Think I'll take an early night," Danny said, just after eight thirty.

"OK darling, and tomorrow's Saturday so we can go somewhere, maybe to the movies," Juanita said.

"That'd be great," Danny muttered.

"'Night, son," Walt said.

"Good night. Oh, and guys? Keep the garage light on, please. I've put a sheet out there with some glue on it to catch moths; it's for a school project," Danny said, and retreated to his bedroom to wait.

Walt and Juanita were early risers and both of them went to bed early these days. He didn't have to wait long for Juanita. She was worn out by all the problems of the casino, and Danny heard her stomp along the landing shortly after nine. He heard her fuss for a bit in the bathroom and heard her on the landing once more.

Then, nothing.

Danny dressed himself in black jeans, black T-shirt, black sweater, black socks, black Converse sneakers, and got his black leather jacket ready. He killed the bedroom lights and put black tape over the reflectors on his shoes.

He opened the bedroom window.

Of course what he'd told Bob was a lie; he couldn't actually see the *back* of Tony's house from his bedroom. If this was going to work, he'd have to go outside.

He waited for Walt, and finally at a quarter to ten he heard Walt come up to bed.

Walt did a lot more fussing than Juanita, but by 10:05 the house was silent.

Now the hard part.

Explaining his plan to Jeffrey.

He took Jeff's furry orange face in his hands and stroked his head.

"I'm sorry, pal, but I'm going to try and get this guy, and you're going to have to help," he whispered.

Jeffrey didn't understand.

"It's like this, buddy: Snowflake's a house cat, kind of pathetic . . . Have you seen him? He's all white and furry. He'll go to pieces when the cat ki—the uh, the bad guy grabs him. He'll probably have a heart attack and die on the spot. But you? You're a street cat; you can handle yourself in a fight, and anyway it's only going to be until I get some video evidence and then I'm gonna reveal myself. Maybe do a citizen's arrest. I got some pepper spray that I can use if things get rough, which they probably won't, 'cause it's a kid that's doing it. A kid from our school, and believe me I can handle any of those jerks. We're both from Vegas, remember!"

Jeffrey yawned.

"OK, I've got to do it now. I'm not going to let him hurt you, I promise. I love you," Danny said. He scooped Jeffrey up and carried him to the cat carrier. Poor Jeffrey still didn't understand. He began to purr.

Danny started to have second thoughts.

"Look, Jeff, Bob said that you have to look within and all that crap, but I can't really do that. When I look within, it's just confusing. I gotta act, I gotta do something. Do you see what I'm saying? It's like this, old buddy, I can't let anything happen to her cat. You see that, don't you? And you can stick up for yourself. I know you can. Like when you took on that coyote."

Danny placed Jeffrey gently into the cat carrier. Jeffrey, perhaps thinking he was going on a trip somewhere, curled up and closed his eyes.

Danny grabbed the carrier by the handle and, wiping away a tear, went downstairs on tiptoe. He checked his flashlight and his Handycam and pulled on his coat. He went into the kitchen cabinet, and behind the sink cleaner he found the can of pepper spray that Juanita still kept from the days when she was working the night shift at the Glynn and walking home from the Strip. He got his mini backpack and chucked in some rope and the rest of the gear.

"Cat, rope, flashlight, camera, pepper spray. Check," Danny said.

He zipped up his jacket and walked across the street to Tony's house.

He knew he was safe there; if the killer was already watching the house from the woods, he wouldn't be able to see this little maneuver. He opened the cat carrier, took out Jeffrey, and pushed him through the cat flap. He took Jeffrey's favorite toy, a squeaky mouse, and threw that inside too.

The mouse would keep Jeffrey busy downstairs for hours, and if Snowflake played true to type, he'd be snoozing in his basket upstairs; the odds were pretty good that the catnapper would get Jeffrey. Of course, you couldn't predict it, but it made it more likely.

Danny went back across Johnson Close and killed the garage light in front of his house.

The darkness, immediately, was profound.

"Have to hurry now," he said to himself. He ran to the back gate, opened it quietly, and slipped into the woods.

He looked at his watch. The window for a burglary couldn't be very long. Maybe an hour, but not much more. You couldn't afford to wait until all the lights were off in all the houses in the cul-de-sac, but now that the powerful garage light was dead, any unseen watchers could seize their chance. I mean, how long did it take to drive to Denver? How long was the musical? You couldn't be certain, but if you were going to kidnap a cat you'd do it well before midnight just to be on the safe side. You'd go over the fence, squeeze through the cat flap, grab poor Jeffrey playing with his mouse . . .

"Jeffrey!" he whispered to himself, fear coursing through him. "Oh my God, Jeffrey. What the hell was I thinking? This is madness. I've got to stop this. I'll make a noise, scare him off . . ."

But he didn't shout, he didn't turn on the flashlight, he didn't climb over the Meadowses' fence, he didn't retrieve Jeffrey. Instead, he retreated deeper into the forest and turned on the night vision of the Handycam.

"He'll be OK . . . He's taken on coyotes and snakes in his time," Danny said to himself.

He remembered what Dan Flight of Eagles had said.

Was this the grown-up thing to do? Was this a responsible thing? Or was this an attempt to get glory for himself?

He didn't have an answer.

He waited.

Snow began to fall.

He looked at his watch.

Nothing happened for a long time.

Minutes went past.

Perhaps an hour.

Heavier snow began to fall.

But then, movement.

On the fence to the east of Tony's house.

Someone was there. Was there someone there?

Then they were gone. Danny lifted the camera lens to his eye. He scanned the fence. Nothing. Had he seen someone?

He thought of Jeffrey and his heart sank like a stone. "What have I done, what have I done, what have I done?" he whispered like a mantra.

A minute passed that felt much longer. Then another and another and then more movement by the fence and then it was over. Whoever had been there was now in the backyard of Tony's neighbors, the Allens. The catnapper hadn't come over the fence into the woods; he had seen an easier way through the Allens' house. Danny wouldn't be able to track him. He had screwed up!

"Oh no!" Danny said, and stuffed the camera in the backpack, shouldered it, and began running through the trees. He made it to the Allens' just in time to see the intruder walking along the side of the Allens' house and making his way around to Johnson Close.

The street?

Danny didn't understand.

He was going to walk down the middle of the street? But didn't he always use the woods to navigate? Had he already gotten Jeffrey? What was going on?

His whole plan was falling apart.

He ran out of the forest and alongside the Allens' house.

Someone inside was watching Letterman, the blue light from the tube casting weird reflections on the ground in front of him.

Danny made it to the street just in time to see the burglar ride off on a mountain bike with a large rucksack on his back.

"Holy crap!" Danny said, and sprinted back across Johnson Close to his house.

He ran upstairs, burst into his bedroom, grabbed Sunflower, and ran back downstairs again.

He bomb-dropped on the board and kicked hard but the bicyclist was far ahead of him. It was all downhill, and any bike could generate a much greater speed than even the most powerful skateboarder.

Danny kicked hard five times goofy-foot.

The wind licked his face. Light snow flew into his eyes. He kicked every two beats and didn't allow himself to freewheel at all.

"Faster," he said aloud. "Faster!"

Danny reached the junction at Alameda and there was no one to be seen.

Raw panic.

The guy was gone.

Jeffrey was gone.

Jeffrey was going to be murdered and it was all his fault.

Alameda went either left or right. Right took you to Manitou, left toward the prison road.

Left was more isolated. Had to be left.

Danny dead-leg kicked along Alameda for ten seconds and then changed his mind and stopped.

"No. He went right," he said to himself.

He slash-curved the board, boneless-jumped, and kicked it toward Manitou, almost getting sideswiped by a car coming down the hill.

In thirty seconds he knew that his change of mind had paid off.

There, ahead of him, far in the distance, was a shadowy form on the road. A bike. They were on level ground and Danny pulled back some of the distance between them.

Yeah, that was him.

The cat killer.

Was it a man on the bike or a *boy* on the bike? Hard to tell, because he was wearing a big coat, a ski mask, gloves. Definitely a male, though?

No, Danny didn't even know that for sure.

This part of Cobalt had few houses, and the woods on either side had been cleared for grass. Across the barbwire he saw haystacks covered with snow that looked like odd brooding monsters out there in the darkness.

He was shaking with fear—no, with excitement, or

maybe both—and at a runoff ramp for trucks he found himself doing an Andrecht invert just for the hell of it.

Suddenly the bike swerved to the left and went up a lane that Danny had never even noticed before.

"Where are you going, pal?" Danny said, landing after the invert and wiping the snowflakes from his face with the back of his glove.

He kicked up the lane and almost fell.

The wheels spun. There was no traction. He jumped off and touched the ground. It was a dirt road. There was no way Danny could ride it.

He got off the board, tucked Sunflower under his arm, and ran to keep up with the bicyclist.

A sign ahead of him said something about a State Park, but he didn't have time to read it.

The dirt trail came to a small parking lot, and then gigantic rocks loomed out of the darkness and the landscape appeared to assume a parched, desertlike quality.

The dirt under his feet became a packed sandstone, and although the trail was wide, it was unnerving to walk between gigantic unseen boulders that he knew were on either side of him. Big sandstone pillars weathered into strange shapes a little like pictures he'd seen of Stonehenge.

What is this place? Danny wondered as he walked along the sandy canyon floor. Is this the Garden of the Gods? He'd heard about that weird rock formation from Tom, but he thought that was in the Springs.

Perhaps this was another outcrop of the same formation?

A landform from the time when Colorado was an ancient seabed and the Front Range hadn't yet been born.

Suddenly he became aware of all the noise he was making.

His feet were stomping along on the gravel and the echo was reverbing off the canyon walls.

He stopped and listened.

Had he given himself away?

He stood still for a full minute and then began to move.

He had to go on. Jeffrey or Snowflake or both of them were up there somewhere. In danger.

Around the next bend he saw the cat killer's bike leaning against one of the boulders. He tiptoed over to it and examined it. Standard mountain bike—no clues.

One thing he could do was deflate the guy's tires.

Let's see you try and get away now, Danny thought as he unscrewed the tube cap and released the air from both tubes.

He went around the next bend.

The path was still quite wide and his eyes had adjusted to the dark enough to let him see the whole canyon. It reminded him a little of places he'd visited in Arizona— Indian settlements in the desert, pueblos. It was strange to find a little microclimate like this in Colorado. Especially since it was still snowing and cold.

The gravelly trail took a wide bend and terminated in a large open space—a natural rock amphitheater bounded by sandstone columns.

It wasn't a true circle, but it was close and looked even

more like Stonehenge, except that all of it had obviously been created by geologic rather than man-made forces.

The cat killer was twenty yards ahead of him, standing by a large flat stone.

His back was to Danny, his hood still up.

Danny thought about the pepper spray. Maybe he should have tested it first. How far would it shoot? Could he aim it at night? His mom had bought it from a guy on Craigslist and just assumed that it was the genuine article. Maybe she'd been scammed.

Once this doubt began floating in his brain, other doubts formed.

Perhaps he should have brought a cell phone, or left a note for his parents or told Tony herself.

No, not Tony.

But maybe his mom.

In his mind Danny measured the distance from himself to the killer. About twenty-five feet. Beyond the range of the pepper spray for sure. He would have to get closer.

He stepped out from the sandstone rock just as the moon finally appeared over the canyon walls.

The cat killer looked up. He was ecstatic. "The moon, perfect, perfect," he muttered.

The cat killer picked up a flashlight and a knife.

Because of the muttering and the weird acoustics, Danny still had no clue who he was.

The cat killer opened a bag and lifted out a cat.

It was Jeff, not Snowball.

Jeff was hissing and fighting.

The cat killer had Jeff in one hand, the knife in the other.

His plan was obvious. He was going to kill Jeffrey here in this place, this place that maybe had some kind of religious significance for him or his deranged cult friends.

Kill him here and then display him here or transport the body to some other shocking location.

Danny wondered what this lunatic was thinking.

Was he thinking at all?

Maybe he too was on drugs.

Danny knew that he had to act.

He reached into his jacket pocket, fumbled for an anxious few seconds, and found the pepper spray.

As he took it out he noticed that his hands were shaking uncontrollably.

"Gotta keep it together, Danny. Got to keep it together, bro," he told himself.

He looked at the pepper-spray can and tried to read the instructions on the side but it was much too dark for that. The cat killer was talking to himself through his ski mask.

Danny took the cap off the pepper spray. Probably you just aimed and pushed.

Danny walked closer.

Jeff was struggling.

The cat killer pushed Jeff down onto the stone.

Lifted his knife.

"That's enough!" Danny said.

The cat killer turned, startled.

Jeff jumped off the rock and ran straight to Danny.

Danny pointed the pepper spray at the strange hooded figure in front of him.

They were fifteen feet apart.

"The game's up, you little punk," Danny said, his voice steady.

Jeff was rubbing himself against Danny's legs, seeking his approval. "Yes, you're very clever, now scoot. Get out of here. Hide yourself in those rocks over there," he whispered.

Suddenly the cat killer turned off his flashlight.

All was darkness.

For two seconds Danny wondered what to do.

But then he saw the cat killer moving silently toward him as if on rails.

Danny didn't hesitate.

He fired the pepper spray. His aim was good. The cat killer was caught completely unaware. He yelped as hot pepper scalded his face and stung his eyes.

"We got him, Jeff!" Danny yelled.

But then the killer fired his weapon.

There was a scream.

Danny's scream.

And then his body was on fire.

Danny convulsed in pain. He threw up. And then the pain came again.

The air was sucked from his lungs. He couldn't think. All he could do was feel pain. Pain in every joint and muscle, pain in every nerve ending and synapse.

A terrible, white molten torment as a thousand volts traveled from the Taser along its wires and into Danny.

When the full charge was used the cat killer threw the Taser to one side and ran at him. He knocked the can of pepper spray from Danny's hand and Danny felt fists thumping into his body. Heavy, measured, deliberate blows that clubbed the air out of him. A punch in the face, another in the throat, one in the gut.

Danny's leather jacket did little to protect him.

Another punch in the face.

White spots before his eyes.

He went down.

Blackout.

More fists. A kick. Kicks.

Red-out.

Blood pouring from his nostrils, his mouth.

Somehow Danny curled himself into the fetal position.

The cat killer paused to regard him and get his breath. Irritation over the lost cat had transmuted into triumph.

This was a special day, after all.

This was graduation day.

This was the day he made the cross-species jump. Like a virus. Like a deadly virus. From bugs to cats to, finally, people. A fourteen-year-old boy called Danny Lopez.

Danny tried to wipe the blood from his face but he couldn't move.

Everything hurt.

Tears had cleared the blood from his eyes. He tried to lift

his head but it was wedged into one position like the closed-circuit camera directly above a blackjack table.

He stared along the canyon floor. He saw the killer's combat boots and, through his legs, the desert terrain and the distant red and blue lights of Colorado Springs blurring into one long smear of color.

And on the edge of his vision a pair of slant eyes staring at him from the darkness.

Run, cat, run, he thought wearily.

But Jeff was caught up in the moment and he crouched there, behind a cactus, transfixed.

Curiosity will be the death of both of us, Danny thought.

The cat killer bent down over him.

Danny felt his breath.

The cat killer put his hand on Danny's cheek, turned his face toward him.

He grabbed Danny's long brown hair and pulled it back, exposing the jugular vein to the fleeting moon.

Danny blinked.

He blinked moon, desert, canyon, mountain, and truck lights on the I-25.

The last thing he'd ever see.

Danny knew it was the end. Now was the time for prayer. He sought words in English, in Spanish, in Cherokee. He fumbled for words, he drowned in words, but no words came. He thought about everything that had happened in the past couple of weeks, ever since they had arrived at Denver International Airport. Could he have done things differently? Of course. He could have gone with the flow. Hidden. Dissolved. That's what he should have done. More like his levelheaded mom, less like his screwup "father."

He thought about Nevada and L.A. and all the places he had been in his short life. He would never get to see any of them again. And he would die not knowing who did this to him.

It didn't seem fair.

At the very least show me your face, Danny thought.

The cat killer smiled under his ski mask.

His thoughts were very different from Danny's.

Elated.

Triumphant.

Graduation day at last! And the boy's heart as a trophy. Better than a cat heart by far. A candle against the dark. A chance to live, a chance to—

He heard a sound and looked up. It was nothing, just a flock of geese tugging into the blue water of the infinite night . . .

His head was swimming with adrenal hormones. Perhaps he should calm down. Do this right. Danny wasn't going anywhere. He reached into his pocket for one of his morphine pills.

The opium fell into the lining of his stomach and the acids worked on the chalky exterior of the pill, dissolving it. Slowly the opiates seeped through his stomach wall and into his blood.

Everything relaxed. Everything was good.

Nothing bad had happened in his life.

Nothing bad was going to happen.

There was only the present.

The Master said so.

The Master was right.

Where was the Master?

He looked around him.

Geese, knife, snow, desert, rock.

Beneath him, Danny.

Groaning.

Take a deep breath, Danny Lopez, deep enough to carry you across the Styx.

It is time to die.

The blade went up.

The boy's throat was bare.

The blade swung down into the headlights of a car accelerating hard toward him along the gravel path.

Headlights.

A car.

People.

A trap!

Forget the cat! Forget the boy!

Run.

Run!

Into the woods. Deep into the woods.

The trees will hide us. The trees are our confederates.

Master, are you there?

Yes, come on.

The trees . . .

Keep going. This way!

More trees. Another hill. Finally, the mountain.

Rest here for a moment and then we'll run again.

They'll bring in the FBI for this one.

But they won't catch us.

Distant flashlights.

Cop cars.

But they were miles below on the lower slopes.

And gradually the conversation of mankind grew fainter and fainter, until it was lost completely and he was in the woods, *his* woods, among bear and fox and wolf and other predators, other allies of the dark, and before he knew it he was on the old familiar trails and as dawn rose red and gold on the eastern horizon he was back at his house and, at least for a while, safe.

Letter VII

Who is *Indrid Cold*? Who indeed? Indrid Cold is a pseudonym
that has been used many times in America over the last
century and a half.

I became aware of it through the Pennsylvania Mothman
Prophecies from the 1970s.

But in the *National Archives* there is a letter from
an Indrid Cold who warned Abraham Lincoln about an
assassination attempt that was to be made on his person at
Ford's Theatre.

There was a photographer called Indrid Cold at the
opening of the tomb of King Tutankhamun.

An Indrid Cold was late for, and was not permitted to
board, American Airlines Flight 77 on September 11, 2001.

Some have speculated that Indrid comes from Indra—the
god of fire. The name would therefore be a kind of oxymoron.
A joke.

I don't know.

I am not *the* Indrid Cold, but in a very real way I am
indeed *an* Indrid Cold.

Does this make sense?

Someday perhaps you will understand.

TWENTY

The Visitors

Danny woke suddenly and breathed in great gulps of air.

He gasped and opened his eyes.

Stars.

Stars through a skylight.

There was something in his arm.

Sheets, coolness, a hum of machines.

He was in a hospital.

Someone had saved him.

He lay for a while. Thought. Was Jeffrey OK? Had the cat killer got away? How come nothing hurt?

He closed his eyes and when he opened them the room was filled with light and his mom was holding his hand.

"They told us you were awake," she said.

"Jeffrey?" he said.

"Your dad found him and brought him home."

"My dad? From Chicago?"

"Walt. He followed you in the electric car."

"Silent but deadly, the Tesla," Danny joked.

Juanita smiled and stroked his forehead.

"The guy? . . . The cat killer?" Danny asked.

"I'm afraid he got away. I'm sorry. There's a police officer outside who wants to . . . No, that can wait. How are you feeling?"

"I feel fine. What happened? I mean . . . Why am I in here? What happened to me? Am I hurt? Did I have surgery?"

"No. A concussion and three broken ribs, but everyone says you got off lightly."

"He Tasered me."

"They told me that. Are you OK?"

"It was terrible. It hurt so bad, Mom. It really hurt." Danny bit his lip.

"You're OK now," she said. "You're OK now."

"But they didn't get him, did they?" Danny asked.

"Not yet. But they will. It happened on the Ute Reservation, so of course the FBI are involved, not that idiotic sheriff."

"I broke some ribs?"

"Three ribs."

"I can't feel anything."

"Painkillers through the drip in your arm."

"There's a drip in my arm?"

Just then the door opened and a nurse asked him how

he was doing. Danny said he was doing fine and the nurse asked if he would like some ice cream. He said yes and she brought him a cup of delicious vanilla ice cream with a little wooden spoon.

"I've never been in a hospital before," Danny said as his mom fed him.

"I know."

"I like it."

"That's good."

"What day is it?"

"It's Saturday."

"So, I wasn't in a coma?"

"No. Why?"

"I didn't have any dreams. They say you don't have any dreams in a coma."

"You talked up a storm."

"I did?"

"Who's Indrid Cold?" his mom asked. "You were babbling about him or her."

"Uh . . . nobody," Danny said.

Juanita sighed. "You need more rest."

"Are they going to fix my ribs?"

"Danny, Walt's waiting outside. He's been worried sick. Can I send him in to see you?"

Danny nodded.

Juanita got up and opened the door.

Walt came in. He was pale.

He sat next to Juanita.

"You're not mad at me, are you, son?" Walt said.

Danny shook his head and started to cry.

He cried for a long while and Juanita took one hand and Walt the other.

"Thank you, Dad," Danny said when the tears had stopped.

Walt nodded and swallowed hard. "Oh God, here come the waterworks," he said.

"Are they going to fix my ribs?" Danny asked, to help Walt out.

Walt smiled. "They say there's not much they can do about ribs. Ribs just kind of fix themselves. But you'll be OK." His voice was frail and he looked old.

"You followed me, didn't you?" Danny said.

Walt nodded. "Yeah, I followed you."

"Bob told you I was going to stake out Tony's house, didn't he? He's a traitor."

"Bob did the right thing."

"He lied to me."

"Bob was really concerned about you. I called him this morning. He was so relieved that you were OK."

Danny knew Bob and Walt *had* done the right thing, but even so it was still a betrayal and that hurt a little.

"I'm never talking to him again," Danny said.

"I hope you change your mind about that. Bob really likes you," Walt said.

Danny nodded. "We'll see."

"Do you want to hear the details? Are you strong enough?" Walt asked.

"Sure. Spill. I'm listening."

Walt explained that he had snuck out after Danny, but lost him when he went off on the skateboard. He had fired up the Tesla and chased after him, almost killing him at the junction on Alameda. Then he'd tracked him, arriving just in time to stop the cat killer from cutting Danny's throat.

The cat killer had run off into the trees.

Walt had called 911 and Jeffrey had come sauntering out of the shrubs as if nothing had happened.

"You saved my life," Danny said.

"We found this near you; it must have fallen out of your jeans," Walt said, giving Danny a little postcard of the Eiffel Tower painted in watercolors.

Danny didn't get the significance of it and merely nodded. Juanita put it up next to his water jug, where it looked nice.

"There's a whole roomful of people waiting out there for you," Walt said.

"Like who?" Danny wondered.

"Like cops and a couple of your friends from school and your principal, too."

"Mr. Lebkuchen?" Danny said, surprised, and then let out a yawn.

"Let them all wait," Juanita said.

"Yeah," Danny said, and closed his eyes.

When he woke the next time a nurse was there, reading his chart. "How are you doing?" she asked.

"OK," he said.

"Would you like anything?"

"Could I get more ice cream?" he wondered.

"Sure."

Juanita came in with the ice cream and after the ice cream was finished she asked him if he was strong enough to talk to someone.

He said he was.

A woman came in.

She was an FBI agent named Anna Ford. They talked for half an hour. Danny couldn't give her a description and he said that although the killer had spoken to him he hadn't recognized his voice. Anna asked if he might be able to pick it out from a group of samples, and he said maybe. Anna gave him her card and told him that if he remembered anything at all he was to give her a call, day or night.

"You'll catch him, though, won't you?" Danny said as she left.

"We'll do our very best," she replied. "Copycats—er, no pun intended—are sometimes more violent than the actual perpetrators."

"What do you mean 'copycats'?"

"Well, you know, kids or whoever, trying to get some of the limelight for themselves," Anna said.

"I don't understand. This was the cat killer, I tracked the actual guy," Danny said.

Anna shook her head. "We have that guy in custody. We got a confession out of him. This must be someone trying to poach on his territory. It's still very dangerous, of course, but don't worry, we'll catch him."

Danny said nothing until Anna had gone.

"They still don't get it. Nobody gets it but me!" Danny said.

"Don't excite yourself, darling. The FBI are on the case; they'll take care of it," Juanita said soothingly.

Danny decided to get Mr. Lebkuchen over with next. He came in, warmly greeted Juanita, sat by Danny, and asked if he was OK. He was wearing his coat and his driving gloves and Danny had a feeling that he was in a hurry, that he'd only come because he had to, not because he was genuinely concerned about his welfare.

"So how are you doing, young Daniel?" Mr. Lebkuchen asked far too loudly.

Danny said he was fine. Mr. Lebkuchen told Danny that he was an example of everything that was good about CJHCS and that his parents must be very proud of him. Juanita assured him that they were. Mr. Lebkuchen further explained that whenever Danny was well enough to return to school, they would have a special assembly in his honor.

With a pleading look to his mother, Danny begged Mr. Lebkuchen not to do such a thing and to treat him exactly the same as before.

"I really don't want any special attention or treatment. Please," he insisted.

"But you're a hero, a very special boy," Mr. Lebkuchen said, as if he were talking about Pinocchio.

"No, please. I'm just the same kid as last week who was in detention. What I did wasn't heroic. It was stupid. I risked my cat, I let the guy get away, I got Walt involved, and I can't even give the FBI a proper description. I'm a big screwup."

Mr. Lebkuchen did not reply, but after a moment Juanita asked, "You were in detention, Danny?"

"Yes," Danny and Mr. Lebkuchen said together.

"Of course," Mr. Lebkuchen said unctuously, "there will be no more talk of detentions or punishments. Danny will be getting the gold-star treatment from now on and I'll make sure that everyone—"

"No, no, no, no!" Danny begged. "Please. Don't do any assemblies. Give me the detention. No special treatment. Please, Mom, tell him," Danny said.

"Danny's always been a little introverted," Juanita said, as if he weren't there. "He, uh, never knew his real father. That might have something to do with it."

Mr. Lebkuchen smiled. "Yes, we've talked about that. Danny and I are quite close. My father died when I was quite young. It can have an effect on a boy."

"Oh, I'm sorry to hear that," Juanita said. "Was he ill or . . ."

"Yes. I'm afraid so. He had Alexander disease, and unfortunately it's hereditary."

"Oh, I am sorry," Juanita said.

There was an awkward silence before Lebkuchen stood up and made his good-byes. "I'm afraid I must be off. I've got an interview with Channel 7 in Denver. CJHCS is being given the governor's award for best school in the state next week," he said happily.

That's all he cares about, not me, not the madman running around the country killing cats, Danny thought.

"Should I send in your little friends?" Juanita asked after Mr. Lebkuchen had left.

"You might as well," Danny said.

There were surprisingly many of them. Hector, Tony, Cooper, Olivia, Charlie, and Tom. For a kid who didn't make friends easily, Danny suddenly had a lot of friends.

They asked the usual questions. Danny tried to answer some of them, but was too exhausted to explain things well.

The kids talked among themselves. Tony, Olivia, Cooper, and Charlie talked about *The Lion King*, but neither Hector nor Tom had gone so they couldn't contribute much.

When everyone had told him what a cool dude he was and how brave he was, and after Charlie and Tom had shaken his hand too hard and Olivia had kissed him on the cheek, Danny asked the others to leave and give him and Tony a minute.

Juanita hustled them all out and gave Danny an embarrassing smile.

"You too, Mom," Danny said, and she went with the others.

"What is it?" Tony asked, a little embarrassed herself.

"You left me a message. You said you've got vital information," Danny said.

Tony's eyes widened with excitement. "There were two things."

"Go on."

"I used to get these weird anonymous letters. Crazy stuff. Anyway, I stopped getting them a few months ago and I figured it was just some creepy boy trying to impress me. One of the letters said something about a cat. I don't remember what, exactly."

"What was in these letters?"

"Oh, I don't know, I threw them all out as soon as I opened them. The last was months ago. They were all crazy stuff. Boy stuff. Space and war and how I was the coolest chick ever."

"That doesn't really sound like it's got anything to do with this. Except for whatever that cat thing was."

"No, it doesn't, does it?" Tony said with a little smile. "I didn't think anything more about it. But then while you were sleeping, your mom asked if we knew who Indrid Cold was; you've been babbling about Indrid Cold. The letters I got were all signed Indrid Cold."

A chill went down Danny's spine and he told her about the note that had lured him to the science room.

"I Googled Indrid Cold," Danny said.

"Me too," Tony replied. "It didn't get me anywhere."

"Me either."

"Do you think that they're the same person? The cat killer and the letter writer?"

Danny shook his head. "I don't know. When did the letters stop?"

"Before Christmas."

"And when did the cat killings start?"

"After Christmas?"

"Yeah, January."

They thought about this for a couple of minutes, but they didn't get anywhere with it. Indrid Cold was probably a boy who had a thing for Tony. Was he also the cat killer? It was impossible to say.

"What was the second piece of information?" Danny asked.

Tony smiled again. "OK, so I was thinking about what you were saying about Mr. Lebkuchen, so I called up Jenny, that's Dr. Precious's secretary—he's our dentist—and I told her that I was Mr. L.'s nurse from Kaiser Permanente and said that we were running a double prescription check to see if his dentist had prescribed him any painkillers. They do that, you know. In case you go doctor shopping. I saw it on *60 Minutes*."

Danny was flabbergasted. "You did what?"

Tony fumbled in the back pocket of her jeans for a sec, took out a piece of paper, and continued. "So Jenny's pretty trusting, and she comes back on the phone and she's got the list of all the prescriptions he's been taking, and I ask her to read it back to me and I write them down and thank her and hang up. And then I go to the Internet and look them all up. So he's taking some hayfever medication and he got a prescription of Ambien once—that's a sleeping pill. But he's also taking Zenapax, which is used in the treatment of multiple sclerosis, which is not a fatal disease at all. But he's also taking Teriflunomide, which, combined with Zenapax or a generic equivalent—I'm reading this, by the way—is the only known treatment for adult-onset dysmyelogenic leukodystrophy, or Alexander disease. So the upshot of *that* is that—"

"He's got Alexander disease."

"Yes."

"He just told us that. Me and Mom."

"He did?" Tony said as all the excitement drained from her face.

"Yeah."

"So it's not a secret?"

"I guess not."

"So we're sort of back to, uh—"

"Square one," Danny said.

Letter VIII

Computer power doubles every eighteen months. A logical conclusion of this is that in the coming centuries computers will be powerful enough to simulate entire worlds. Logically, in that time too computers will be able to simulate consciousness. Sims of entire worlds with conscious beings living within them will be relatively easy to run. There will, inevitably, be trillions of sim worlds with trillions of conscious beings living within them. Biological consciousness is expensive; simulated consciousness is cheap. The probability that you, a conscious entity, are one of the few biological consciousnesses in the universe is extremely remote. You are almost certainly a sim. We are all, almost certainly, living in a sim run by beings from the future or from other worlds. Interestingly the same mathematics applies to them and they, too, are almost certainly living in a sim whether they realize it or not. This is not The Matrix. This is far worse. There is no ultimate biological body to be freed. None of us even has a biological body. We are merely conscious sims, living in a machine, and there is nothing we can do about it. This is the gnosis! This is the Secret! This is our curse, but also our liberation!

In a sim world everything science frowns upon—prayer, sacrifice, and so forth—are all perfectly reasonable propositions. Instead of praying or sacrificing to an imaginary God, of course, we are in fact praying to the sim runners who are watching our every move. Pray or sacrifice if you must, but the real question we must ask ourselves is this: How should we conduct our lives, knowing that we are living in a sim?

I have come up with the answer.

The only way the Sim Watchers will save us from death is for us to distinguish ourselves from the other entities in the sim. The only way the Watchers will save us from annihilation is if we do something extraordinary.

I, Indrid Cold, have already taken the first steps down this road.

TWENTY-ONE

L Is for . . .

The mountain, always the mountain. The mountain in winter, covered with ice and snow. The mountain in summer, golden in the long twilight. The mountain in spring, dense with wildflowers. For the past 450 days Bob had woken in his narrow cot with the view through his small window of the famous Pikes Peak.

The mountain was never the same, and he appreciated that.

He knew that he was lucky to be in a minimum-security prison with a view. The Supermax prison right next door might as well be on the moon. Its celebrity prisoners exercised in an enclosed yard, the only windows too high to see out of and the temperature controlled so that it was impossible to tell what time of year it was or even whether it was day or night.

Bob reflected on this as he surveyed the work detail for the day and put another X through the date on his calendar. Only forty-one days to go and then he was free. Then he could rejoin society and travel where he wanted and do what he liked. He had made mistakes early in life and he had been punished for those mistakes, but he was thirty-five years old now and he wanted freedom.

Forty-one days.

In forty-one days he would leave Colorado Springs and never come back. In fact, he thought, he would probably avoid the whole state.

He screwed the top back on his marker pen and brewed his coffee.

He walked to the guardhouse and asked Officer Rodriguez if he could borrow his *Denver Post*.

"Sure," Rodriguez said—it was only a formality. The *Denver Post* came for the prison and Rodriguez never read it. Bob got the paper, tucked it under his arm, and walked back to his cell, looking at the mountain.

He thought about Danny. He had heard what had happened to him and he thanked God he'd told Walt about his suspicions.

Kids always did the dumbest things possible.

If Walt hadn't followed him . . .

Danny's story had been in the Saturday *Post* and a little

bit in the Sunday *Post,* but in today's paper, the Monday edition, there was only a statement that the investigation was "ongoing."

So the killer was still out there. Or the copycat, if you preferred the FBI's version of events.

"Kids," Bob said to himself. Danny's plan had been good, but it had gone wrong and he had nearly died. He was lucky to be alive.

Bob sat on the edge of his bed. The coffee cooled. Grew cold. Time passed.

"Phone call for you, Bob," Officer Rodriguez yelled from the guardhouse.

He ran to the guardhouse, thanked Rodriguez, and took the phone.

"Hi, Bob, it's Walt. I guess I will be coming out today after all. So you better tell your boys."

"I thought you were staying home with Danny?" Bob said.

"Yeah, that's what we thought. But Danny wants to go to school. 'No special treatment,' he says. And you know what the funny thing is? He has to go in early because he's got detention with Mr. Lebkuchen. Can you believe that kid? He should be going to the White House to see President Obama. He is some special kid, huh?"

Bob laughed. "Yeah."

"Anyway, so you better tell your boys to get the work detail sorted. I'll be over presently."

"OK, Walt, I'll see you in a little bit."

Bob hung up the phone and gave it back to Officer Rodriguez, then he told him that they were going to need to authorize the chain gang after all.

Officer Rodriguez wasn't happy. "First you say it's on, then you say it's off, and then you say it's on again . . ."

But Bob knew Rodriguez didn't really care. Chain-gang work counted as "hardship duty," and you got double time for that.

Bob went back to his cell and stared at the mountain.

"Forty-one days and I'll never see you again," he said with a chuckle.

He looked at the picture in his cell of *Hunters in the Snow*, and he looked at the empty space on his wall where someone had taken one of his postcards, and he looked at all those gloomy books on serial killers on his bookshelves.

"I'm going to leave all of those here. I never want to see them again either," Bob said to himself, and he climbed up to his bunk.

After a few minutes he found that his brows were knitting together. His foot was tapping. Something was troubling him. What was the matter? Something he ate? No, he hadn't even had chow yet.

No, it was, it was . . . something Walt had said, something about—

Danny?

No.

The work gang today?

No.

What was it, then?

A name. President Obama, no, the—

Mr. Lebkuchen. Yes. *Lebkuchen.*

He'd read it in the paper, of course, but Walt saying it out loud like that had made it resonate in his mind. He'd seen that name before somewhere.

Where?

In one of his books, that's where!

He'd seen it here in this cell . . . Where? He snapped his fingers. When that weird kid, that friend of Danny's, had left the *Encyclopedia of Serial Killers* open at the letter L!

Bob took the grisly *Encyclopedia of Serial Killers* from the shelf and thumbed through the index.

"Leba . . . Leber . . . Lebkuchen, Arthur J., page 466."

Bob turned quickly to the page. It was only a one-paragraph entry:

Arthur John Lebkuchen, Staff Sgt. US Army, 1948–1988. Staff Sergeant Lebkuchen was accused of killing a fellow soldier while serving at Kadena Air Base on Okinawa, Japan, in a dispute over the ownership of a stray cat. Lebkuchen hung himself before trial. Lebkuchen cannot be considered a true serial killer since there was only one victim. Although in a bizarre echo of his crime for several weeks after his death, Kadena AB was inundated with dead cats.

Bob read the paragraph again and shut the book. "I

thought it was a kid!" he said aloud. "I thought it was a kid and I was wrong." It wasn't a kid. It was an adult whose emotions had been arrested in childhood. Bob tossed the book, jumped off his bunk, and ran to the guardhouse just as Walt was arriving.

He climbed into Walt's car.

"Rodriguez, sign me out!" Bob yelled.

"What's going on?" Walt asked.

"We've got to get to the school! We'll be there before the cops can get up from Colorado Springs!"

"What's the matter?" Walt asked.

"Drive to the school! I'll call the cops on your cell phone and have them meet us there!"

"What is going on?"

"I'll explain on the way! Drive!"

TWENTY-TWO

The Coil

On the other side of Cobalt, Colorado, Danny became aware of a faint siren in the distance.

"What is that?" he would've liked to have asked, but of course in school no talking was allowed.

He studied the math problem in front of him.

"If John and Mary have six apples and Mary and Tania have three apples, how many apples belong to—"

"Daniel," Mr. Lebkuchen said.

"Yes?"

"Can you help me with something?"

"What?" Danny said, still not entirely sure if he was allowed to reply or not.

Mr. Lebkuchen was standing next to the big machine that was covered in tarpaulin at the back of the classroom.

"Can you help me lift this?"

"Sure," Danny said.

They pulled the tarp off the enormous Tesla coil.

Danny was impressed by the machine. It was like a mad scientist's experiment kit in an old black-and-white movie. Two tall, terrifying-looking electrodes with thick wires coming from them and a spark box where raw electricity would leap between the electrode poles.

"What do you think of that?" Mr. Lebkuchen said.

"It's cool," Danny said.

"Wait till you see what it looks like when it's plugged in."

Lebkuchen fumbled with a dazzling array of plugs and then pulled a large lever that said, clearly, DO NOT PULL.

For a minute there was a humming sound that increased in decibels until, suddenly, blue fire leaped between the electrodes.

"My God," said Danny. "Are you sure we should be messing with this thing?"

"I didn't do anything, Danny," Lebkuchen said innocently.

"Sure you did. You just turned it on."

Mr. Lebkuchen laughed. "*I* didn't touch it. I left you alone in here and you must have turned it on. I should never have trusted you after what happened with the gas taps, but you seemed to have really grown up since then. I was in my office, getting some paperwork. I heard a scream, I came running, but unfortunately you were already dead."

A chill went through Danny.

He looked at Mr. Lebkuchen, who had that little smile on his face that did not always mean that something was funny.

"Are you joking?" Danny asked.

"Unfortunately for you, Danny, not this time, no."

Danny looked for an exit, but the windows were closed and Lebkuchen had locked the only door.

"Why?" Danny said.

"It was only a matter of time, Danny. You were bound to recognize me sooner or later. Really, I was lucky to get you in here so soon. You're such a good boy, insisting on no special treatment. I could have laughed out loud when you said that. You should have seen me running out of that hospital room with some nonsense about TV. Of course, I would have found another pretext to get you alone in here, because you could have blabbed at any time."

"I didn't get a good look at you."

"I'm afraid I can't take any chances."

"What are you going to do?" Danny asked.

Mr. Lebkuchen frowned. "Oh, don't worry. I'm not a complete sadist. It will be quick. I'll throw you between the poles and those things are charged to twenty thousand volts."

"What will happen to me?" Danny said.

Lebkuchen shook his head and laughed. "You'll be killed instantly, of course. Electrocuted, burned—it will all be over in a second. Like the other night, when I hit you with the Taser. But this will be much cleaner. It will be a win-win for everyone. You'll be dead, I'll have completed the pentagram, and we'll get rid of this ghastly Tesla device, which has been clogging up this room since we opened this school. It was endowed to the old school by the Ford Foundation, so we can't really get rid of it without a reason."

Danny feinted to the left and tried to make a run for the door, but Lebkuchen was watching him like a city cat watches a country mouse and he feinted at exactly the same time.

"You can scream if you like; we're pretty well sound-proofed and there's no one around here this early," Lebkuchen said.

"I'm meeting Tony. She's going to be here any minute."

"In a minute you're going to be dead!" Lebkuchen laughed.

"Just let me go, I won't say anything."

"You won't say anything? Ha! Look, Danny, you might as well compose yourself. There's no escape. I won't tell you to pray because, well, I suspect your soul will be taken by the demons."

Danny swallowed hard. "Demons?"

"Of course. Why do you think we're doing all this?"

"Because you're nuts?"

Lebkuchen grimaced. "That's what they always call those who see farther than others. Our world is controlled by beings more powerful than you will ever be able to comprehend. We are mere shadows, you and I. It has all been explained to me and now I understand."

"But—but why me?"

Mr. Lebkuchen shook his head impatiently. "Because you'd have recognized me, or more likely my voice, sooner or later. I was talking to myself the other night. I've always said far too much. Talking . . . it gets you into trouble. I used to have a stutter, but my voice coach helped me get rid of that. My old dad used to say to me, 'Children should be seen and not heard.' That's what he said. He believed that. He was old-school."

"And why the cats? They can't talk."

Lebkuchen blinked as if momentarily thrown.

Behind them the Tesla coil fizzed and spat like a monster in a cage.

"Well, that's the whole thing, of course, Danny. I need to be better. This machine is a good metaphor. I need to draw the power from the earth. Do you see?"

"No."

"We're making an exchange with the underworld. The cats and a child for more life. The Master told me this. But the cats first. Cats feed the demons. Everyone knows that. The Ute knew it. The Egyptians knew it."

Danny nodded calmly. "You know that doesn't make any sense at all?" he said.

"It makes sense to me," Lebkuchen said, removing his jacket and flexing his arms. He was small but wiry and strong.

"Seriously, did you ever consider the possibility that you might just be completely insane?" Danny said.

Mr. Lebkuchen shook his head. "Me, insane? I run the best school in the state. Maybe the country. Look at my results. I'm going to be on the Oprah channel. Michelle Obama is going to visit us later in the year. And then what? Who knows where I could go! We need more schools like CJHCS. We need Direct Instruction. The silent system. The Chinese are getting ahead. Do you read Tom Friedman? I could be the savior of America. If I live. Education secretary, perhaps? Yeah, I know its only education secretary, but it's a Cabinet posting. It's nothing to be sneezed at. And when you look where I came from . . . Of course, yes, the FBI will turn up all that old stuff in their background check. I know what you're saying. So maybe I should lie low for a few years, maybe you're right, keep my head down, k-keep out of the h-headlines."

His eyes had glazed over and the stutter had returned to his voice. Mr. Lebkuchen was one of those people who could compartmentalize their insanity most, if not all, of the time. They could pass for sane, only letting it out with those they trusted or those they thought were worthless. Since he was about to die, Danny figured he obviously fell into the latter category.

"But you're an intelligent man . . . You've got to know that there are no demons," Danny said.

Mr. Lebkuchen rubbed his chin and danced from foot to foot. "I am not an expert in demonology. The Master is. That's why we must complete the pentagram. It's a pity we won't complete the pentagram in order. A human child should have been last, but I don't think that matters too much."

"Oh, it does. You're going to screw everything up," Danny said, changing tack. "If you kill me now, the plan will be ruined."

Lebkuchen's eyes widened for a moment but then his smile and equanimity returned. "You're just trying to talk your way out of this. You don't know anything about demons or the Great Controllers."

"Neither do you. You don't believe any of that; you're running the Secret Scripture Union. You've got the God squad on your side. What would they say about all this?"

Mr. Lebkuchen shook his head dismissively "Those idiots? What do they know? They think Noah's Ark is literally real. If it rained for forty days, there would be so much moisture in the atmosphere you would literally drown in the air. Those fools. Useful to have an inside track, of course, so we can keep tabs on the teachers. Easy bunch to manipulate. Give them a little info here and there, make them feel special. The Master's idea, of course, like this school, like all of it. I will ride his coattails."

"You don't even realize that you're a lunatic, do you?" Danny said. If he could keep him talking long enough, kids would start showing up for school . . .

"No, not a lunatic. Rash, perhaps. Some of the ideas have been mine. Like this one."

Mr. Lebkuchen took a step closer and Danny backed up against a desk.

"Wait a minute," Danny said. "Let's talk about this—"

"We've talked enough. Now it's time for you to die."

"No!" Danny said, throwing his backpack and pencils and notebook at the crazed principal, but Lebkuchen swatted them away like King Kong swatting at biplanes. Nothing was going to stop him.

Danny looked around desperately for something else to throw, but the room was clean and the science cupboards were padlocked. He made a dash for the windows but Mr. Lebkuchen lunged forward, grabbed him by the tail of his blazer, and threw him to the ground.

"Heard you broke some ribs. Bet they're pretty painful, eh?" he said, punching Danny hard in the chest.

Pain tore through Danny, winding him, doubling him up on the floor.

The Tesla coil sizzled and made sharp, loud snapping sounds.

Surely it was making so much noise that eventually someone was bound to come and see it. There were always early birds, and even one witness would ruin Mr. Lebkuchen's plan. That was Danny's only chance.

"Please, I'm nobody. I'm innocent."

"No one is innocent. Your mother works in a casino, no? What kind of a place is that? You are the symbol of the decline of this nation. You and your family, building a casino in a holy place. Colorado Springs—the great nexus of America. You . . . innocent? Who do you think your real father is, Danny? Have you ever thought about it? I'll bet it's Mr. Glynn himself. And he's the real criminal, a feeder on human weakness."

"I don't care about that guy. Walt is my dad," Danny said.

"Oh, is he? Well, he's no innocent either, I'll bet. And you're no innocent. And besides, you should think about me. It won't be easy. It's one thing to kill a cat, another to kill a man or a child."

"Mr. Lebkuchen, I—"

"Enough talk."

Mr. Lebkuchen kicked Danny in the ribs to cripple him with pain and then bent down, wrapped him in a bear hug, and lifted him up. He carried him toward the massive, spitting Tesla coil. The smell was of raw electrical energy as it singed atoms in the air, burning molecules and leaving lightning in their wake. What purpose, Danny wondered, could this machine have had but to frighten and to kill?

Danny tried to wriggle from Mr. Lebkuchen's grip, but he was being held too tightly.

"A little closer," Mr. Lebkuchen said, and carried Danny to within a few feet of the machine.

White electron fire whipped terrifyingly from pole to pole in great buzzing arcs of death, like some dreadful, future serpent mankind might discover in deep, deep space. The noise was horrible, the heat intense, and already the static had lifted Danny's hair from his scalp.

"Demon, I cast thee out!" Mr. Lebkuchen said, planting his feet on the ground and shoving Danny toward the coil.

Danny felt weak and hurt and part of him wanted to just let events carry him along to a quick death.

But then he thought: *No!*

What would Dan Flight of Eagles do?

What would the samurai in Japan do?

What would Jeff do back at the Tropicana Wash?

They would fight to the very last.

He would fight to the very last.

Danny bit into Mr. Lebkuchen's wrist; he bit hard into tendon and bone.

Mr. Lebkuchen screamed, and at the same moment, behind him, a window smashed as a brick came hurtling through it.

Tony Meadows climbed through the broken frame a moment later.

"Danny, what the hell is going on in here?" she yelled.

"Better yet!" Mr. Lebkuchen cried. "Two birds with one stone!"

"It's Lebkuchen. It was him all along! He's crazy!" Danny said.

"I will cast thee into the fire too!" Lebkuchen cried, walking toward Tony.

"Cast this," Tony said, throwing her backpack at him.

"And this!" Danny said, freeing himself. He spotted a heavy wooden chair and tossed it.

The chair and backpack caught Lebkuchen in the stomach, tripping him and sending him clattering into the Bunsen burner gas taps at the back of the classroom.

He got to his feet quickly just as they heard a car screech to a halt outside the building.

Tony tried to dodge him, but he was too fast for her. Mr. Lebkuchen grabbed Tony by the scruff of the neck.

"No!" she yelled, and began clawing at him.

"Perhaps it should be ladies first," Mr. Lebkuchen said, and carried her toward the Tesla coil.

Danny jumped him and tried to tackle him to the ground, but Lebkuchen was far too strong and threw Danny away from him, hurling him almost all the way into the hissing coil.

Danny landed awkwardly on the floor just in front of the machine.

"I'll blame you for both of your deaths," Mr. Lebkuchen said to Danny. "And you won't be able to contradict me because you'll be dead."

With Tony under one arm he walked purposefully toward Danny.

Danny tried to get up but his leg gave way under him.

"Wait a minute! You smell that? You fell against the gas taps and turned them on. That's gas! If we don't get out of here we're all going to go up in flames!" Danny said.

Mr. Lebkuchen laughed. "All the better. The Controllers, the Masters of this false reality, will reward me for this in the next go-round. But first you, the two of you, into the flame."

Suddenly they heard banging at the classroom door.

"Open up, Lebkuchen, the game's up. The cops are on their way!" Bob was yelling as he shoulder-charged the door.

Mr. Lebkuchen's eyes widened for a moment, but then he shook his head and continued walking toward Danny. "So be it; we will all of us go together!" he snarled.

"Come on, Lebkuchen, open up. It's over!" Walt yelled through the door.

"Shut up!" Mr. Lebkuchen yelled back.

"Why did you do it, Lebkuchen? To impress your father?" Bob yelled.

Mr. Lebkuchen was taken aback. "What do you know of him?" he snapped, dropping Tony to the ground in his rage.

"We know everything. Okinawa, the murder, the suicide. That's how it started, isn't it? But then you came back to the States and it all stopped for a long time. What got you started again? What gave you the push? Did something happen? Did you meet someone?"

"You know nothing! You are ignorant!" Mr. Lebkuchen screamed, and advanced the last two paces toward Danny. "Come, boy, let us enter the coil together!"

He bent down to pick Danny up, but before he could reach him, Tony grabbed a piece of broken glass from the window and tossed it underhand to Danny, who caught it in his outstretched T-shirt.

The glass glittered in the Colorado sunlight.

It was long and sharp like a dagger.

Mr. Lebkuchen grabbed at Danny and the boy stabbed the glass into his principal's shoulder.

Mr. Lebkuchen screamed, clutching his shoulder, and fell backward, tangling himself in the snake pit of cables at the base of the Tesla coil.

Tony helped Danny to his feet just as the classroom door burst open and Bob and Walt rushed into the room.

"I smell gas! Kids, quickly, we've got to get out of here!" Bob yelled.

Mr. Lebkuchen was desperately trying to free himself from the cables. His eyes were wild and panicked.

"We've got to help him!" Danny said, pointing at Mr. Lebkuchen.

"No time! We've got to run!" Walt said as he and Bob helped Danny to his feet.

All four of them ran out of the classroom and sprinted across the playground.

They dived into the snow just as the Tesla coil ignited the room full of gas.

There was an almighty explosion that sent fragments two hundred feet into the air and whose percussion wave set off every car alarm in Cobalt and Manitou Springs.

Burning splinters and liquefied glass rained down on Tony, Bob, Walt, and Danny.

"Cover your eyes!" Bob yelled.

Yellow fire licked the sky, and the Tesla coil, which had taken off like a rocket, landed with an enormous crash.

The fire burned and the debris came down like snow in a nuclear winter.

People were pouring out of their houses now. In the distance Danny could hear a fire truck already on its way from Manitou and a cop car coming up from the Springs.

Danny was still dazed. "Bob? What are you doing here?"

"Saving your bacon," Bob said with a smile.

"Well, thank you," Danny said.

"You did well, son," Bob said.

"I was lucky," Danny said.

"Nah, you weren't lucky; you were smart—both of you," Bob said, and winked at Tony.

Walt was talking now. Danny nodded, but he couldn't really hear anymore because of the ringing in his ears.

Seeing was enough.

An exploded classroom.

Burning drywall. Upturned desks. Fizzing electric cables.

And all around, smoke—tight corkscrews of smoke curling from dozens of little debris fires into the impossibly blue sky.

TWENTY-THREE

Spring

Sirens. More sirens. A news helicopter. Firefighters. Cops. FBI.

Danny and Tony were taken to the hospital.

For Tony this was the first time ever.

For Danny it was the second time in a matter of days.

They were both released the following day.

Interviewed.

Their picture in the local paper.

Their picture in the *Denver Post*.

Of course, the school was closed.

First for a week and then for two weeks.

At an emergency parents' meeting it was decided that Mrs. Sanchez, the Spanish teacher, would take over as principal and run Cobalt Junior High along traditional lines until they could figure out what to do next. Only the science classroom had been destroyed and it seemed a shame to let the rest of the buildings go to waste.

But Direct Instruction was scrapped and the silent system was scrapped.

The uniform was kept, but they lost the gloves.

Newspapers speculated about Mr. Lebkuchen's motives, but no one really knew the answer. Was it about his father? Was it about some satanic religious cult? Was it about his terminal illness? Or was it simply the fact that he was insane?

He had kept a journal, on the cover of which he had written the line "It was written that I be logical to the nightmare of my choice," but, frustratingly for the investigating officers, all the other pages had been torn out and presumably destroyed.

It came out about Bob's part in the rescue.

He was released early and said good-bye to everyone at a meal at Casa Bonita and hopped a bus for anywhere that wasn't Colorado.

Life slowly got back to normal.

February.

March.

April.

It wasn't quite as cold.

Daffodils were everywhere.

The casino was open and doing a roaring trade.

Danny and Tony held hands as they walked to Tom's house.

Her hair was short, boyish, spiky. It would always be like that. Eventually she would get a nose ring.

Danny wouldn't like it, but he'd put up with it.

They walked up Hill Street and rang Tom's doorbell.

"Poor Tom. He hasn't been the same since the SSU collapsed. No one to spy on, no big conspiracies . . . His life's pretty dull," Tony said.

Danny rubbed his chin.

Coming to Cobalt had changed him. It had deepened him. He had grown up and he had become a more astute observer of himself and everyone else.

He could acknowledge Walt and accept him, flaws and all.

He could look within himself and see his own flaws.

And sometimes this self-knowledge helped him understand others, too.

There was something about Tom that he didn't quite like. Something—

"What is it?" Tony asked, concern knitting her brows together.

Danny shrugged. "Sorry, what were you saying?"

"I was saying poor Tom, his life is empty now."

"Don't worry about Tom. He'll find something else, you'll see," Danny said.

"He's going to give us that awful hot chocolate," Tony said.

"Don't you like it?"

"I like this," Tony replied, and kissed him. He kissed her back. Her lips were soft, salty.

A thought occurred to him. "Hey, you ever been to the ocean?"

"No, I haven't."

"Next time I go there with Mom and Dad, you wanna come? I've got cousins in L.A.," Danny said.

"I'd like to meet them," Tony said.

"You will," Danny replied, and rang the bell again.

TWENTY-FOUR

I, Indrid Cold

A sunrise. A gag of gray light through the webs of haze. I can smell the forest. I can see birds, planes, clouds on the mountaintop. But I am in the city. The pavement pushes up coins and paper and the rings from plastic bottles. My coat is heavy, my ski pants thick.

I am lonely.

People disappear as they pass behind me. It's all darkness back there. I don't turn to make sure. I just know.

I walk through the north wind. Through the empty streets.

The school is deserted at this time of the morning.

The science lab bulldozed. The police tape gone.

It's as if the whole planet has been evacuated, with only one person left behind.

Me.

I sigh and leave the school and walk home.

A long walk. I miss Lebkuchen. It was almost as if we shared one mind, so similar were our thoughts. The two of us, together. And now I am here by myself. Stuck here. On this scratch of land. Alone. I walk through Colorado Springs to Hill Street, to my house, and up three flights to my room.

I think about the FBI.

I think about them with contempt.

They've solved nothing. They are idiots.

Of course, how could they know? They couldn't know. It didn't match their profiles. Serial killers worked alone. They didn't take apprentices. Or disciples. One case in a hundred was like that. They worked by themselves, enjoying their personal fetish. A world of their own making that they didn't want to share.

But Lebkuchen had shared.

I had been in on every kill, including that last one in the rock canyon.

Yes, the FBI were wrong about a lot of things. They made a big deal about the report from Lebkuchen's doctor that his hands were covered with lesions from his Alexander disease. That's why he made *everyone* wear gloves, they said. It wasn't true. He really believed the gloves were a good idea and would promote discipline within the school. And they were wrong about the trophies, too. The missing cats' hearts. They weren't trophies. I only wanted the cat hearts to grind into my hot chocolate like the ancient Maya had done.

My secret recipe!

They never did explain how Lebkuchen got through spaces only a child could fit through. And they never figured out the Tesla connection either. Tesla, like Newton, was a scientist who believed in the paranormal, and he'd picked Colorado Springs as a place to do his experiments because of the supposed "flux energy" of Pikes Peak.

They'd only scratched the surface of this case. They were lazy. Everyone was lazy.

Still, what did it matter? Lebkuchen was dead. The cat-killer case was closed. They had nipped it/him in the bud. A serial killer grown in youth, reformed in adulthood, grown again, but caught in the early stages. Before he had a chance to move up that phylogenetic scale.

Of course, it was exciting news for a small place. They'd splashed it on the front page of the *Cobalt Daily News*, the front page of the *Colorado Springs Gazette*, and the second lede of the *Denver Post*. It was silly. What was the big deal about a man who killed cats? The Colorado Springs municipality kills twenty or thirty cats a week and nobody kicks up a fuss about that.

Poor Lebkuchen. I'd directed him so well. Controlled him. Gave him the drugs to tranquilize the cats, told him about those falconer gloves he'd loved so much. He'd been so easy to manipulate. Sharing his secret and me sharing mine.

The gnosis.

The secret.

In retrospect, it would have been better to keep him out of it. He was a sad, deluded man, driven forward by his ambition and his fear. I'd peeled him like the layers of an onion; first when he was my private tutor and then when I suggested he reopen the Tesla school.

And of course when I told him about the Other World and that I could save him from his disease, that I was the Chosen One and that cats were a familiar for him and a sign for me . . .

Poor Lebkuchen. How his head had been turned with my stories of magic and sorcery.

He really must have been crazy.

Anyway, all that was in the past. Finished. Over and done with.

The page-one story had become a page-two story had become a page-six story. It wasn't picked up in the national press or the TV news. Now even the school was open again with many of the same teachers, almost all the same students. The events of January were like a bad dream.

It was all so neat and pretty.

Danny and Tony together. Danny and his dad reaching a new understanding. My own dear father due back in a few weeks. Lebkuchen and his father united in death. Of course, if Lebkuchen hadn't botched that whole operation in the rock canyon, I was going to use the postcard I stole from Bob's cell to set him up. Bob would have been the perfect victim instead of a hero!

Oh well . . .

At least I'm safe up here. I can see the whole town from up here.

"The whole world," I mutter sarcastically, and turn the periscope viewer through 360 degrees, looking at Pikes Peak, the US Olympic Training Center, Goose Gossage Field, Colorado College, the Air Force Academy, Fort Carson, the entrance to NORAD over at Cheyenne Mountain . . .

I look for a while and then, bored, put the lens cover on the device. I flick through my DVDs, briefly consider *The Invisible Man* or *A Matter of Life and Death,* aka *Stairway to Heaven,* but finally decide on nothing.

I lean back in my chair and wonder if the only thing this whole episode has taught me is the value of patience. Lebkuchen's problem was that he was impulsive, quick-tempered. He didn't see that life was counted in years and decades, not weeks and days. Even with his condition he could have waited a little longer.

I certainly will not be carrying out any acts of violence for a long time now.

I'll probably wait until I join the army.

I'll be a pacifist until then. (Except of course for the rodent hearts I now put in my hot chocolate.)

Perhaps, though, it is time for a new letter to Tony?

I begin scratching on a piece of paper: *I, Indrid Cold, the Grinning Man, the Seeker, the Believer, wish you to know that I have only the greatest respect for you and that I wish you no harm . . .*

The doorbell rings.

I crumple up the paper and throw it in the trash can.

"Mother!" I yell, but then I remember that she's visiting the graveyard today. This is the anniversary of the accident. My poor brother, John, killed on the way to his job at the animal shelter. A random accident on I-25. A job he'd only taken so it would look good on his Harvard application, and possibly because our own dear kitty was accidentally poisoned.

Cleaning and inoculating all those stray cats and dogs—what a bore.

Poor John.

John, who really raised me when Dad was off with the Army or lobbying in Washington DC, leaving his family on that awful ranch that no one liked. Least of all me.

It was after John's death that I had run away, been expelled from Colorado Academy, had run away again and got private tuition.

That, I suppose, was when it all began.

The doorbell rings a second time.

"I suppose I'll have to get it myself," I mutter to the unseen listeners. To those Watchers who control everything in this wicked, fallen sim that we call the earth.

I get up from my chair and walk down those three flights.

I open the door. It's Danny standing there with beautiful Tony.

Smiles on both their faces.

"Hiya, Tom," Tony says.

"Come in," I reply, and grin so hard that it actually hurts.

"We will," Danny says.

"So," I ask with more forced cheerfulness, "who would like some of my famous hot chocolate?"

ABOUT THE AUTHOR

Adrian McKinty is an award-winning crime novelist, and his Lighthouse Trilogy series of young adult novels was published by Amulet. He was born and raised in Carrickfergus, Northern Ireland. He studied philosophy at Oxford University, and in the early 1990s he immigrated to New York City, where he found work as a construction worker, barman, and bookstore clerk. In 2000, Adrian relocated to Denver, Colorado, where he taught high school English for nine years until moving with his family to Melbourne, Australia.

This book was designed by Maria T. Middleton. The text is set in 11-point Sabon, an old-style typeface designed by the German typographer Jan Tschichold in the mid-1960s. Sabon's elegant design was inspired by the work of the sixteenth-century French punchcutter Claude Garamond and his protégé, Jakob Sabon, for whom the font is named. The display face is Matrix Bold, designed by Zuzana Licko in 1986.